PLAIN MURDER

PLAIN MURDER

EMMA MILLER

KENSINGTON BOOKS
www.kensingtonbooks.com

KENSINGTON BOOKS are published by

Kensington Publishing Corp.
119 West 40th Street
New York, NY 10018

All Kensington titles, imprints, and distributed lines are available at special quantity discounts for bulk purchases for sales promotion, premiums, fund-raising, and educational or institutional use.

Special book excerpts or customized printings can also be created to fit specific needs. For details, write or phone the office of the Kensington Special Sales Manager: Kensington Publishing Corp., 119 West 40th Street, New York, NY 10018. Attn. Special Sales Department. Phone: 1-800-221-2647.

ISBN-13: 978-0-7582-9172-1
ISBN-10: 0-7582-9172-8
First Kensington Trade Paperback Printing: January 2014

eISBN-13: 978-0-7582-9173-8
eISBN-10: 0-7582-9173-6
First Kensington Electronic Edition: January 2014

10 9 8 7 6 5 4 3 2 1

Printed in the United States of America

Plain Murder

Chapter 1

Stone Mill, Pennsylvania

Rachel Mast was the most unusual person in town, a party of one. She had one foot firmly planted in her Amish youth, the other reluctantly planted in the "college grad, Phi Beta Kappa, Wharton MBA, corporate-ladder-climbing junior partner" of her adulthood. This morning, the Amish girl won out as she walked barefoot across the wide lawn and jammed the *OPEN* flag into the grass. Satisfied that the flag would not block the modest wood sign—

STONE MILL HOUSE, 1798
BED & BREAKFAST
AMISH GIFT SHOP

Rachel gave herself a minute to simply enjoy her leap of faith . . . her B&B.

Built from fieldstone, the house was a nearly square, solid, gabled two-and-a-half-story structure with a wide center doorway, eleven windows, and two perfectly matched stone chimneys. There was a recessed two-story addition in the back, and attached to that, the stone summer kitchen, with its tiny windows and its own enormous chimney.

Approaching the house, she couldn't help but admire the

Federal-blue shutters and black door that tied everything together. It had taken her days to scrape those shutters down to their original 1798 color and several hours of mixing paint to match it, but every minute had been worth it.

Two years earlier, nearly eleven months had gone into work on the main house, which still wasn't a hundred percent done. It had turned out to be a huge money pit. Her 401(k) was empty. All the stock options used up. Nearly every penny of her savings—along with the traditional blood, sweat, and tears—had gone into the building, which had been neglected for thirty years.

This was not just a house, however; it was artwork, worthy of the finest canvas. The huge oak trees framing the home stood like ancient sentinels, their broad branches forming a canopy of green leaves that shaded the house, the thick lawn, and the cobblestone drive. No one knew if the property got its name from the town or the other way around, but both the house and the historical village now shone like new pennies.

Off to the west, mist rose off the rolling farm fields in ghostly shrouds. A cool breeze coming down the mountain would dispel them soon enough. Mountains surrounded this valley of rich, loamy soil. Those same mountains had both protected the farmland and shielded the inhabitants from the outside world for generations too many to count. This morning, the May air smelled of climbing roses and jack-in-the-pulpits.

By the time Rachel was seventeen, she had no longer felt at home here in the world of the Amish that she'd been born into. She'd thought there was too much to do, too much to see, too much to learn beyond the valley. Now, after fifteen long, stubborn years trying to fight the ties that bound her here, she was back home. Not Amish, probably never to be Amish again, but home nonetheless.

Rachel walked back toward the house, the cool, damp

grass under her feet. She had plenty of work to do, but the first hour or two of her day was always hers alone. There'd be plenty of time later to see to her guests and wait on the customers in the gift shop—tourists she hoped would come.

She had eight guest rooms. She was happy that she'd never had to turn someone away, but it would have been nice to be full, at least once. She'd welcomed a young priest yesterday afternoon, then two middle-aged sisters from Bayonne, New Jersey, later on. None of them had come down for breakfast yet, but Ada Hertzler was already in the kitchen, brewing coffee and sliding a cast-iron pan of cinnamon rolls into the oven.

The coffee and rolls would be just the first course. Ada would follow that with scrambled eggs, sausage, scrapple, and blueberry pancakes with the fresh, warm blueberry syrup Rachel had spotted simmering on the back of the stove when she'd grabbed her first cup of coffee at six. Her stomach rumbled just thinking of Ada's pancakes.

Taking the granite entrance steps two at a time, Rachel swung open the heavy front door. Gooseflesh rose on her arms and she, involuntarily, glanced over her shoulder. "*Naddish,*" she chided herself. *Foolishness*.

She had every right to use this entrance. She wasn't a barefoot Amish child with skinned knees delivering eggs and butter. She *was* barefoot, but there was no one here, Englisher or Amish, to scold her and send her around to the kitchen door. She owned Stone Mill House. Or, at least, she and Bank of America owned it.

She was learning that the values one grew up with were hard to shake. The Amish didn't borrow money from banks. An Amish member of Stone Mill never bought anything—not a house, not a horse, not a jar of jam—unless he or she had the cash to pay for it. "The borrower is a servant to the lender," any one of her friends, family, or neighbors would gladly quote.

Taking the mortgage on the Stone Mill House and property had set tongues wagging for months. No matter how many times she tried to explain to her father, her siblings, her uncles, her aunts, or her cousins that mortgages were sometimes necessary, no one bought it. Of course, her mother wouldn't discuss it with her. Her mother didn't discuss anything with her.

Starting a B&B in a nontourist town in depressed central Pennsylvania during an economic downturn would have distressed her Wharton professors as much as the mortgage did her family. But she was convinced that her clientele would grow as the tourist trade found its way to this secret Brigadoon. With large families and the scarcity of farmland for sale, the town had found itself forced to transform from a strictly agricultural area to a tourist destination. Business had already picked up over the last year at Wagler's Grocery, Elijah's Furniture, the Seven Sisters Quilt Shop, and Russell's Hardware and Emporium.

Stone Mill was a picturesque Amish village with none of the commercial ugliness of Lancaster—no strip malls, no outlet stores, no neon signs proclaiming *Gut Food* or *Dutch Miniature Golf*. There were no twenty-foot-high plastic Amish figures luring tourists into T-shirt marts or big-box discount stores. The nearest Dairy Queen was twenty miles away.

The Old Order Amish of Stone Mill were strongly conservative, and had been reluctant to listen to Rachel when she had told them that they needed to change or see their way of life disappear, along with their children. Eventually, both Amish and Englishers, over the course of more town meetings than Rachel could recall, agreed that this was the only way to keep the town from dying out. People didn't have to leave their farms and their businesses and move away. They could change what Stone Mill was without changing themselves or their values.

The citizens of Stone Mill gave visitors what they had to offer and that was a sliver of the idyllic life of yesteryear. For a few hours, a few days, or even a week, guests could buy homemade crafts, visit a farm that had been run the same way for the last hundred and fifty years, and taste food prepared the way their great-grandmothers had made it.

Rachel walked across the original wide-plank flooring of the spacious center hall with its ten-foot-high plaster ceiling and broad walnut staircase. She hung a left into the onetime parlor, now a gift shop.

Here, she displayed authentic Amish crafts: hand-stitched quilts and braided rugs and delicious jams, jellies, relishes, and candies. There were also a few carefully chosen pieces of pottery, hand-woven reed baskets, and traditional, faceless Amish dolls. Along one wall, she displayed books on the history of the area and Amish culture, written by a professor at Penn State University. There were no T-shirts, no sunglasses, no bobblehead Amish farmers. Nothing made of plastic and nothing made in China.

Golden rays of sunlight spilled through one of the two tall, deep-set windows. Bishop, a large seal point Siamese, was stretched full length on the wide windowsill. He was pretending to be asleep, but Rachel knew better. "Admit it," she said. "You think the gift shop is a good idea."

She went to the window to open it and caught a glimpse of her reflection in the wavy glass. She had few mirrors in the house—another throwback from her childhood—but she couldn't resist taking a peek. Her straight strawberry-blond hair fell well below her shoulders, framing her fair-skinned, freckled face. Her hazel eyes were very green this morning.

Was she attractive? It was a question she'd asked herself many times, a question that she'd once asked her Grandmother Mast.

"*Grossmama,* am I pretty?" she'd asked, knowing that just saying it was evidence of pride, or *hochmut,* one of the worst traits a well-brought-up Amish girl could exhibit. She must have been nine or ten, and she'd run home from the one-room schoolhouse in tears because sixth grader Jakob Peachey had called her a "beet-headed puddin' face" and everyone had laughed at her.

Her grandmother hadn't admonished her. Instead, she'd pulled Rachel close to the porch rocker where she'd sat shelling peas and studied her face. Even now, Rachel could remember how her cheeks had burned. She'd tried to pull away, but *Grossmama* had held tight to her sleeve and inspected her features carefully.

Finally, when Rachel had thought she would die of embarrassment, her grandmother had said, "Your forehead is high like your *mam*'s, and you have her nose. Not too big, not too small. Your mouth is wide, a Mast mouth, but you will grow into it, and you have your *dat*'s eyes. *Ne,* I would not call yours a beautiful face, but beautiful never lasts. Yours is *grefta*—strong. It is a face that people will trust." *Grossmama* had tapped her on the forehead. "You have a *gut* brain and a pure heart. Better to be smart than beautiful, Rachel." Her grandmother had smiled, showing small, even, perfect teeth. "So, dry your tears. It is a face that men will like, and of that, you must be ever watchful."

A strong face, *Grossmama* had declared. And better than beautiful. Rachel looked at herself again and shrugged. It would have to do. She reached over the cat and pushed up the window, letting the fresh air into the room.

Bishop deigned to open his slanting eyes and stretched, but made no comment. The cat had no opinion on business matters. It simply wasn't his way. Mundane, petty commerce was beneath Bishop's dignity. He concerned himself with eating, sleeping, and finding the most comfortable spots in the house to perch and observe the goings-on of Stone Mill House.

"I know I'm right." Rachel paused to scratch behind the Siamese's ears. He didn't consent to actually purr, but he did give what could only be described as a tiny rumble of pleasure. "This place is special," Rachel murmured. "People who want a genuine experience will come."

"Excuse me."

Rachel turned to see one of her female guests, either Ms. Baird or her sister, Ms. Hess—Rachel wasn't sure which—surveying the room from the open doorway.

"Good morning," Rachel said, hoping that the woman hadn't heard her conversing with a cat. She assumed her best hostess smile. "Were you looking for the dining room? Coffee's on. But you probably already knew that by the heavenly smell."

Not even the slimmest of smiles.

The woman peered at her through pink, rhinestone-studded glasses. "I rang the desk, but no one answered."

"Sorry, I was outside." There was a wall phone in the kitchen, but Ada wouldn't have answered it. As far as Rachel knew, Ada had never gotten within three feet of the abomination called a telephone. Phones were against the Old Order rules, and Ada never broke the rules.

Ms. Hess—Rachel thought this was the younger of the two women she'd welcomed last night—was tall and thin with short, spiky hair that was an unnatural shade of rhubarb. Her yellow capris, peppered with oversized blue flowers, clung to her like a second skin. Her nearly transparent orange peasant blouse, over a tiger-stripe bra, matched her four-inch-high wedges. "Is this the gift shop?" she demanded in a nasally tone that had all the comfort of fingernails grating on a chalkboard.

Rachel glanced at the open door. *Patience,* she reminded herself. Her *Gift Shop Open* sign still hung there. Her business permit and her MasterCard/Visa placards were plainly displayed. "Yes," Rachel answered pleasantly. "You're welcome to come in."

"I'm a guest here."

Rachel nodded. "It's good to have you. I checked you and your sister in last night."

The woman stared pointedly at Rachel's bare feet and then slowly lifted her gaze, taking in Rachel's worn blue jeans and her raggedy T-shirt that read *Penn State 5K Buggy Run 2012*. "Are you *Aim*-ish?" she asked. "You don't look *Aim*-ish. I thought the pamphlet said this was an *Aim*-ish B&B."

"We advertise that Stone Mill House is in the heart of *Ah*-mish country. I'm not *Ah*-mish. If I were I wouldn't be allowed to run a B&B." She smiled. "But all the men and women who work here are Amish. Our food is very traditional."

Rachel wasn't about to admit that she had once been Amish. She rarely shared that with strangers. Too personal. "You should come in and have a look around. Everything we sell is Amish-made."

"I wanted to know if there was room service. That's why I was calling. My sister and I want breakfast in our rooms. We're taking the Zook buggy ride at nine thirty." Ms. Hess entered the shop and zeroed in on Mary Aaron's "Diamond in the Square" crib quilt on display near the front counter. The counter had once been a teacher's desk from an Amish schoolhouse in the next county over, something Rachel had picked up at an auction.

"I'm sorry. We don't offer room service. Meals are served in the dining room, but you're welcome to take anything upstairs." Rachel kept smiling. Ninety percent of her guests were lovely people, but the other ten could be . . . *interesting*. "Breakfast is already set up there. We have an assortment of fresh fruits, cereal, and pastries, and our cook, Ada, will be happy to make you pancakes, bacon, scrapple, eggs, whatever you'd like. This morning, she made an amazing fresh blueberry syrup. It's so good, I could eat the stuff with a spoon."

Ms. Hess dragged an acrylic fingernail over another quilt and examined the tag. "Pricey, aren't you?"

"Authentic Amish quilts are all hand-stitched, more a piece of artwork than a bed linen. Mary Aaron's quilting is recognized as some of the finest Amish work in the county. Most people prefer to display her quilts as wall art rather than—"

"You said it was sewn by *Aim*-ish." Ms. Hess regarded Rachel dubiously. " 'Mary Aaron' doesn't sound *Aim*-ish to me."

"Her actual name is Mary Hostetler. We tend to use the same names over and over in our families, so to avoid confusion, we use a lot of nicknames. We call her Mary Aaron as in Aaron's Mary. Aaron is her father." *And my uncle,* Rachel thought, but again, that was personal information. Then she realized she'd said "our" families . . . Luckily, the woman didn't seem to have noticed.

"And the father's *Aim*-ish?"

"He is *Ah*-mish," Rachel confirmed with a nod. "And so is Mary's mother."

The woman grimaced. "I've never heard of such a thing. What if they had a son? What do you call him?"

"It depends. Hannah and Aaron Hostetler have a son named Alan. We just call him 'Alan' because it's not a common name. But we call their son John 'John Hannah' because there must be a dozen John Hostetlers in the valley. Hannah's son John"—Rachel made her best *and there you have it* gesture—"is, thus, John Hannah."

Ms. Hess looked at Rachel for a moment over the top of her pink glasses. "That's the silliest thing I've ever heard of." She inspected the quilt again. "Are you certain this is hand-sewn? The stitches are too even. It looks machine—"

"Rachel! Rachel!"

Glancing out the window, Rachel spotted Mary Aaron—black bonnet strings flying—racing up the front drive, her push-scooter left on its side in the grass. Her feet were bare, and she was wearing a rose-colored traditional ankle-length dress with a white apron over it.

"In the gift shop!" Rachel called through the open window, wondering why Mary was in such a hurry this morning.

Rachel turned back to her guest with a smile. "You're in luck. Here's Mary Aaron now. You'll be able to meet her. I know she can answer any questions you may have about her quilt."

"Does she talk English?"

"She *speaks* English perfectly," Rachel assured her.

"Because sometimes it's difficult to understand foreigners."

"I can assure you that Mary Aaron's English is excellent." Rachel stepped into the hall just as Mary Aaron threw open the front door and burst inside.

"Come quick!" she exclaimed. She was breathing hard; beads of sweat ran down her face. She must have rushed the full three miles from her house on her push-scooter.

"You have to come!" Mary Aaron said, switching from English to Pennsylvania Deitsch when she caught sight of Ms. Hess staring at her from the gift shop doorway. "It's Willy. He's been found!"

Willy O'Day's mysterious disappearance had been the subject of conjecture in Stone Mill for the last eight months. The prominent English businessman had vanished without a trace, and no one had heard from him since.

"So the rumors were true?" Rachel asked, also in Deitsch. "He ran off with that blond waitress from the diner?"

"*Ne.*" Mary Aaron shook her head.

For the first time, Rachel realized her cousin's face was pale, despite her rosy cheeks from the effort it had taken to get here on her scooter.

"Get your head covering, Rachel. It's bad, really bad. My *dat* needs you!"

A sense of dread came over Rachel as she realized the extent of her cousin's distress. "What is it? What's happened to Willy?"

Mary Aaron grabbed Rachel's hand. "He's sleeping the long sleep in our cow pasture." Tears welled up in her big brown eyes and spilled down her dirt-streaked cheeks. "And the police think *Dat* put him there."

Chapter 2

"Will you come, Rachel?" Mary Aaron pleaded. "We need your help. *Dat* needs you."

Rachel nodded. "Of course I'll come." She turned back to her guest. "I'm afraid I have an emergency. I have to go."

Ms. Hess frowned as she stepped out of the gift shop and into the hall. "I'm interested in this quilt. Can't your errand wait until—"

"Sorry." Rachel reached around her guest and pulled the gift shop door shut behind her. She flipped the wooden sign around so that it read: *CLOSED. Please come again!* "Family comes first."

"But the quilt."

"We can talk about it later." Rachel indicated the door across the hallway. "Breakfast in the dining room," she said. She turned to Mary Aaron. "Wait for me out front. I'll bring the Jeep around. We can throw your scooter in the back."

The church districts in Stone Mill were Old Order and very conservative. Members weren't permitted to operate any type of motor vehicle; they used horse-drawn wagons and carriages. Mary Aaron was, however, permitted to accept a ride from Rachel.

"We have to hurry! The police are talking to him. You know how *Dat* can be."

"It'll be all right." Rachel gave her cousin's hand a quick squeeze. "We'll straighten this out."

Mary Aaron opened her mouth to answer and then closed it abruptly, but Rachel knew what she was thinking. Willy and Uncle Aaron had been feuding for years. Everyone knew how much the dead man and Uncle Aaron had disliked each other; they'd had a public shouting match at the livestock sale only days before Willy disappeared. It had been such a scene that the bishop, two preachers, and a deacon had called on her uncle that evening—not a particularly pleasant visit for any of them, she imagined.

"Meet you out front," Rachel repeated. Then she went down the hall, exited the main house, and entered the kitchen, where Ada was patting loose sausage into round cakes and dropping them onto a skillet.

"I've got to go to Uncle Aaron's," she explained in Pennsylvania Deitsch. It was an old German dialect used only among the Amish in North America. "Please see that the guests get breakfast and ask the girls to . . . you know, the usual morning chores."

Ada's pale-blue eyes narrowed. She was a tall, broad-shouldered woman with a plump middle and a wide bottom, but she exhibited none of the joviality usually associated with a plus-size woman.

"You'll manage fine," Rachel said with forced cheerfulness as she snatched her keys from a hook near the back door. Ada could be prickly, but she was a capable woman and Rachel couldn't run the business without her. "I'll be back soon," she promised, crossing her fingers behind her back.

On her way out, she paused long enough to snatch an elastic hair tie and a handful of large bobby pins from a drawer. As she stepped onto the back porch and into a pair of black Keds, she began to plait her hair into a single braid.

She couldn't believe Willy O'Day was dead. Not just dead. Dead in her uncle's cow pasture. That chill that she'd felt earlier returned and rippled down her spine. It didn't seem possible. Willy had been missing since October. He couldn't have been lying in the pasture all that time. Someone would have found him. The *buzzards* would have found him.

She hurried across the grassy back lawn. Securing her braid with the hair tie, she took a few quick twists and then used the pins to fix it tightly to the back of her head.

This all had to be a misunderstanding. Things like this happened to strangers on the evening news. Unexplained disappearances and deaths happened in Harrisburg or Philadelphia, not in peaceful Stone Mill. It was ridiculous for the police to even consider that Uncle Aaron might be involved. He was Amish. He'd had the centuries-old canon of nonviolence bred into his blood and bones.

Rachel tugged open the carriage shed doors and entered the semidarkness of the stone outbuilding to climb into her Jeep. In the driveway, she circled the house and braked long enough for Mary Aaron to lift her scooter into the back and climb in beside her.

"Seat belt," Rachel reminded automatically. Amish buggies didn't require seat belts, and whenever she transported one of the Plain folk, she had to remind them about safety.

"Could you get my scarf?" Rachel nodded and motioned toward the glove compartment.

Mary Aaron opened it, pulled out a crumpled men's bandana, and attempted to smooth out the wrinkles.

At a four-way stop, Rachel took a moment to cover her head with the bandana and knot it at the nape of her neck. "You're certain Willy's dead?" She slid the car into first gear and went through the intersection. "He didn't just fall and hit his head or something?"

"If he did, he fell into his own grave and then revived just long enough to cover himself up. Someone working for the power company found him." Mary Aaron grimaced. "No, he's dead all right. *Dat* said it looked like someone bashed in his head."

"He was murdered?" Rachel whispered.

"*Ya.* Willy O'Day was murdered. Right there on our farm. And the way the police are acting, they think *Dat* did it."

Rachel didn't know what to say . . . so she said nothing. The blacktop narrowed and snaked downhill toward the rich bottomland where the Hostetler farm lay. She pointed. "Behind the seat. Would you get my skirt and blouse?"

Rachel wasn't Amish anymore, and everyone knew it. Her leaving the faith was a disgrace that her family lived with every day. She was an Englisher to the Amish, but still, if she expected to be welcome among them, she couldn't show up at her uncle's place in jeans and a T-shirt. And if she wanted any of her family to speak to her, she had to wear a head covering. The modest shirt and calf-length denim skirt was a hard-won compromise, but the best deal she could make.

"What if they've arrested *Dat?*" Mary Aaron held the clothing on her lap so it wouldn't blow out of the Jeep.

"They won't," Rachel replied, but the words felt awkward. "So what if Willy's body is on your property? That doesn't mean your father killed him."

"*Dat* threatened him." Mary Aaron chewed nervously at a ragged thumbnail. " 'If you ever set foot on my farm again, Willy, you'll be sorry.' That's what he said." She hesitated. "At least that's what everyone says he said. I wasn't there."

Rachel glanced at her cousin, then back at the road. "People say things all the time that they don't mean."

Her uncle was known to be taciturn, even gruff, but never violent—at least not to humans or animals. But he had a reputation. He'd once gotten so angry with his windmill when it kept breaking down that he'd hacked at the supports with an ax until the whole thing crashed into the garden. And then there was the incident with the grape arbor when he'd taken the same ax to it in front of a group of women who had gathered at his farm to quilt.

"He wouldn't hurt anyone," Rachel continued. "He couldn't even put his own driving horse down when it broke its leg."

"That's different. *Dat* likes horses. It's people he has problems with. Especially English people."

Uncle Aaron had never been mean to Rachel when she was a child; he hadn't been exactly warm and friendly, either. Since Rachel's return to Stone Mill, however, he'd barely been civil. The Hostetlers had always been sticklers for following the *Ordnung*—the rules—and Rachel had broken the rules. All of them. Her father's people, the Masts, were equally devout, but much more easygoing in gray areas, such as runaway children and dealings with the English.

Rachel and Mary Aaron rounded a sharp curve in the Jeep and climbed a hill to an intersection. It was blocked by a police cruiser. A state trooper stood in the middle of the road and held up one hand. Rachel pulled her Jeep alongside him. "This is Mary Hostetler," she said. "She lives on the Aaron Hostetler farm just ahead."

"The road is closed to all traffic," the officer deadpanned.

"But how do I get home?" Mary Aaron looked like she was fighting tears. "My mother needs me."

"Sorry. No exceptions."

"Can we park and walk in?" Rachel asked. She knew several of the local policemen, but she didn't recognize this trooper.

"Sorry." He waved his hand, indicating she could make a left or a right. "You'll have to move along."

"All right, Officer." Rachel turned down the one-lane road to the left. Once they had gone a quarter mile and were out of sight of the policeman, she turned onto an old logging road.

"The bridge?" Mary Aaron asked.

Rachel nodded. She drove a short distance, far enough so that the trees blocked sight of her Jeep from the road, and stopped. Climbing out, she hastily stepped into the denim skirt. It fell halfway between her ankles and knees. Next, she donned the blue blouse over her T-shirt. "Will I pass?" she asked her cousin in Pennsylvania Deitsch.

Mary Aaron shrugged. "Not as Amish, but you're Plain enough."

Definitely not a compliment, in Rachel's eyes. But Plain was good where she was headed. She tucked the Jeep key into a hidden zipper pocket of her skirt and set off through the woods. She could tell by the crunch of leaves and undergrowth that Mary Aaron was following.

It wasn't far to the river. It was deep, rocky, and, because it was spring, fast-running. No chance of wading across it today—too much water. But downstream were the remnants of an old covered bridge. There were missing floorboards, and it was too rickety for even a horse and wagon, but the stone foundation had survived two hundred years of spring floods. Rachel had crossed it dozens of times as a child, and she was certain they could safely cross it now. Old stand timber grew thick on the far side. The nearest land was Mast property, but just beyond that parcel lay the boundaries of Uncle Aaron's farm.

"So tell me again how Willy was found," Rachel said.

"Someone found him in the pasture. Someone working for the power company. I guess they were checking something on the highline that cuts across our property," Mary Aaron explained.

Rachel pushed through a blackberry bush and stopped to extricate her skirt from the briars. "And they're certain it's Willy?"

"It must be. One of the firemen said it's him. It's awful: fire trucks, police cars, and ambulances. *Mam* didn't know whether to stay with *Dat* or run and hide. You know how shy she gets around Englishers—strangers, anyway."

"*Ya,*" Rachel agreed. At home or at church, her Aunt Hannah would chatter like a blue jay, but when she came to town, she rarely spoke, except in brief sentences, gaze cast downward. Even at Wagler's Grocery, where she shopped twice a month, she pointed at what she wanted in the deli case and one of the clerks just gave her a pound. No matter what she bought—bacon, scrapple, cheddar cheese—she got a pound.

"Rae-Rae, have you crossed here lately?" Mary Aaron asked, hesitation in her voice.

Mary Aaron's use of Rachel's nickname made her look ahead, through the trees. What she saw made her stomach pitch. The bridge had not fared well over the last few winters. The roof was gone, the sides were rotten and gaping, and there was a stretch of beam running out to the first stone piling without any flooring or walls at all. It took a minute to assess the situation and choose the best path across. "You game?" she asked her cousin.

"If you are."

Moments later, they stood at the river's edge. It had rained heavily earlier in the week, and white water foamed around granite boulders protruding from the river. Rachel swallowed, glanced down at the raging force, and sucked in a deep breath. "It looks like it will just be a matter of moving from beam to beam," she said, raising her voice to be heard above the rush of the water. "If the worst happens, we swim."

Mary Aaron stared at the rush of water and gulped. The first beam was broken. They'd have to jump down onto the rocks, then up to the next beam. "It would be awful cold."

"It would be." Rachel took a leaping step, landed on a slippery rock and turned back to her cousin. "So I guess we'd better not fall in."

Ten minutes later, Rachel and Mary Aaron—somewhat worse for wear—climbed a stile over a stone wall onto Uncle Aaron's south pasture and were immediately engulfed by a wave of small Hostetlers, Masts, Beilers, and Bontraegers, accompanied by several dogs. The Zook twins were leading the pack—beating out Zebby Beiler on his black pony.

"No school today?" Rachel asked.

Mary Aaron shook her head. "Teacher had her wisdom teeth out."

The children—all Amish and ranging between six and fourteen years of age—swarmed around them, tugging at their hands and skirts and talking excitedly in Pennsylvania Deitsch. Rachel knew every one of them by name; they were nieces or nephews, cousins, second cousins, or neighbors.

"Rachel! Rachel!" her niece Susan cried. Susan was Rachel's oldest brother Paul's daughter; Paul and his family lived in a small house on the same property where he and Rachel had grown up. "The police have come! And an ambulance car!" Susan's blue eyes were as wide as a startled doe's; her dirt-smudged *kapp* was barely hanging onto the back of her head.

". . . Willy O'Day! Somebody cut off his head!" That was one of her Hostetler cousins, either Toby or Joel. It didn't matter. Both were given to exaggeration.

"They did not!" Sally, Rachel's youngest sibling, protested. At nine years old, she was as thin as a beanpole and always eager to take control of any situation. "You're such a liar, Toby!"

"They broke his head," another boy supplied eagerly.

"And buried him ten feet deep in *Dat*'s cow pasture." That

bit of information came from Mary Aaron's little brother Jesse.

"Hush, all of you," Mary Aaron chided. "You need to go home. You don't belong here."

"Listen to Mary Aaron," Rachel agreed. "This is no place for any of you. You should all go home." She eyed her nephew Naaman, who was Susan's brother. He was sweaty, and his red hair stood up in clumps. Somewhere in his mad dash, he had lost his straw hat. "And be sure you find his hat." Rachel motioned to his bare head. "Or all of you will be in hot water."

"Rachel, please," Mary Aaron urged. "We have to hurry."

Rachel released Susan's hand and strode after Mary Aaron. "They may not want us to get close to your father," she told her, catching up. "You might have to cause a distraction."

"What kind of distraction?"

"You'll think of something."

Rachel took a deep breath and began to jog up the hill beneath the electric power lines strung between highline towers. The highline didn't bring electricity to the Amish farms, but carried it over the mountains to the English towns and country beyond. It had been a bone of contention with the Plain people since the towers had been erected, decades ago, cutting through the cropland and forest. Mostly, the Amish tried to ignore the ugly structures, but today, that was impossible.

At the crest of the hill, Rachel stopped to catch her breath. Below, she spotted two ambulances, three police cars, and a fire truck—why the emergency responders would need a fire truck for a dead man in a pasture, she couldn't imagine. When she glanced back over her shoulder, Rachel saw that the Zook twins, the boy on the pony, and one of the older girls were still running after them, but she doubted if a few more onlookers would make any difference.

Half the inhabitants of the valley already seemed to be there ahead of them. Ahead, besides the emergency vehicles, Rachel saw two buggies, a wagon stacked with bales of straw, a half-dozen horses and a mule, and a collection of pickup trucks and cars. One, an older model Buick, bore the words *The George—Fiction & Nonfiction Bookseller* on one of the doors.

Rachel pressed her hand to her side to ease the stitch. *Poor George.* A wave of compassion for one of Stone Mill's all-time finest educators made her blink back tears. Sixty-seven-year-old George O'Day had been devastated by his twin brother's disappearance, but he'd never given up expecting Willy to walk through the doors of The George. Finally learning that Willy wasn't coming home, that he was dead, would be terrible for him.

After a moment's rest, Rachel and Mary Aaron walked down into the valley to mingle with the crowd of Amish and English gathered outside the ominous *CRIME SCENE* tape that ringed what was obviously the spot where Willy's body had been discovered. They were only ten feet or so from the fence line that divided the Hostetler property from a piece owned by the O'Day brothers.

Rachel caught sight of her father and her brother Paul talking to Aunt Hannah. Hannah's eyes were red and puffy, her nose red, and her mouth quivering.

"Aunt Hannah." Rachel hurried over to them.

Mary Aaron moved to her mother's side and hugged her.

Rachel's father and brother both nodded to her. Rachel met her *dat*'s gaze, then looked away, afraid she might tear up. No words were necessary. *Your family needs you,* he was saying.

"Where's Uncle Aaron?" Rachel began, and then she saw him standing on the far side of the yellow tape barrier, surrounded by police.

"Bad, bad," her aunt muttered, and then, "Englishers. My poor, poor Aaron." She gripped Rachel's arm. "You must help him. You can talk to them Englishers, tell them that Aaron is a good man, not a killer."

"I'll do what I can," Rachel promised, giving her aunt's hand a squeeze.

Aunt Hannah slipped off her shawl and wrapped it around Rachel's shoulders. "So you look proper when you talk to them Englishers," she said.

"Thank you," Rachel murmured, looking for a way to get to her uncle without being stopped by the big officer standing directly in front of them.

From the corner of her eye, Rachel saw Bill Billingsly, editor of their hometown newspaper, holding up his iPhone. She knew very well what he was doing. She could just imagine the front page of Monday's paper. *LOCAL OLD ORDER AMISH FARMER ARRESTED ON MURDER ONE!* Bill was fond of theatrics, and more than once she'd caught him taking pictures of her Amish neighbors even though he knew very well it was against their beliefs.

"All the news that's fit to print," Bill liked to say to anyone who would listen. "And Amish faces sell papers." On any other day, she'd confront him and try to shame him into deleting the photos, but today, it was more important for her to get to Uncle Aaron before he said anything too incriminating.

"Rachel! What am I going to do?"

She looked up to see George O'Day stumble toward her. He was a man of average height and average weight, but he had the brightest, twinkling blue eyes. As always, he was wearing a ball cap over his full head of white hair that read *THE GEORGE.*

"George. I'm so sorry." Rachel took a step toward him and hugged him.

"Who would do such a thing?" he rasped, resting his head

on her shoulder for a moment. "Surely not Aaron Hostetler. I know he wouldn't . . . couldn't." He staggered back and covered his face with his hands. "I can't believe this has happened. I can't believe it."

It wasn't quite as unbelievable as George suggested, but Rachel would never say such a thing. As sweet as George O'Day was, and as many parents, kids, and fellow teachers and administrators had reason to love George, there were an equal number of people who had good reason to despise Willy.

George's twin brother had none of his common decency and little of his charity toward his fellow man. Rachel had often wondered how George and Willy's parents had hatched one son with a heart of gold and another with a heart of stone. While George had lived his life trying to help others, Willy's life's ambition had been to take advantage of them.

"They won't let me see him." George's lower lip quivered. He was in good health for his age, but today, he looked ten years older and fragile. "Maybe there's been some mistake. Maybe it isn't Willy. It could be an old Indian grave . . . couldn't it?"

A woman screamed, and Rachel looked up to see Hannah collapse into Mary Aaron's arms. Immediately, people surged forward, and the policeman holding the crowd back ducked under the tape to reach the fallen woman.

Realizing Mary Aaron had just presented the necessary diversion, Rachel dashed under the yellow crime scene tape. "Don't say another word!" she called to her Uncle Aaron, waving to him.

Her uncle looked up, startled.

"I'm coming!" Rachel bounded forward, and her foot sank into soft soil. She lost her balance, and before she had a chance to catch herself, she pitched forward onto her knees.

Looming just in front of her was a ditch—not a ditch, she realized, with horror. A grave.

Lying in the bottom of the hole was a man . . . or what had been a man. And it was Willy O'Day. There was no mistaking him. He was still wearing his *THE GEORGE* ball cap, and his signature three-carat diamond ring glittered obscenely on his skeleton finger.

Chapter 3

Light-headed, Rachel closed her eyes and fought to keep her stomach from going into full rebellion. When she opened her eyes a second later, Willy was still there at the bottom of the grave, and still just as unpleasantly dead.

"Hannah? Was ist los?" Uncle Aaron's voice boomed from a few yards away.

"Mr. Hostetler," a state trooper called. "Sir, come back."

"Mr. Hostetler!" came another male voice, this one more threatening.

Rachel snapped her head up in time to see her uncle dashing away from his interrogators. He ran past her, breaking through the yellow crime scene tape, and vanished into the crowd of Amish in aprons and black suspenders who were gathering around her fallen aunt.

Rachel was in the process of picking herself up out of the dirt when an authoritative voice boomed above her. "You can't be here! This is a crime scene. Have you lost your mind?" A strong hand closed around her upper arm and pulled her to her feet. "Didn't you see the yellow tape?"

Rachel looked up into a pair of steely-gray eyes framed in a chiseled and all-too-handsome male face. She took a step back.

Evan? Where had he come from? Despite her past—her possible future—with Evan, she became defensive. "That's my Uncle Aaron you guys are strong-arming," she said under her breath so the other police wouldn't hear. "You don't have a right to interrogate him like that. He has the same legal rights that everyone else in this country does."

"No one's trying to *take away his rights,* Rachel." Evan put an arm around her shoulder and guided her away from the edge of the pit. His wide shoulders looked even bulkier in the state trooper's uniform: light-gray shirt with black epaulets, black tie, dark-gray trousers, and the trademark campaign-style hat with the strap secured beneath his chin. He blocked her view of what was going on, but—from the shouted English commands and the explosion of Pennsylvania Deitsch—she could guess.

"And no one's being strong-armed." Evan released her. "We're only questioning—"

"Questioning?" She cut him off, meeting his gaze. "Or *questioning* questioning?"

Evan hesitated, looked away, then back at her. "This is serious, Rache."

She softened her tone. "You really think my Uncle Aaron murdered Willy and buried him on his *own* property? *Really?*"

The look on Evan's face told her there was no sense trying to reason with him right now. For one thing, seeing her in a long skirt and head covering always set him off. He just didn't understand where she was coming from. More importantly, he took his job as a law enforcement officer very seriously. It had taken him many years and many failed exams to reach the state police academy in Hershey. To Rachel, it meant Evan was better than most, but to him, it meant he would always have to prove himself.

"Evan, I'm here because Uncle Aaron needs an advocate. You know that. Everyone needs an advocate at times like this."

Evan hesitated, then gestured toward the commotion where she supposed her uncle must be. "You need to be on the other side of the tape. Not contaminating a crime scene." He lowered his voice again. "Rache, you nearly fell in on top of our unidentified victim. You could be arrested for interfering with police procedure."

"Unidentified?" Rachel exhaled and continued in a hushed whisper. "I just saw him. The dead man is Willy O'Day. You know it. I know it. Everyone here knows it." She frowned. "And who's going to arrest me, Evan? You?"

He had the decency to blush, and for just an instant, a hint of uncertainty clouded his gorgeous gray eyes. A muscle twitched along the left side of his jaw, and she caught a faint scent of the Cartier Pasha cologne she'd given him for his birthday—the cologne he'd complained was too expensive but which she knew he secretly really liked.

"I don't suppose it will make any difference if I tell you to stay out of this, will it?" Evan asked.

She shook her head. "No. Uncle Aaron is a hothead, but he's not a murderer. And he doesn't understand your world. He needs my help."

The two were silent for a moment, just standing there, him looking down at her with a stern look in his eyes. Then, Evan stepped aside, and she hurried to find Uncle Aaron. As she'd suspected, her peaceful relatives and neighbors were deliberately causing confusion for the investigators. The Amish were nonviolent, but that didn't mean they were always cooperative or easy for outsiders to deal with. Somehow, without offering a harsh word or raising a hand in protest, the group had managed to fend off five policemen long enough for Uncle Aaron to reach his wife's side. How long this delaying tactic would last before the officers' patience ran out and she was swallowed up in a mass arrest, Rachel wasn't sure.

"Excuse me," she said, inserting herself in front of a red-faced sergeant. "May I ask, who's in charge here?"

"Who are you?" the trooper demanded.

"Rachel Mast. I represent Aaron Hostetler, my uncle."

The policeman scowled as he took in her tattered attire, even more disreputable after her jaunt through the briar patch and near tumble into the grave. "Are you his attorney?" he demanded brusquely.

"No," she answered. "I'm not, but he has a right to an attorney. English is Uncle Aaron's second language. He doesn't understand the implications of what you're asking him. And he's not going to answer any more of your questions until he has legal representation."

"We asked Mr. Hostetler if he understood—"

Rachel shook her head, interrupting. "He doesn't. And—" She broke off as Uncle Aaron abruptly appeared at her shoulder.

"My wife is sick," he said, tugging at his straw hat. "No more questions. I'm taking her home." He switched to Pennsylvania Deitsch. "Your aunt's dizzy-headed. She should be in bed. All this"—he waved toward the place where they'd discovered Willy's body—"is too hard on her nerves."

The trooper cleared his throat, obviously feeling awkward that they were not conversing in English. "Mr. Hostetler, you can't leave. We have more questions for you."

Uncle Aaron turned hard eyes on him. "I want to take my wife home," he said.

"You can't leave," a second trooper insisted. "We're waiting on a detective." He looked to Rachel. "Can you make him understand that he can't leave a crime scene without police permission?"

Eli Rust, an Amish man in his late forties, pushed through the group. "I will take your Hannah home," he said to Aaron in English, ignoring the two state troopers standing beside his neighbor. "I have my wagon. Your Mary Aaron says she will ride with her mother."

Rachel looked at the two state troopers. "Are you arresting my uncle?"

One shifted his weight uncomfortably. "We . . . have more questions."

"He doesn't have to answer your questions without a lawyer present. If you have cause to arrest him, do it. Otherwise, we're going. Uncle?" Eli took her cue and led the way through the crowd toward his wagon.

Someone had already helped Aunt Hannah into the back, and Rachel could see she was lying on bales of straw. Mary Aaron was kneeling beside her mother.

Eli climbed up onto the seat and untied the reins. Without either man speaking, Aaron joined him on the other side of the wagon bench. Rachel grasped the side of the wagon and put her foot into one of the spokes. As she started to hoist herself up, Evan appeared behind her and caught her around the waist and lifted her up.

"This is a mistake, Rache, him leaving the scene," Evan said quietly. "It makes him look guilty."

As she landed in the wagon, she turned to him, keeping her voice down, too. "It's not right that they should be questioning him without the presence of an attorney. He could accidentally incriminate himself."

"It's the way it's done around here and you know it." Evan shook his head. "There's no way your uncle will hire a lawyer."

"You don't think so?" she shot back as Eli slapped the leathers over his team's backs and the wagon lurched forward. "We'll just see about that."

There wasn't a chance on God's green earth that Uncle Aaron was going to hire an attorney. Rachel closed her eyes for a moment, trying to figure out what she should do next.

"Drink this."

Rachel opened her eyes as Mary Aaron pushed a glass of cool water into her hand.

Aunt Hannah's kitchen was as spotless as ever. No one who wasn't Amish would believe that her aunt, aided by her oldest daughters, prepared three meals a day here for a family of fourteen—and often more, if there were visiting guests.

The counters were bare, the two stoves shiny, and the worn linoleum floor clean enough to eat off. In the center of a long, scarred trestle table stood an oversized, old-fashioned oil lamp. Another, smaller one rested on a mantel above the potbellied stove, and a third lamp was tucked onto a corner shelf on the far side of the propane-powered refrigerator.

Even by Old Order Amish standards, Aunt Hannah's kitchen was devoid of style and color. Her cooking utensils—tucked out of sight—were serviceable, old, and dented. Her chipped dishware was uncompromisingly white, and the bleached wisps of thin cloth that passed for curtains were so threadbare you could almost see through them. Compared to her own mother's domain, Rachel had once overheard her father remark that Hannah's kitchen was almost prideful in its Plainness.

Still, the shadowy kitchen was a cool retreat from the warm sun and the ordeal that Rachel had experienced that morning. Rachel took a long swallow of water and sighed. "Thanks."

Her cousin nodded, finished her own glass, and poured them each another from a tin pitcher. "Come on," Mary Aaron urged and led the way onto a side screened porch, where they both dropped into wicker chairs. "What did you think? *Mam* did a good job of pretending to take sick, didn't she?" she asked.

Rachel nodded. She'd guessed Aunt Hannah hadn't really fainted, but it was still a relief to see her bounce up and climb down out of Eli's wagon under her own steam when they reached the farmhouse. Aunt Hannah and Uncle Aaron were still out in the yard talking to Eli Rust.

"I know you told me to cause a commotion so you could get to *Dat,* but *Mam*'s more convincing. If I passed out, they'd all just step over me." Mary Aaron's mischievous grin faded. "You got him away from the police, but it's not over, is it?"

"I'm afraid it's not." Rachel shivered as she remembered

seeing Willy's body at the bottom of the grave. "Someone killed a man and buried him on your *dat*'s farm. Given Uncle Aaron's history with Willy, suspicion would naturally fall on him until the police have the opportunity to fully investigate."

Mary Aaron placed her empty glass on the floor beside her chair. "*Dat* didn't do it."

"I know that," Rachel assured her, "but we have to convince the authorities of that."

"You told Evan that he wouldn't speak with them without a lawyer, but you know very well he'll never agree to hire one. It's not our way."

Rachel grimaced. "I know. I just said that to get them to stop asking him questions. He should hire one, but I know he won't."

"Was Evan mad that you were there?" Mary Aaron wiped her sweaty face with the corner of her apron.

"He wasn't happy, but he—"

Raised voices from the yard cut through their conversation, and Rachel stopped in midsentence. Aunt Hannah was obviously upset with something one of the men had said or done. Rachel looked at Mary Aaron, and they both got up and went to the edge of the porch. Because of the lilac bushes that grew up around the house, they could see into the yard from where they stood without being immediately seen from outside.

"Mind your tongue," Eli said. "Do you want everyone to—"

Rachel couldn't hear the rest of what Eli said, but she could clearly see that he and Aunt Hannah were having words. Uncle Aaron was nowhere in sight.

Aunt Hannah had lowered her voice, but she shook her finger and stepped closer to Eli. Rachel couldn't imagine what they were arguing about; it wasn't like her aunt to disagree openly with a neighbor, especially a man. What had Eli said to make Aunt Hannah so angry? And where was Uncle Aaron?

"You don't suppose he thinks *Dat*'s guilty, do you?" Mary Aaron whispered, staring at the two of them, her eyes wide.

"If he did, he certainly didn't act like it on the ride back—not from the way he and Uncle Aaron were talking. The two of them were sitting in the front of the wagon, friendlier than I've ever seen them."

"*Dat*'s coming out of the barn," Mary Aaron said. "And I think Eli's leaving."

Rachel stood on tiptoes to peer through a break in the bushes. Eli was climbing back up onto the wagon seat. "I wonder what's going on," she said. Then her heart sank as movement in the distance caught her eye. Beyond the cow pasture, a car turned off the hard-top road onto Uncle Aaron's dirt driveway—a police cruiser.

Her cousin craned her neck to see. "You don't think they're coming for *Dat,* do you?"

Rachel watched as the white car with the gold-and-black keystone on the door slowly crawled toward them. "Maybe they're coming to say it's all a mistake, that Willy was involved with the mob and they offed him for cheating them in a Ponzi scheme."

"I don't know what that means," Mary Aaron said. "But I don't think that's what happened." She ducked down. "*Mam*'s coming into the house."

"Uncle Aaron, too." Rachel grabbed her cousin's hand, and they stepped away from the edge of the porch. "We're getting ahead of ourselves. It might be Evan coming to talk to me." She tried to sound confident, but she had the sinking feeling that whoever was in the police car, it wasn't going to be good news for her uncle. She tried to think fast. "I've got to talk to your *dat*. Right now."

Mary Aaron nodded, and they hurried back to the kitchen, where her aunt had grabbed a broom and was sweeping the already spotless floor. Uncle Aaron stood in the center of the room, stroking his whiskers and looking thoughtful.

"Uncle Aaron," Rachel asked, "could I please speak to you?" She glanced at her aunt. "Privately?"

Aunt Hannah sniffed loudly, propped the broom against the wall, and picked up the coffeepot. "This is just grounds," she said. "I'll make a fresh pot, if it suits you, Aaron."

"It does."

"Uncle Aaron?" Rachel repeated. She motioned toward the hall that led to the interior of the house.

"Strong, Hannah," he said. "I think we all need a strong cup of coffee."

Aunt Hannah pursed her mouth, took down a canister, and began to ladle tablespoons of coffee into the black coffeepot.

Rachel walked out of the kitchen toward the parlor, used only for visits from the bishop and church services. Mary Aaron followed. In a strict Amish home, a private conversation didn't mean an unchaperoned one between an unmarried *English* woman and a married man, even if that man was her uncle. Technically, Rachel didn't consider herself English, but like many situations in her life, it was complicated. She expected Mary Aaron to understand and come with them, and she did so without being asked.

All the windows were closed in the parlor, and the room smelled musty. It wasn't dirty; she doubted anyone could find a speck of dust in Aunt Hannah's house. But the parlor was warm and she felt a little claustrophobic. A lone fly buzzed overhead, and sweat beaded under Rachel's T-shirt and heavy blouse and trickled down her back. She waited for what seemed like a long time before her uncle joined them. *Hurry,* she wanted to shout. *The police are coming!* For once she was grateful that Uncle Aaron's lane was long and full of potholes.

"*Ya,*" he said. "What is it, Rachel? What is so important that you can't speak in front of your aunt?" He ignored Mary Aaron, who tried to make herself invisible and didn't utter a peep.

"This is a terrible thing that has happened to Willy," Rachel began.

"*Ya,* terrible."

"I know that you've been unhappy with me since I made the decision to leave—"

"Since you were a baby," he cut her off, "I have known you, Rachel Mast. Always, I tell your mother, that one is too headstrong for a girl." He pointed at her. "Trouble she will be, and as much as I hate to be right in this instance, it's true. You brought great shame to your parents and to your family when you chose to abandon the faith of your father, to live a fancy life among the English."

"Uncle Aaron—" she began, but he wouldn't let her speak.

"I know you have thought me too strict and too harsh, but it was to me your father came when you ran away like a thief in the night. Not speaking to your parents of your wayward thoughts, not trusting them to help guide you, but leaving a note and sneaking out of the house."

She tried again. "I know you don't understand why I had to leave, that you don't approve of my choice. But you must believe that right now I want only what's best for you and Aunt Hannah, for your children. You need my help, Uncle Aaron."

"You think I did such a thing?" he demanded gruffly. "That I could crush a man's head? What manner of monster do you think I am, Rachel Mast?"

"That's not what I'm saying," she protested. "I don't believe you had anything to do with his death, but what I'm trying to make you understand is that the police think you did. You have to have an attorney. That's how the world works. You need a lawyer to prove your innocence."

"This is God's world, and as His child, I will put my faith in Him. He will protect me, not some English lawyer. I am not speaking another word about this, not another word, child."

"This isn't a matter of faith; it's a matter of—"

Rachel was met with the unmistakable gesture of a single wagging index finger in her face. Her uncle looked sternly into her eyes, turned, and walked away, leaving her with . . . not another word.

Rachel followed him back into the kitchen to find her aunt opening the door to two state troopers, one she recognized as the sergeant whom she'd exchanged words with earlier. The second man, standing behind his superior, was Evan, his face a solemn mask. Rachel's heart rose in her throat.

"Aaron Hostetler?" the police sergeant demanded.

"*Ya,*" Aunt Hannah answered, bristling. "You know his face. Who else would it be in his house?"

"Aaron Hostetler," the trooper repeated. "You'll have to come with us."

Chapter 4

Rachel took a deep breath before she entered her mother's kitchen, letting her little sister Sally scoot in ahead of her. Rachel was torn. She needed to get back to Stone Mill House to see to her guests before Ada drove them all away, but she also had to deal with Uncle Aaron's crisis. There was no choice, really. Family had to come first.

Since Uncle Aaron refused to discuss Willy O'Day with her, the next best thing was to talk to her mother and father. *Mam* was Uncle Aaron's favorite sister and might know something of value in proving his innocence. Talking to her mother, however, wouldn't be easy because Rachel and her mother had been estranged since Rachel left the Amish community fifteen years ago.

Rachel swallowed, summoning her courage as she scanned the dining area of her former home. Her *dat* was already seated at the head of the table for the midday meal. Her two brothers, Danny and Levi, were on the bench closest to the wall. Two of Rachel's sisters were helping their mother bring food to the table.

When her mother saw her, she put down a bowl of applesauce, came to her, and hugged her tightly. But she didn't speak. She never spoke directly to Rachel, not since Rachel had left the faith fifteen years ago. The two stood for a moment, arms wrapped around each other, and then *Mam* let go of her and went back to setting the table.

"Daughter, sit." Her father's weathered face creased into a smile, and he motioned toward a smaller table beside the window that was reserved for her and any overflow of visiting children. "Break bread with us. It's good to have you here, even on such a sad day."

"Set another place, Lettie," *Mam* said.

Sixteen-year-old Lettie took down another plate from the old Welsh cupboard and grabbed a fork and knife from a drawer. She stepped around Amanda, fourteen and wide-eyed, and arranged the lovely plate with the rosebud pattern and the everyday silverware at the children's table.

"Thank you, no." Rachel shook her head. "I didn't mean to intrude on your meal. I just came to—"

"Sit." Her father's soft order left no room for discussion. "Whatever trouble has come to our family, we need strength to persevere. You especially. You're too thin. You need food, and your mother has cooked plenty."

Rachel washed her hands at the kitchen sink and winked at Lettie. Her sister grinned as Rachel took her place in the straight-backed chair that generations of heavy use had worn down to a child's height. Feeling foolish, Rachel had to stretch her long legs out under the table.

Sally exchanged glances with their father, and when he gave an almost imperceptible nod, she left her place at the family table and joined Rachel at the smaller one by the window. Sally didn't utter a peep, but her eyes—the exact hazel shade of Rachel's own—sparkled with mischief.

Mam and Rachel's siblings sat down, and everyone bowed their heads for silent grace. As soon as that was observed, her father complimented her mother on the chicken and dumplings. That was the signal for everyone to begin eating. Sally rose, took both her own and Rachel's plates, and filled them from the food still on the counter and stove.

Rachel's position in her family and in the Amish community was complicated. If she'd been baptized into the faith and then left for the English world, she would have been publicly shunned. No members of the church or their children would have been permitted to speak with her or share meals with her. Shunning wasn't meant as punishment, but as a time-honored method of bringing the lost sheep back into the fold.

Rachel, however, had left home before she'd made a commitment to the Amish faith. In some families—because she hadn't been baptized—she was welcome at the family table, at weddings, funerals, and other gatherings. Most of her relatives accepted her as a stray lamb, but not entirely lost from the fold. It was only here in her mother's kitchen that she was isolated from the adult family. It wasn't her father's wish, and he obviously didn't approve, but the kitchen was traditionally the woman's domain. It was Esther's choice to have their daughter sit at the *lower* table, and so she did.

There was little discussion during the meal to suggest that today was any different from any other weekday. Dinner was a time for eating and sharing general conversation, such as the promise of rain or the birth of a neighbor's new colt. Exchanges between adults might touch on last Sunday's sermon or a planned school auction, but the fact that a citizen of Stone Mill had been murdered and buried in *Mam*'s brother's cow pasture would definitely be ignored. Young children were expected to remain quiet at the table, and Lettie, who might have been considered old enough to have an opinion, sensed that with the tension in the room, she'd be better off paying attention to the chicken and dumplings on her plate.

Sally remained silent, but the sparkle in her eyes and her delighted expressions spoke volumes. Auburn-haired Sally was clever, spirited, and devoted to her oldest sister. Little Sally, Rachel feared, was somewhat of a rebel and bound to clash with their mother when she grew into her teens. If any of her siblings followed her out of the Amish fold, it would probably be Sally.

"Pass her the biscuits," *Mam* directed Amanda. "And the butter dish."

Rachel checked herself from saying *thank you* and nodded. Her *dat* had adopted the Englisher habit of this small and sometimes meaningless courtesy, but her Hostetler-born mother considered the practice *fancy*. Kindness and generosity were expected, and to mention what was a given was prideful, not Plain, behavior. Thus, Rachel and all her brothers and sisters had grown up saying *thank you* and *please* to the Masts and Englishers and omitting the same to the Hostetlers. As for the other Old Order Amish families in the valley, *you had to know the rules to play the game*.

"The dumplings are fantastic, *Mam,*" Rachel declared. Just because her mother wouldn't speak to her didn't mean Rachel couldn't speak to her mother. "Better than usual, and yours are always the best."

"Tell her that I used the same recipe I've always used, the one I learned from my mother." She gave Lettie a *look,* and Lettie dutifully repeated their mother's statement.

"No . . . something's different," Rachel insisted. "The chicken just falls off the bone. Must have been a young fryer rather than an old hen."

"I think the dumplings are especially good, too," her *dat* put in. Her *mam* didn't comment, but Rachel was sure that she saw a look of pleasure in her mother's eyes. "And the biscuits are *gut,* too," he added, patting his stomach. "I think our Amanda made those."

"I did, *Dat.*" Amanda's chubby, freckled cheeks warmed to a rosy red. "But Lettie helped," she quickly added. She glanced at their mother. "Too much salt, though. I think."

"Practice," her *mam* said. "Make them another twenty years, and then you can expect to get it right. It took me that long to make them like my mother."

Rachel looked at Sally, who stuffed another mouthful of mashed potatoes into her mouth to keep from giggling, and then nearly choked on them. It went without saying that Amanda, the most dutiful of all the Mast children, would never claim credit for any task well done, for fear of appearing *proud*. Lettie always said that Amanda would make a perfect wife for a bishop, and Rachel didn't doubt it one bit.

After the apple pie and tall glasses of fresh milk, Rachel's *mam* and *dat* retired to the parlor while the girls cleared away the dishes and began to wash up. Normally, Rachel would have pitched in, and once her mother was out of the kitchen, no one would have minded. But today, she needed to talk to her parents, so she followed them into the family parlor.

The sliding double doors, which opened up the parlor and adjoining formal sitting room to make a large single space for church services, were open wide. Rachel entered the front parlor and slid the doors closed to keep the children from hearing. She hadn't been in this part of the house she'd grown up in for months. It was exactly as she remembered, as it had been for years.

She felt a twinge of nostalgia as she glanced around the familiar area. Everything was the same as it had always been: the navy-blue sofa and matching chairs, benches along two walls, a small, vintage oak table with turned legs, and a bookcase containing more than a dozen large Bibles of varying ages. The walls were white plaster, and the only decorations in the room were her parent's marriage certificate and a family tree done in cross-stitch hanging between the two windows.

Dat had taken off his work shoes and put his feet up on a stool. He settled back with the latest copy of *The Budget,* the weekly Amish and Mennonite newspaper published in Ohio. Her mother had taken a rocker by the window and pulled her mending into her lap. Her *mam* pretended not to notice her presence, but her father's eyes lit with curiosity when Rachel entered the parlor and closed the doors behind her.

She didn't keep him in suspense. "What are we going to do about Uncle Aaron?"

"Pray for him. Samuel," her *mam* added hastily, "I think you should ask the bishop to hold a special prayer meeting."

"Prayer is always good," Rachel responded, "but Uncle Aaron really needs an attorney. I'd be willing to contact one on his behalf, but I may not be able to cover the entire fee. It could run into tens of thousands. Do you think that his legal defense is something the community would be willing to contribute to?"

Dat's brow furrowed as he gave the question consideration. "I can't speak for others. For me, *ya*, I would give money."

Mam drove a needle into a boy's worn blue shirt. The garment was small and probably belonged to Levi. "Tell your daughter that she well knows her uncle would never accept such a thing. He is innocent. What need does an innocent man have of Englisher lawyers?"

"It's not that simple." Rachel perched on the end of the sofa. "They could take Uncle Aaron to prison. He'd be locked up with all sorts of ungodly people, some of them hardened criminals. Anything could happen to him there. We have to convince him that he has to defend himself against this charge."

"Tell *her* that Aaron is in God's hands, Samuel," her *mam* said, not taking her eyes off her neat, even stitches. "It's what we believe. It's what she believed once."

Rachel considered her mother's words. "Maybe God wants us to help ourselves. In the eyes of the legal system, saying nothing might mean that he's guilty."

"Do you think your uncle could be guilty of murder?" her father asked. He folded the paper and laid it across his lap.

"No, of course not. But *someone* is."

"Not Amish," *Mam* put in. "Tell her that it wasn't Amish who would do such a dreadful thing. We are peaceful people."

"Your mother says . . ."

Rachel nodded. "*Ya,* and I agree with her." She looked at *Mam,* then back at her *dat.* "When have any of our people been violent? Violence resulting in a person's death," she corrected herself, thinking of an Amish domestic abuse case Evan had told her about a few months ago. But as terrible and unusual as that was, it hadn't happened in Stone Mill, and it hadn't resulted in serious injury, let alone a death.

Rachel looked at her mother. "Did he say anything to you? Uncle Aaron? I know that he and Willy didn't like each other."

"Samuel, that is true." As usual, her mother refused to address her directly. "My brother didn't like Willy O'Day, but with good reason. Did you know that Willy shot Aaron's sheepdog, the black-and-white one?"

Her father sighed. "I am not yet so forgetful, Esther. I helped Aaron bury the dog. I know they argued about it at the auction. Willy laid hands on your brother and pushed him up against the wall."

"It was a good dog," her mother said. She looked up from the mending. "Ask her if she knows about the cows. Aaron's cows. They got through the fence onto Willy's property." She knotted the thread, bit it off close to the cloth, and searched for the matching spool of thread in her sewing box.

"Twice, I think," her father said. "Got out. There's that pond on the O'Day acreage. I think Willy meant to sell it as a farmette, for an Englisher. It's not big, five acres maybe, but level ground, *gut* for a house." He shrugged. "It seems Aaron's cows left footprints on the bank." He looked at Rachel and chuckled. "More than tracks. Patties. Lots of patties."

"I heard about that," Rachel said. "Willy's brother, George, mentioned it once when I was in the bookstore. Apparently, Willy met some prospective clients out at the property, and they weren't pleased to find"—she chuckled—"*evidence* that the cows had been there. I think George said that the client stepped in a pile. And when they got back into their car, some got on their mats."

"So much fuss over a little cow pie." *Mam* held up the shirt, found a seam that had come unraveled, and began to stitch the sides together. "But you tell her that an argument over stray cows is a long way from killing someone."

"Do you know how they discovered the body?" Rachel asked. "The kids said it was someone from—"

"Does it matter, Samuel?" Her mother's voice was brusque. "I don't wish to talk about such an awful thing. We should be praying for Aaron, not taking pleasure from idle gossip about such an awful act."

"I don't know who it was who found the . . . the grave," her father said, "but your brother Danny said that a groundhog had dug a hole into the . . . depression. I don't know any more." He shook his head. "It's a bad business. Everybody wondered why Willy O'Day had run off without saying a word to his brother about where he was going. But nobody thought he was dead." He glanced at his wife, then back at his daughter.

Her father's expression told Rachel that they'd probably discussed the matter long enough, for now at least. She made the excuse of getting back to her guests at Stone Mill House, said her good-byes to her family, and left.

She'd walked over from Uncle Aaron's farm, where Mary Aaron had remained with her family. The Jeep was still on the other side of the river, and she didn't want to push her luck by attempting to cross the dilapidated bridge again. She'd just walk the long way back to the Jeep.

She'd reached the end of the lane and started along the road when a police car approached. It slowed, then stopped. It was Evan.

"Where are you going?" he asked, rolling down his window.

"Home."

"On foot?"

"I couldn't get to Uncle Aaron's in the Jeep. The cops had closed the road. I left it on the far side of the river."

He pushed up his sunglasses and peered at her, his face stern. "How did you get through the roadblock?"

"You don't want to know."

Evan grimaced. "Get in the car. This road's still closed to traffic, but I'll get you through and back to your vehicle. That was a crazy stunt you pulled, you know. The *distraction*. You could have gotten yourself arrested for interfering in an investigation."

Rachel pulled the handkerchief off her head, balled it up, and stuck it into her skirt pocket. "Won't you get into trouble for having a civilian in your vehicle?"

"Will you just get in, please?"

She did as she was told, sliding onto the seat and snapping the seat belt in place. "He needed someone," she said softly. "He doesn't understand."

"Your uncle will be given a fair trial like any other citizen. If he can't afford an attorney—"

"One will be provided for him," she finished. Then she turned to him. "Do they really think Uncle Aaron—"

"I can't discuss this with you, Rache. It's an open investigation."

"He's innocent. Uncle Aaron could never do anything like that." She looked straight ahead. "I remember that Willy's truck was found in town, parked near the post office."

It had been easy to find; Willy was the only one in town who drove a twenty-five-year-old Ford F-150. Two-tone. The body was blue, one door red. He'd never bothered to have it repainted after being involved in a fender bender years before.

She glanced at Evan. "Anyone have any idea how the truck ended up in town and Willy in a cow pasture?"

He shook his head. "No idea. The truck was on the street, unlocked, but the keys were missing. It was impounded, looked over, and released. George came and got it—had a spare key, I imagine. He still drives it once in a while. There was no evidence of foul play. The only thing they found unusual was a big ham in a cardboard box in the bed of the pickup."

She frowned. "A ham?"

"A ham. Like ten pounds." Evan pushed down his visor and drove west. "You know," he said after a few minutes of silence, "if your uncle's innocent, he has nothing to worry about."

"And now you're the innocent, Evan. You know better." She rubbed her eyes. "I don't even know where they've taken him. He may be on his way to prison as we speak."

"He's at the station. He'll be held and questioned there."

"I have to talk to him."

"They're not going to let you do that."

"But that's not fair. English isn't even his primary language."

"Your Uncle Aaron speaks English very well."

"But he doesn't understand what's happening, or what he might be agreeing to. If his first language were Korean or Greek, they'd allow him an interpreter, wouldn't they?"

"And that would be you?" Evan lowered his sunglasses. "Sit there and don't say a word," he said firmly as he approached a roadblock. "Nada."

Rachel held her tongue and kept her eyes averted as Evan stopped the police car, got out, and spoke to the trooper at the barrier. There were a few back-and-forth exchanges, and then the other trooper stepped aside and waved them through.

"Thanks," she said as Evan got back into the car.

"So where's your Jeep?"

She told him, and she was pretty certain he swore under his breath. "You crossed the old bridge, didn't you? With the water still this high. If you'd fallen in, no one would have known until it was too late, Rache."

"Mary Aaron was with me," she admitted sheepishly. "She'd have fished me out."

"So you endangered her life, too?"

She decided to take that as a rhetorical question and was silent until he pulled up beside her Jeep.

He didn't speak until she got out of the cruiser. "You're probably right about Aaron Hostetler needing an interpreter. I'll see what I can do about getting you in to see him."

She broke into a smile, walked around the car, leaned in, and kissed his cleanly shaven cheek. "Thank you. I'll see you at the station?"

He stared straight ahead. "See you there. But do me a favor?"

"Sure."

He glanced at her long skirt and properly Plain shirt. "Change out of that getup."

Chapter 5

An hour later, Evan was standing in the parking lot of the local state police station as Rachel wheeled her Jeep into the area reserved for visitors. She forced a smile. What was she going to do? Uncle Aaron couldn't be forced to give incriminating evidence against himself, but how could she make him understand that by not cooperating with the police he appeared guilty?

"They didn't buy the 'he needs a translator' strategy," Evan said as he stepped closer. "Half the men out of this station have Amish or Mennonite relatives, and they all speak a little Pennsylvania Dutch."

"Deitsch," she corrected automatically. It wasn't Dutch at all, as many Englishers believed, but a form of German. "It's more complicated than the language; he isn't of your world."

Evan placed a hand on the hood of her Jeep. "I did what I could, Rache. I called in a favor and got you five minutes with him. It's the best I could manage. If I were you, I'd use the time wisely. Find a way to convince him to accept legal counsel." His normally pleasant features were drawn into a grim expression. He stepped back and motioned for her to pull into one of the vacant parking spaces.

"We can go in by the side door," he said. "I've asked the sergeant to have your uncle brought to the conference room rather than the interrogation room." He raised a dark brow. "I'll be right outside the door."

Rachel got out of her Jeep. She'd traded her unconventional skirt and kerchief for a designer-knockoff gray tweed business suit with a pencil skirt, jacket, and black silk shirt. It was a little dowdy, left over from her corporate days, but it was modest enough not to offend her uncle.

An odor of cedar closet clung to the wool, courtesy of her attic storage. However, she'd known better than to try to cover the scent and anger Uncle Aaron by radiating Marc Jacobs Lola. The use of perfume was definitely a worldly practice, and not one of which he would approve.

Evan pushed a button that looked like a doorbell, and someone unlocked the door from the inside. Rachel and Evan entered a short hallway. The interior of the station reflected the economic depression of the area: 1970s wood-grain paneling, faded green tile, and old fluorescent light fixtures.

"In here." Evan waved her into a windowless room containing a table and four chairs. A corkboard took up most of one wall, and on the opposing one hung framed photographs of uniformed troopers and a wall clock. The room smelled of floor wax and . . . corn chips.

"You all could use an interior decorator," Rachel quipped, in an effort to lighten the atmosphere.

Evan didn't even crack a smile. "Have a seat."

She nodded. On the scarred table lay a yellow lined tablet.

"Mr. Hostetler will be here in a few minutes," Evan advised. "He's still being questioned."

"Has he been arrested?"

"Not yet, but it doesn't look good. He can only help himself by—"

"Cooperating with the investigation," she finished. "I know." Neither of them voiced the unthinkable: *unless Uncle Aaron* did *murder Willy O'Day.* She knew that wasn't possible, but her heart was beating quicker than it should have. She took a seat on the side of the table farthest from the door.

"Five minutes," Evan reminded her before he left the room.

Rachel waited. Twice she tensed at the sound of heavy footsteps in the hall, but both times the source passed the room, and she heard the click of the outer doorway.

Come on, come on, she thought. *What's taking so long?* The room felt overly warm, and she tugged at the neckline of her blouse. She was glad she'd remembered to put on more deodorant.

To pass the time, she removed a pen from her bag and began to doodle on the top sheet of the yellow pad. She still had no idea what she would say to Uncle Aaron. She wondered why the authorities were rushing to point the finger at him simply because the body was found on his property.

Willy's disappearance the previous fall had caused quite a stir in the community. It was definitely out of character for a man who had lived his whole life in the town and owned several businesses there. Dawn Clough, a waitress at Junior's Family Restaurant, out on the interstate, had gone missing the same weekend. There'd been some idle speculation that Dawn, who was spoken of as a "hot dish" by some, had run off with Willy.

Rachel doubted that. Dawn was a newcomer to the area who'd only worked at the restaurant a few months. The most reasonable explanation was that she'd gotten sick of her abusive boyfriend and gone back to Florida, where her kids lived with her mother.

Willy was a confirmed bachelor, and although he dated occasionally, his usual ladies of choice were plump, churchgoing, middle-aged widows with nice homes and solid bank accounts. Willy was infamous for being tight, and a waitress, especially one with all the curves of a cheap broom, could expect her tip in small change. Rachel couldn't see how any attraction between the struggling thirty-something waitress and the tightfisted entrepreneur would have developed. It had to be a simple coincidence that Dawn and Willy had vanished the same weekend.

Willard Calvin O'Day, Rachel scribbled across the top line of the blank sheet of paper. Other than his brother, George, no one in Stone Mill had loved Willy, and few admitted to being his friend. But she couldn't think of anyone who disliked Willy enough to do him bodily harm. It still seemed impossible that someone had killed him and buried him in a field. It was more than frightening . . . it was something out of a horror movie. And what about his truck? She remembered that it had been found in town, but she couldn't recall any other details. How had he gotten separated from it?

The door opened and Rachel looked up to see her Uncle Aaron standing on the threshold, framed by two troopers: Evan and an African-American female. Rachel was relieved that her uncle wasn't in handcuffs, but was dismayed by the demeanor of his escorts.

The woman, tall and solidly built, with a flawless caramel complexion, scanned the room. "I'll have to ask you for your bag," she said.

Rachel glanced at Evan, and he nodded.

Rachel handed over her bag. Uncle Aaron stepped into the room, and the door closed behind him.

"Are you all right?" Rachel asked.

Her uncle folded his arms and stared at her. "Why wouldn't I be well? I was not sick when I left home."

"Sit down."

He looked at her.

"Please." She patted the table. "We only have five minutes."

He reluctantly took the chair across from her.

"What kinds of questions have they asked you?" She planted her hands on the table and leaned forward. "Why do they think you would know what happened to Willy?"

"What did I tell you?" he asked in the Deitsch dialect.

She stopped short. "I'm sorry?"

"Enough." He brought his weathered palm down on the table sharply, and she sat back in the chair. "No more." He was a big, square-framed man with a stern Old Testament face and a long, graying beard. She had known him all her life, and not once had he ever laid hands on her in anger, but he still intimidated her. "Did I not tell you that I would speak no more of this matter?"

She nodded.

"And have you ever known me to say that which I do not mean?"

"*Ne.*" She switched from English to the same dialect. "But you have to defend yourself against these charges. Otherwise, people will think you're guilty. You must let me find you an attorney."

"I never thought you a stupid girl, Rachel Mast. Foolish, but not stupid. Can it be that you are so lost to the world that you can no longer understand me? I will have no Englisher of the law to speak for me. I put my trust in God, and that is that. Now, think no more of me. Go home and pray for your salvation. Look to your soul, and allow me to look to mine."

"But Uncle Aaron . . . you can't do this. You have to give the police reason to believe that you're innocent."

Hooded eyes glared back at her with a fierce gleam. His hands clenched into fists on the table and his body stiffened. He did not utter another word.

Thirty seconds passed. Another.

A knock came at the door. "Rachel." It was Evan's voice. "You'll have to go now."

"Please consider what I've said," Rachel murmured, looking into her uncle's eyes. "For Aunt Hannah's sake. For your children and your community. If you don't know anything about Willy's death, you have to tell that to the police. But only with your attorney present. Don't say anything to anyone without an attorney present. Not even to Evan," she added in a whisper.

Evan walked in.

Her uncle scowled, but didn't answer Rachel. With a sinking heart, she left him, retrieved her bag from the female officer in the hall, and exited the station by the same side entrance.

In the short time that she'd been inside, the sky had clouded over. She hoped she'd get home before it rained. The road over the mountain was narrow and tree-lined. Leaves and pine needles made the surface slick, and too many drivers didn't heed the caution signs on the steep curves.

As Rachel reached her vehicle, Evan came out the door and walked over to her. "No luck?"

She shook her head. "I don't know what to do. If he's charged, will the court appoint counsel whether he wants it or not?"

Evan shrugged. "I'm not sure how that works. Him not wanting an attorney, but not wanting to represent himself, either."

"I know he didn't do it, but he thinks that it would indicate a lack of faith to accept an attorney. He's certain God will protect him and prove his innocence."

"Let's hope he's right."

Teatime at Stone Mill House was at three o'clock on Tuesdays, Thursdays, and Saturdays. Rachel pulled into the driveway at five. If any of her guests had been expecting her to be present for tea, they had been disappointed.

She'd left Ada in charge. Ada would have baked the scones, the miniature cheesecakes, and individual gingerbreads with a cherry on top. She would have made fresh coffee and hot tea and hand-squeezed lemonade. She would have closely supervised her kitchen assistant and grandniece Minnie. The sixteen-year-old's duties included putting together chicken salad sandwiches and ham on tiny cheese biscuits. But neither of them would have opened the dining room and welcomed the guests in.

Ada didn't serve. Ada cooked and directed the housecleaning staff. She purchased groceries and sent her nephews to find the freshest fruits and vegetables and the finest country-cured hams for Stone Mill House. What Ada *didn't* do was interact with the Englishers who came to stay at the B&B.

Ada went home at four sharp, no exceptions. When Rachel walked into the dining room, with its deep windowsills and heavy walnut sideboard, she found sandwiches, fruit, and sweets on the table. A teapot and French press stood ready for hot water. No one had touched anything, which meant her guests hadn't made it back to the inn. It happened often; guests certainly weren't required to attend tea. But usually, on weekdays, she checked with everyone. In all the confusion of the day, she'd forgotten. She picked up a miniature biscuit-and-ham sandwich and took a bite.

Grabbing a chicken salad triangle, Rachel pushed open the door to the hallway. The ham was delicious, and she was famished. She'd go back for another after she checked her answering machine. Then she'd start packing up the goodies. The sweets, fruit, and ham could be served the next day; she'd just have to eat the chicken salad. Or maybe take it over to Aunt Hannah's tomorrow.

"Rachel? Is that you, dear?"

"Hulda?" She ate the chicken salad sandwich in two bites.

The thin voice—that of her next-door neighbor Hulda Schenfeld—had come from the small parlor that Rachel used as an office.

Rachel walked into the parlor, licking her fingertips.

A smiling face, framed in white hair, peered up from a laptop on the desk. "Good, good. Glad it's you and not a burglar sneaking around the house. I think I've done this right." She pointed to the screen. "A wedding party. The mother of the bride called and said they would need seven doubles for the nights of the fourteenth through the sixteenth. Next month. Three nights. I told her that you would get back to her within the hour."

Rachel chuckled. "You're taking calls for me?"

"And who else? Certainly not your Ada or that silly little Minnie Stoltzfus. And the mother wants to know if there's a discount, seeing as how they're taking so many rooms. I told her there would be. I hope that's all right." She raised a sheet of paper. "I wrote her name and the phone number here. I'm not sure about these lap computers. I use a desktop. Six years old, but runs like a tomcat."

"Seven rooms?" Rachel shook her head. "I should mind? I should put you on the payroll."

"Rooms aren't paid for yet. She wanted to leave a credit card number, but I said, no, you would do that. I didn't want to make a mistake, not with someone's credit card. I'm not as sharp as I used to be."

Rachel took the paper. The name and number and other details were written clearly in beautiful penmanship. *I should be so sharp at ninety-three,* she thought. "You're a lifesaver, Hulda Schenfeld. Thank you."

"Hulda Schenfeld." She chuckled. "Still sounds funny. Kline was my maiden name. My father was Joseph Kline. Maybe you've heard of him? He was an old-time family doctor in Huntingdon."

"I *have* heard of him," Rachel said, not bothering to remind Hulda that she told the story often. She was a treasure. Rachel wondered, though, how it was that she'd been here to answer the office phone.

Almost as if she'd read her mind, Hulda continued. "I came hoping something would be left over from tea. The phone started ringing before I made it to the dining room. You have a single next weekend, a regular, a Miss Harper, and a couple for Friday, Saturday, and Sunday. I checked your calendar, saw you had plenty of rooms open, and confirmed both."

"That settles it. I am putting you on the payroll, payment is an open invitation to come to afternoon tea whenever you like, no charge. And I insist you take some of those ham-and-biscuit sandwiches and gingerbread home."

"I won't say no," Hulda replied with a chuckle. "Most fun I've had in days. If I weren't here interfering in your affairs, I'd be home ordering something off a shopping network. I got the most beautiful scarf Monday, silk. You can wear it five ways. It's multicolored. Goes with everything. You must come over and see it when it arrives." She rose and came spryly around the desk. She was a small woman, no more than four feet ten or eleven inches tall, wearing a pink-and-white jogging suit and tan Birkenstock sandals. Bishop strolled after her, long tail curled over his back.

"I wondered where you were," Rachel said.

"Curled up in my lap. Knows how I love cats. You know I have an Abyssinian. Thomas. A lovely creature, but very particular about his diet." Hulda stooped to stroke Bishop. "Oh, and you had visitors, dear. John Hannah and your sister Annie. I told them that you had gone to see what you could do to get your uncle out of that horrible prison."

"He isn't in *prison* yet," Rachel said. She sighed. If Hulda knew, then Willy O'Day's homecoming was already common knowledge. "He's at the state police station."

"Terrible tragedy," she said with a shake of her head. "How could they ever believe one of your people would do such a thing? A stranger did it, I'm sure. Murdered for the money in his pocket. Everyone knew Willy liked to collect his rents in cash on the first of the month. George told me that Willy would sometimes come home with several thousand dollars on him. Cash money." She made a clucking noise with her tongue. "I'll not be able to rest easy in my bed tonight, I can tell you that."

"I'm sure you'll be safe enough. You have your son and grandsons in the house. And your daughter-in-law." Hulda's grand old home next door provided ample living space for her extended family and a never-ending round of relatives.

"True, I have them there."

"See, you're well protected. And well loved by the whole community." Rachel led the way back through the hall into the dining room. "I'll make you a basket of goodies to take home." She opened the right-hand door on the sideboard to remove a basket just as the kitchen door popped open.

"Rachel." It was Mary Aaron. "I'm sorry I didn't get back in time to serve the tea. The house was in an uproar. What did you find out about *Dat?* Are they going to bring him home?"

Rachel motioned, and Mary Aaron came into the dining room. Mary Aaron greeted the older woman, who smiled and asked about her mother.

"Like you'd expect," Mary Aaron said. "Heartsick that anybody would think *Dat* could harm someone. Upset that anyone would think him foolish enough to bury him in his own cow pasture."

"Exactly," Mrs. Schenfeld agreed. "Just what I told Rachel. Some stranger, probably high on pills or maybe an escaped convict from that super-max prison in Waynesburg."

Rachel murmured something appropriate and finished making the basket of goodies for her neighbor. It would be easier to think that it was a stranger who'd murdered Willy, but if it was a stranger, how did he know that Willy regularly carried large sums of money? And if it *was* a robbery, why hadn't the perpetrator taken his diamond ring?

Once Hulda was on her way, Rachel turned to Mary Aaron and relayed what had happened at the police station, which was, basically, nothing. "Evan thinks that they will charge him with Willy's murder, but no one, including your *dat,* will say why."

"*Dat* could never do such a thing."

"I know that, and you know that. It's convincing the authorities that will be difficult, especially since your father refuses to even consider a lawyer and won't talk to the police or to me."

Mary Aaron grabbed two plates and followed Rachel to help put the food away. Her normally pink and rosy complexion was a pasty gray, and the worry showed in her eyes. "Will they let him come home? After they question him?"

"I don't know," she mused, giving Mary Aaron's shoulder a gentle squeeze.

Rachel felt an overwhelming sense of responsibility, not just to Mary Aaron and her father, but to the whole community. When she'd returned to Stone Mill two years ago, the town had been in decline. It had been *her* idea to make Stone Mill a destination for tourists and to advertise it on the Internet. It had been *her* idea to produce income with tourist dollars. *She* had been the one to encourage both Amish and Englishers to have market days, to build roadside stands to sell their organic fruits and vegetables, and offer wagon and buggy rides to visitors. Her family and neighbors had put their trust in her, and the town really did seem to be taking a turn for the better. But with that trust had come responsibility. One that she felt heavily on her shoulders today.

Chapter 6

The following morning, Ms. Hess and her sister checked out early. They refused the free breakfast, saying that they'd eat on the road. They did, however, ask that she open the gift shop so that Ms. Hess could look at Mary Aaron's "Diamond in the Square" crib quilt again. And Ms. Baird requested rooms for the coming weekend for the two of them.

"Are you certain the price isn't negotiable?" Ms. Hess asked as she fingered the quilt. "Everyone dickers at flea markets."

Rachel forced a smile, but before she could utter a suitable comeback, the sister filled the void.

"This is hardly a flea market, Tina, and this would be perfect for Sasha's baby. The blanket could be displayed on the family room wall near their stone fireplace. It will become a family heirloom in days to come."

Ms. Hess's red lips puckered, and she peered over the rim of her pink glasses. "Did you see this?" She tugged at the cloth tag with the price worked in cross-stitch. The previous day's tight yellow capris were nowhere in sight. Instead, she wore a pink-flowered, see-through top over the now-familiar tiger-striped bra, white shorts with *Hottie* spelled out in rhinestones on the back, and, of course, the four-inch wedges. Balanced on her arm was a high-end zebra-striped bag, presumably to match her bra.

Dealing with Ms. Hess this morning was almost comic relief after the previous day and the sleepless night Rachel had had. She'd wanted to go to her aunt's this morning, but she knew that the police must still be holding her uncle, as she hadn't heard otherwise from Evan. If she left Stone Mill House before seeing to her guests, Ada might make good on her threats and quit. And if Ada quit, Minnie and the other girls would go with her. Then where would she be? Without staff, that's where. Without altering her uncle's fate one iota.

"So leave the price on," Ms. Baird suggested to her sister. "Aunt Dot will be impressed. A pity you didn't snap a picture of the *Aim*-ish girl yesterday, the one she"—Ms. Baird pointed at Rachel—"said made it. It would have made the gift more special. You know, with the *Aim*-ish woman holding the blanket."

"Rachel!" Ada called from the kitchen. "Minnie's not here and . . ."

Rachel couldn't hear the rest of it, but she did see her one remaining guest, Father Young, coming down the stairs. "I think I just need to pop into the dining room for a moment," Rachel said to the two women. "Feel free to look around."

"No," Ms. Hess said. "We want to be in Lancaster for lunch. I'll take the blanket. You accept credit cards, don't you?"

Rachel motioned to the sign. "MasterCard and Visa."

"Not American Express? That's inconvenient," Ms. Hess grumbled, but she produced a suitable credit card.

By the time Rachel had rung up the quilt and wrapped it, Ms. Baird had picked out three jars of Ada's jam, a copper tray, an antique butter dish, and an original eight-by-ten watercolor of a one-room schoolhouse with a stream of children in the foreground. The figures were small and all painted from the back so that no faces were revealed.

"You want all of these?" Rachel asked, stunned. Apparently, she did. Ms. Baird paid in cash without a quibble over the prices.

Rachel waved as they hurried out the front door, overnight

cases in hand. She couldn't believe that she'd just sold Mary Aaron's quilt and a painting at the same time. Mary Aaron would be ecstatic about the quilt. This was her first big sale, and it made the months of work worthwhile, something a lot of the Amish hadn't expected.

"Use the sewing machine," Aunt Hannah had advised. "It's faster. The stitches are more even, and the Englishers won't know the difference. No one makes quilts the old way anymore."

But Mary Aaron did make it the old way, and it had paid off handsomely. And best of all, this sale might influence other women to emulate her. Even among the Amish, skills were being lost as the old people died. Maintaining centuries-old artistry was vital to their community and their faith. Few large families could survive on farming alone in these difficult economic times, and people all over the country were coming to appreciate Amish artistry. Women, married or unmarried, didn't have to choose between picking apples, working behind the counter at a fruit stand, or cleaning other people's houses. Thanks to the Stone Mill Heirloom Arts website, the possibilities for real alternatives were unlimited.

But Rachel didn't have time to savor this small success. Father Young would want his breakfast. With Minnie not there, Rachel would need to see to her guest personally. Ada cooked, but she didn't serve. And she spoke only Deitsch to the visitors, pretending that she didn't understand English. If she hadn't been such a miracle worker in the kitchen, Rachel might have rethought her decision to hire Ada in the first place.

Father Young was both pleasant and hungry. He drank most of a pot of coffee and devoured scones, strawberries, pancakes, eggs, toast, and bacon. Today, he'd planned a hike up Black Mountain onto state game lands, and he asked if it was possible to purchase a bag lunch. She assured him that it was no trouble, and no charge. It was the least she could do since he'd missed Ada's wonderful afternoon tea.

Rachel was just clearing away the breakfast dishes when her brother Levi walked into the kitchen from the back door. Rachel waved him into the dining room and told him to help himself to the breakfast goodies. Levi was always hungry, and although their mother was a good cook, her baked goods didn't come close to Ada's.

"Watch out," Levi warned between bites of almond scone. Rachel handed him a napkin, and he wiped the ring of milk off his mouth. "*Mam*'s set on sending the deacon around to try and convince you to give up this house and come home for good." Eleven years old, he was the dark-haired one of the brood, but he had the same color eyes as Rachel. He was a good-natured scamp, and she thought he might be the brightest of all her brothers.

"Aren't you supposed to be in school?" Rachel asked. "Does *Mam* know you're here?" Her mother disapproved of the younger children visiting Stone Mill House.

Rachel supposed her mother thought that she would try to lure them away from Amish ways with television cartoons and iPads. What *Mam* didn't know, and would probably dislike even more, was that Levi came to read. He'd just finished *Twenty Thousand Leagues Under the Sea,* and he was halfway through *Treasure Island*. One of the rooms upstairs had been a library, and she'd taken immense pleasure in filling the floor-to-ceiling shelves with secondhand volumes of classics that George O'Day acquired for her.

"No school this morning." Levi grinned. "Teacher's not feeling good from having her teeth pulled. I have to be there at eleven, and we won't get recess in the afternoon."

"And *Mam* didn't have chores for you?"

He shrugged. "She thought there was school. She went to Aunt Hannah's." He stuffed a strip of now-cold bacon into his mouth. "Did Uncle Aaron really kill Willy O'Day?"

"No, he didn't. How could you ask such a thing?"

"Jesse said they took his *dat* away and locked him in a

prison, just like the old martyrs. He said Uncle Aaron couldn't come home until he was a hundred years old."

"Jesse is wrong, too. I don't know what happened to Willy, but Uncle Aaron would never hurt anyone."

"Oh, and Jesse said to tell you that Mary Aaron can't come today. Her mother needs her. And . . . and . . ." He stuffed another slice of bacon in his mouth. "She's sorry." He stood up. "Can I go upstairs and read?"

She considered, knowing that she didn't have the heart to forbid him access to the books that she'd loved when she was his age—children's favorites that she would never have known existed if it hadn't been for kindly Mrs. Schenfeld. "For a little while, but listen for the clock on the landing. When it chimes ten thirty, you scoot." She reached out and brushed down his cowlick. "How did you get here? Did you come on your scooter-bike?"

Levi headed for the stairs. "Zebby Beiler's pony. I cut through the woods. I won't be late."

Once Levi was gone, Rachel stood for a moment gathering her thoughts and making a plan for the morning. Since neither Minnie nor Mary Aaron was coming today, she'd have to make up the guest rooms and do the laundry herself. She'd start with Father Young's room so that if he returned early and wanted an afternoon nap, she wouldn't have to disturb him.

She went to the kitchen to gather the cleaning supplies. Changing linen, vacuuming, and dusting three guest rooms were only a start to the day's housekeeping. There was the staircase, the landing, and the upstairs hall to sweep, the bathrooms to scrub. And while she was at it, she took the opportunity to air out the scatter rugs and replace the vase of flowers that stood in the downstairs entranceway. By the time she'd thrown the last load of sheets into the commercial washer in a laundry room, it was after two.

Did she have time to drive over to Aunt Hannah's? There was an electric bill to be paid, but she could do that online.

She needed to check her email to see if there were any more inquiries or, hopefully, reservations.

"Rachel!" Ada's voice called from the kitchen. "An Englisher to see you!" The last bit of information was yelled in Deitsch.

In the kitchen, she found Ada, barefoot, her back to the visitor, kneading dough on the butcher block island with all her might.

"Evan?" Rachel looked at Ada with her back to him and rolled her eyes. Ada had known Evan since he was no older than Levi, yet for the most part, she ignored him because he was English.

Evan wasn't wearing his uniform, which meant it wasn't an official visit, but his expression was grave. "Good news, I hope?" Her tone was one of false cheerfulness.

"Can we talk?"

"Sure." She opened the refrigerator and took out a pitcher of lemonade. She filled two tall glasses. "Listen for the dryer, would you, Ada? When it rings, take out the load and fold it, if you don't mind."

"Sun's out," Ada replied, again in Deitsch. "Why didn't you hang the towels out on the line?"

"Maybe next time," Rachel answered. She loved the smell of towels hung in the sunshine, too, but guests, she'd learned, preferred their towels fluffy and smelling of fabric softener.

She picked up the glasses and motioned to Evan to bring the pitcher. He held the door open for her, and they went out into the back and crossed the yard to the seating area under the grapevine arbor. It was one of her favorite spots around the house. She'd strung twinkle lights over the arbor and planted shrubs and flowers that attracted butterflies and hummingbirds.

Evan sat on the cushioned glider, and she handed him his lemonade and took a seat beside him. It never failed to amaze her how comfortable she was with him and how much they enjoyed each other's company. Sometimes, when weather permitted, they would sit out here in the evening and enjoy a glass of wine. It was too early in the afternoon to offer Evan wine, but she almost wished that it weren't.

"It is good news, isn't it?" she urged. "They've realized that they've made a mistake. They're going to let Uncle Aaron go home?"

"I just dropped him off at his farm," he said. "They haven't arrested him yet, but you've got to get over there, Rache. You've got to talk some sense into him."

Suddenly, she didn't want her lemonade. She felt as if the swing were falling and the ground were a long way off. "But if they let him go, surely—"

"Listen to me," he said quietly. It wasn't Evan's way to raise his voice. He was a gentle man. He'd been soft-spoken even when they were kids. He didn't talk a lot, but when he did, he commanded attention. "This is serious. Someone . . . I can't say who . . . told me that an arrest is imminent. And if he doesn't accept legal counsel—and post bail—he'll end up in county prison. I don't think I have to elaborate on what that would do to a man like Aaron."

She exhaled, thinking. "Do we . . . Do the police know how long Willy's body has . . . you know, been there?"

"ME's initial report will take another day or two, but the coroner who came for the body confirmed that it looked as if it had been there about eight months."

Rachel bit the inside of her lip. "Did anyone say why Uncle Aaron was going to be arrested? I mean, specifically."

He frowned. "No, but I have an idea it has something to do with the book they found on the body."

She glanced at him. "What book?"

"A notebook. A journal. Whatever you want to call it," he told her, obviously wrestling with whether or not he should say even that much.

She waited.

"Apparently, he kept track of things. Groceries to pick up. Phone calls to make. Whatever." He took a sip of lemonade.

"There was a page dated the day he disappeared. Across the top were the letters *A, T, B, R.*"

"*A, T, B, R,*" she repeated. "What does it mean?"

"We don't know. Not yet. I'm sure someone will ask George."

She swirled the ice in her glass, stared down at it. *This isn't happening.* In a few minutes, she would wake up and discover that it had all been a bad dream. But reason told her that she was refusing to face reality. "He's no killer. Uncle Aaron."

"That said, there was bad blood between him and Willy O'Day. The whole valley knows it. Everyone knows they argued at the auction a week before he disappeared. And the year before that, there was a disagreement over where the other's property line started and ended. I know that for a fact because I was called to calm them both down in the grocery store parking lot."

"Having an argument isn't proof of murder. They can't arrest someone for murder without proof." Her gaze met his. "There isn't proof, is there?"

"I've already said too much, Rache. I'm risking my career by discussing the case with you. It's unprofessional, to say the least." He stood up and placed his lemonade on the table beside the wooden glider. "If your uncle's innocent, why won't he cooperate? Why won't he answer our questions?"

It was a sunny May afternoon. The temperature was seventy degrees, but Rachel suddenly felt chilly. Goose bumps rose on her bare arms. "He doesn't understand. It's a matter of faith. The way Uncle Aaron sees it, he didn't do anything wrong. Denying it or accepting the help of a lawyer would be admitting to a lack of faith in God's plan."

"This could destroy his life."

She hugged herself. "Even if he's innocent? I thought you believed in our legal system—innocent until proven guilty."

"I do believe in it. You know I do. You know how long I wanted to be a cop, to do something positive with my life.

But you're not like the rest of your family. You know enough about the world to know that bad things happen to good people. Justice is blind, Rache. It doesn't make exceptions for Amish acts of faith. You need to convince him to accept help, or it may go very badly for him."

"I've tried. He wouldn't listen," she protested.

"Try harder."

"I don't know that I can do anything to change his mind. He doesn't trust me." She looked up at him. "To him, I'm a lost soul."

"That may be true, but he trusts you more than he trusts me." Evan placed a hand on her shoulder. "Maybe you could talk to your aunt. Get her to work on him. They have young children and a farm. What will happen to her and his family if he goes to jail?"

"Can you at least find out exactly what evidence they have against him?"

Evan shook his head. "I can't." He took a step back away from her. "I shouldn't even have come here." A muscle twitched on the side of his jaw. "But I had to. You might be his only chance."

"I'll go and try to talk some sense into him." She rose. "Into all of them. Of course, I'll go." She always thought of Evan as being a big man, but standing beside him, he wasn't all that much taller than she was. "It means a lot to me that you would care enough to come to me."

He nodded. "You're special to me, Rache," he admitted huskily. "You know that . . . Always have been."

"You, too," she answered.

As they gazed into each other's eyes, something passed between them. Something that suggested maybe it was time to take their relationship to the next level. Or to at least admit that there *was* a relationship, for starters. But this wasn't the place. It certainly wasn't the time. And they both knew it.

* * *

Half an hour later, Rachel stood outside her Uncle Aaron's enormous two-story stone barn with Mary Aaron and her Aunt Hannah. The double doors were open, and inside the center hallway, her uncle and Mary Aaron's brother John Hannah were putting the harness on a team of workhorses. Her cousin Elsie, nineteen, was sweeping the back step. Rachel saw none of the younger cousins and assumed that they hadn't gotten home from school yet. It seemed a normal workday, one that Rachel had witnessed hundreds of times before in her own childhood. But it wasn't.

"You just missed your *mam,*" Mary Aaron said. "She and Lettie left not ten minutes ago." She touched her *kapp* and looked at Rachel meaningfully.

Understanding the silent warning, Rachel adjusted her kerchief. It had slid backward, revealing more of her hair than was appropriate. "I didn't see the buggy."

"They walked across the fields. You know your mother," her aunt said. Aunt Hannah's eyes and nose were red, as if she'd been crying. She seemed agitated, which Rachel could certainly understand. Having a body discovered on her farm and having her husband questioned for the crime must have been terrible for her.

"It was good of Aunt Esther to come and stay with *Mam,*" Mary Aaron said. She glanced at her father and brother and then back to her mother. "*Mam*'s been beside herself."

"My nerves can't take much more, I can tell you." Aunt Hannah looked down at her everyday apron and brushed at the stains. "The bishop's wife came and prayed with us."

"She's a kind woman." Rachel glanced in the direction of the barn again. "I was hoping to talk to Uncle Aaron—"

"He doesn't want to see you." She shook her head for emphasis. "'Keep Rachel away from me,' he said. 'I've told her that I don't need her help, and I don't want any English lawyer speaking for me.'"

"But I just want to help," Rachel replied. She'd been afraid of this. Her uncle hadn't been happy that she'd come to the police station. They'd never been close, even before she left Stone Mill. And since her return, he'd openly expressed his disapproval that she'd not yet rediscovered her Amish faith.

"You don't believe this is over, do you?" Mary Aaron reached for her mother's hand. "*Mam,* isn't there anything you can say to make him listen to her? She knows way more about the English world than *Dat* does."

"If your father is innocent, the Lord will protect him."

"She doesn't doubt *Dat,*" Mary Aaron hurried to say. "We know he didn't do this terrible thing."

Rachel stood there for a moment, then turned away from them and walked to the barn door. She didn't need her aunt's permission to speak to her uncle. And she couldn't leave here without at least trying. "Uncle Aaron," she called, "it's Rachel."

"I know who it is. I heard that car of yours. Go away," her uncle called. "This is none of your affair."

"Please, just listen to me. I—"

"*Ne.* Enough. Best you leave before I say things that cannot be unsaid." He turned his back on her and strode deeper into the interior of the barn. John Hannah cast a sympathetic look in Rachel's direction, but his father called back. "John!"

He followed his father into the barn.

Her uncle's glance had carried such dark anger that she felt as though she'd been slapped. Stunned, she turned toward her aunt, but Hannah was already walking toward the house.

Mary Aaron came to her and put her arms around her. "You see how he is? How they both are? You have to help us, Rachel."

"If he won't help himself—"

"He won't," her cousin whispered. "You can see that. But we're your family. You have to do something."

The back of Rachel's eyelids stung. She wasn't a crier, but she wanted to weep now. She felt so hurt . . . so helpless. She looked into Mary Aaron's eyes. "If there was anything I could do, you know I would. But we have to trust that justice will prevail. This is a matter for the authorities."

"But you're smart. You know how the English world works. You could find the man who is truly guilty of this. If you learn who killed Willy, they'll let *Dat* go."

"Mary Aaron, I don't know the first thing about investigating a murder. That's a police detective's job."

"You're as smart as any policeman."

Rachel sucked in a ragged breath. Thought for a moment. "I guess I could ask a few questions."

"*Ya,* you can. And I'll help you. I'll talk to our people . . . the ones who don't want to talk to you. Together . . . we could do this." Mary Aaron's eyes were pleading. "Please, Rachel."

She found herself nodding. "I'll do what I can. It won't hurt to nose around a little because . . ."

"Because if *Dat* is innocent," Mary Aaron murmured, saying what they were both thinking, "the man who killed Willy is still out there, and he . . ."

"Might kill again," Rachel finished. She shivered. One murder in Stone Mill was terrible enough . . . but what if Willy's death wasn't the end of it? She knew every person in this valley. Who else might be in danger?

Chapter 7

It was a little before seven that evening when Rachel approached the main entrance to George O'Day's bookstore. She hadn't expected to find The George open, but she'd spoken to Hulda when she was pulling out of her driveway, and the elderly woman had assured her that George was at work.

"I can't blame him, poor man." Hulda made a clucking sound with her tongue as she shook her head. For her age, she had remarkably few lines in her face, and the expression in her faded blue eyes was as kind as ever. "What would he do? Rattling around in that big, empty house, just him and Sophie. Better he be with his books and his friends."

Stone Mill and the surrounding valley were small enough that most people here had known George for years. Many had been his students, and those who hadn't had relatives who had either worked with him or gone to the same high school where he taught for twenty-five years. Hulda was right, Rachel decided. Despite the shock and grief at losing his twin, being at the bookstore was probably the best choice for George.

Normally, Rachel would have walked. It wasn't that far to the intersecting streets that composed the downtown business section of Stone Mill, but she was taking George a big tray of Ada's raisin-cinnamon rolls, his favorite. So she'd taken the electric golf cart. Inside town limits and on private country lanes, she often used it to give her guests tours of the town. It made no noise and moved at about the same pace as a horse and buggy; Hulda and several other business owners had acquired carts for their own use.

The bookstore sat on the corner of Main and Poplar and had been constructed, originally, as an opera house in 1904. In the '30s, it became a theater, but fell into disrepair in the '70s and was closed. It was George who, after retiring from teaching, had repurposed it as a bookstore and opened the doors again three years earlier.

Rachel parked the golf cart in front of The George, picked up Ada's cinnamon rolls, and pushed through the brass-handled double doors. What had once been a refreshment area was now the checkout desk, commanded by George's right-hand girl, Ell. She glanced up from her computer, waved, and smiled.

"Hi, Ell," Rachel said, balancing the tray of cinnamon rolls in her right hand. "Is George here?"

The young woman with the head of short, spiky black hair motioned to the winding staircase on the right side of the reception area. "Upstairs, checking in a package of books just in from Dublin." Ell was just beyond her teens, with a long, thin face, dark eyes, and a pale complexion marred by acne scars. Her round Irish nose was adorned with a shiny piece of hardware, vying for attention with the multiple piercings in her eyebrows, lower lip, and ears. The voluminous black tunic, tights, and black lace-up leather boots didn't quite match her shy but eager-to-help nature.

"How is he?" Rachel asked.

Ell sighed. "About how you'd guess. Nobody expects death to come knocking. We all thought Willy had run off with Dawn . . . you know, that waitress." Ell spread her long, thin fingers. "Unless . . . maybe Dawn was with him, and she's been murdered, too."

"I suppose that's something the police will look into," Rachel said, though she doubted it. The most logical answer was that Dawn had simply gotten tired of putting up with her boyfriend's abuse and gone back to where she'd come from. But . . . could they have had a lover's quarrel that ended in Willy's violent death? Maybe the waitress and her jealous boyfriend should be suspects. Rachel nibbled at her bottom lip. She'd have to start taking notes so she could keep all the possibilities straight in her mind.

"You can put the goodies in there with all the others," Ell said with another wave. "People have been coming by and dropping things off all day." She walked out from behind the counter. "Wait, I can do it for you. Ada made these, right?"

Rachel nodded. "You wouldn't want them if I'd baked them."

Ell chuckled as she took the tray. "I just made coffee. I want to get one of these before the customers zoom in on them."

"Busy?"

Ell rolled her eyes. "You know it! Business has doubled since . . . well . . . since they found him. It's all anyone wants to talk about. Like, like maybe your uncle didn't do it, and there's a murderer stalking the valley. I . . . oh! Take this!" She handed the tray of cinnamon rolls back to Rachel, turned away, and sneezed. "Sorry." She pulled a tissue out of her tunic pocket and blew her nose. "I swear I'm allergic to that dog."

"Impossible." George came down the curved steps, followed by a plump, white fifteen-pound dog that looked very much like a miniature poodle. The dog barked, a high-pitched yip-yip-yip that pierced Rachel's eardrums. "The bichon frise was bred to be hypoallergenic."

Ell cut her eyes at George. "'It is important to note that human sensitivity to dog fur, dander, and saliva varies considerably. Although hair, dander, and saliva can be minimized, inhaling the allergens, or being licked by the dog, can trigger a reaction in a sensitive person.' And I quote," she said, "Wikipedia."

Rachel chuckled as she placed the tray of rolls on a pillar that had once been the station of a uniformed ticket taker. She extended her arms to hug George. His eyes were swollen, his cheeks sunken, and his signature smile was missing under his ball cap. "I'm so sorry," she murmured as she embraced him.

"Rachel, Rachel." He held her for an instant before releasing her. "I still can't believe it, you know." He shook his head. "I was worried, naturally, but I kept expecting the phone to ring and Willy's voice to boom out on the other end. I thought . . . anytime now, I'll look up, and he'll come walking through the stacks. But he won't. He's gone, Rachel." George's voice broke. "He's all I had, and . . . he's really gone."

"I can't imagine what you're going through," Rachel said. George smelled faintly of Calvin Klein cologne, and his button-down shirt and tie were fresh and unwrinkled. His clean white hair was knotted at the back of his neck in the style of another age. But then George had always insisted that this wasn't his century—he was better suited to the life of a Victorian gentleman.

Sophie bounced up and down, her razor-like nails scratching Rachel's shins through her jeans. She tried to ignore the assault.

"Stop that, Sophie," George ordered. "Behave yourself." Sophie kept barking and bouncing until Ell broke off a tiny corner of cinnamon bun and tossed it on the marble floor tiles. Immediately, Sophie abandoned the attack and went after the crumb of food.

"She's so spoiled," George apologized. "Willy always said she was spoiled rotten. He never took to her."

"Took to her?" Ell made a face. "He *hated* her. Used to say he was going to wring her neck."

George blanched, as if speaking so of his brother cut him deeply. "My fault, I admit it. We were never allowed to have pets, growing up, and now that I can, I'm hopeless as a disciplinarian."

"Maybe obedience classes would help," Rachel suggested.

"Boot camp," Ell put in. "Definitely doggy boot camp. We could ship her out to California to the Dog Whisperer. He'd whip her into shape."

Three teenagers entered, and one of the girls called out to Ell, "Did my book come in?"

"I think so. 'Scuse me, Rachel. Duty calls." Ell hurried back to the desk.

"I don't want to bother you," Rachel said to George. "I know this is a terrible time for you, but I wanted to come by and . . . say hi."

"I was just going to make a pot of tea," he said. "Join me, please." He led the way into the huge room that housed the books. Most of the original seating had been removed to make space for the tables and shelves, but groups of two or three remained scattered about. At the far end, on what had been the stage, heavy drapes framed a comfortable reading area with sofas, easy chairs, and a self-serve coffee bar. Ell was right. People had been coming all day. A table groaned under the weight of coffee cakes, cookies, pies, brownies, and plates of homemade candy. Rachel counted two coconut cakes, a pineapple upside-down cake, and three chocolate cakes.

Teresa Ridley, Ell's mother, was the only customer in the reading lounge. She was seated at one of the small tables in the back corner, pretending to be engrossed in a mystery. Rachel wasn't convinced that Teresa was all that interested in her book because her reading glasses were perched on her forehead. Teresa had a reputation for being a loner.

Rachel put on her innkeeper smile and offered a cheerful "Hi."

Teresa returned a tepid greeting and gathered her purse and a pile of crumpled tissues. Leaving the novel on the table, she murmured regrets to George and made an awkward retreat. As she passed, Rachel noticed that she looked as if she'd been crying, too. If Willy's death had upset the unflappable Teresa Ridley to the point of tears, it had certainly knocked Stone Mill for a loop.

Rachel offered to make the tea, but George insisted that she was his guest. "It gives me something to do with my hands," he said. "Otherwise, I'm afraid I'd have to take up smoking or something. I just seem so . . . so out of sorts." He sighed. "It still doesn't seem real. I can't believe it. I saw . . ." He swallowed. "Saw his remains . . . but I still can't accept it." He looked up from measuring tea into a white porcelain teapot. "All these months, I hoped . . . And now . . ." His voice trailed off.

Rachel felt so bad for him that her chest actually ached. "George, I don't know who could have done such a thing, but it wasn't my Uncle Aaron. You know that, right?" She took a seat at one of the café-style tables.

George raised a hand to his forehead and absently rubbed his temple. "I'm so sorry about that. Aaron wouldn't do such a thing. He couldn't. He's a stern man, your uncle, but not a vengeful man. He couldn't have killed Willy."

"I'm glad to hear you say you believe in Uncle Aaron's innocence. He couldn't have murdered anyone. He doesn't even butcher his own pigs. Sends them all to Reuben's and picks them up all wrapped neatly in paper bundles marked *pork chops* and *sausage*." It wasn't until the words were out of her mouth that she realized how insensitive they sounded; his *brother* had been butchered. Fortunately, George didn't seem to be offended; in fact, it seemed as if he had barely heard her.

He removed a little carton of half-and-half from a small refrigerator and carried that to the table. Honey and a bowl of raw sugar were already there. "Do you want that artificial stuff? I have it, but not many people—"

"No. I like mine with honey," she said. The container was a plain pint-size canning jar with a bee sticker that read *Fresh Local Honey* on the side. She recognized the container; the honey had been collected from hives in her sister Annie's backyard. Rachel sold the honey in her shop, and they used it exclusively in the kitchen at Stone Mill House.

"I know I've got arrangements to make." George took a chair across from her. "But I haven't had the heart to start. McCloud's, of course. They've buried the O'Days since . . . well . . . for a long, long time." Sophie began to whine, and George lifted the dog into his lap, where she curled up, tucked her nose under her paws, and closed her eyes. "The trouble is," George said as he scratched behind the bichon's ears, "I don't know how long before the authorities will release the . . ." He swallowed again, and moisture glistened in his eyes. "The remains."

"I don't know, either," Rachel said. "I could ask, if you like . . . if it would help. Evan might know."

"Yes, your young man. He might know."

"Oh, he isn't . . ." she began, and then decided to let the subject of Evan drop. No need to go into a detailed explanation of the relationship between her and Evan Parks, a relationship that was . . . well . . . complicated. Was he her boyfriend or not? They were certainly friends . . . but maybe more. "I'll see what I can find out," she promised.

"I'd be grateful." George stroked the dog in his lap. "Sophia Lazzaro's all I have now. Aren't you?" he crooned. He looked up at Rachel again. "Willy and I lost our parents when we were young. A train wreck. They were vacationing in Europe."

"I'm so sorry," Rachel said. "I didn't know that."

"It was a long time ago." He sighed and stroked Sophie's head. "A maiden aunt raised us. She loved us, in her own way, but Aunt Helen had never considered marriage nor wanted children. She'd wanted to join a cloistered order of Catholic nuns, Order of the Most Blessed Virgin Mary, in Philadelphia. As you can imagine, a pair of boys were a great trial to her."

"I know you and your brother were close," Rachel said, wondering if it would be offensive to ask the questions that were troubling her. She didn't want to be insensitive, not when George was grieving so, but her uncle's future, maybe even his life, was at stake. "Were you concerned when Willy didn't come home that night?" she ventured. "If you don't mind me asking."

"I don't mind. I like—" He stopped and started again. "Talking about him. We'd breakfasted together that morning." The teakettle sputtered, and George put the dog gently on the floor and got up to pour the water into the pot. "I made Assam," he said. "If that's all right with you."

"Love it," Rachel answered. "You say you and Willy had breakfast together the day he disappeared. At Junior's?"

George nodded as he poured the hot water. "Friday mornings we always had breakfast out. It was a tradition. Usually, it was my treat. You know how Willy was with his money. Frugal. Between you and me, there was no need to worry. Our Grandfather O'Day made his money in the railroads . . . and in mining. Coal. He left us . . ." George hesitated as he came back to the table with the teapot and set it down. "Let's just say that we never had to worry. It's how I could do this after retiring from the state." He waved at the expanse of bookshelves. "Bookstores are a dying institution, so they tell me. Everyone purchases e-books on the Internet. But it's not the same. I like the feel of books, the smell of them."

"Did Willy seem different in any way that morning?" Rachel asked, trying to gracefully steer the conversation back to Willy's murder. "Anxious? Worried about anything?"

George shook his head. "No, to the contrary, he was in the best of moods. It was the first of the month—when Willy collected his rents. It always cheered him up." He glanced at his watch, the vintage Montblanc she'd never seen him without. "Almost ready. Three minutes exactly. Some people leave tea leaves in the pot after it's finished brewing, or let the water get too hot. Like it's coffee." He shook his head again. "Completely wrong for good tea."

"So—"

"I think I'd like to establish a scholarship in Willy's name," George went on, not seeming to hear her. "For college. You know how it is with most of our young people in Stone Mill. Money has been so tight for families in the valley that many bright kids are falling through the cracks. The only thing is . . ." He hesitated. "I'm concerned that our Amish neighbors would feel slighted . . . because their children couldn't benefit." He looked at her questioningly. "I wouldn't want to cause hard feelings."

Rachel considered. "I think a scholarship fund would be a fine idea. And it wouldn't occur to the Amish families that they were being slighted. They don't consider themselves part of your—" She corrected herself. "Part of *our* world." She, again, tried to steer the conversation back to Willy. George had a reputation for being a talker. Not that that was bad; ordinarily, she enjoyed her chats with him immensely. It was just that today . . .

George poured the tea into the two pottery mugs he'd brought to the table. They were handmade here in Stone Mill by Coyote Finch, one of their newest residents. Coyote was a potter. She and her husband had discovered Stone Mill on the Internet and moved here with their four children in the spring, setting up shop down the street from The George.

"You were telling me about your breakfast with your brother?"

"Willy was quite pleased with himself. He didn't say why, but he was in such a good humor that he gave our waitress, Dawn, a twenty percent tip. Even she looked shocked. And she liked Willy. The ladies did, you know. They all liked him, in spite of his wandering eye and his frugality. They saw him as he really was, not as a lot of men saw him. Willy had a good heart. Under that tough business exterior, he really was a sweet person." George spooned sugar into his tea. "He was always good to me, looked after me when we were kids. He was the oldest. By only twenty minutes, but the elder, nevertheless, and he took his position seriously." George uttered a muffled sound of grief, quickly smothering it with a napkin. "I'm sorry, Rachel. Forgive me, but this is so hard."

"I can't imagine losing one of my brothers," she said. "And I have four of them."

"It's not something anyone should ever have to do," he said. "I always thought it would be me that went first . . . I inherited a faulty valve in my ticker from my father. Kept me from playing school sports. Not Willy, thank God. He was healthy as a horse. He was a quarterback in college. Did you know that? I was so proud of him. I never missed a game."

"George," she said, "after breakfast, you didn't see Willy again?"

He shook his head. "No. Friday, October first, rent day." He added half-and-half to his cup. "The more I think about it, the more I'm afraid it was a robbery."

"You think someone robbed him and killed him?" she asked, stirring the honey into her tea.

"Makes sense. He would have had the money from the rent. In cash. Just in a rubber band. The cash wasn't found on his body."

"A robbery," she mused. She glanced up at him. "You think it could have been a robbery even though they didn't take his diamond ring?"

He stared into his mug as he stirred.

She gave him time to think.

"It was tight on him. Hard to get off. I think he'd put on a little weight." He went silent for a moment. When he spoke again, his voice was full of regret. "I told him it was dangerous. That someone would hit him over the head and rob him. I tried and tried to convince him not to collect the rent personally or take cash. But he wouldn't listen."

"And a lot of people knew that Willy had that cash on the first of the month," she said, thinking out loud.

"Exactly."

She added a splash of half-and-half to her tea. Willy had been missing for seven months; she was now vague about some of the details. "So he didn't come home that night?"

"No. He never came home."

"Did he often come home late on rent days? Could you have been asleep and missed . . ."

"No. I was awake. I'd recorded an old John Wayne movie. We liked to pop a frozen pizza in the oven and have a glass of wine with it as we watched a little TV." He offered the first hint of a smile she'd seen all evening. "Willy loved John Wayne."

"I imagine you went over all this with the police."

"Of course, when he went missing. Then again yesterday, and again this morning. I really didn't have much to tell them."

"You must have been worried when he didn't come home."

"A little. I sat up until . . . oh . . . a little after one a.m. Then I took Sophie out for her late-night duty, and we went to bed. When I woke up, Saturday morning, there was still no word from Willy."

"And that's when you called the police?"

"No." George flushed and looked away. "I thought . . . well, I thought that Willy had . . ." He raised his head and met her gaze. He looked as if he was about to start crying again. "Willy had lady friends. I'm not judging him. He was just that way."

"And you assumed he'd spent the night with one of them?"

"He and Dawn had been friendly at breakfast." George took another sip of his tea. "Honestly, Rachel, I thought he and Dawn had taken off for the weekend. He sometimes did that. Atlantic City . . . Dover, Delaware. Willy liked to gamble. Not to excess. He'd set aside a certain sum, and win or lose, he'd play with that."

"When did you decide that something was wrong? That you needed to contact the authorities?"

"Monday morning. He should have been back by Sunday afternoon. Even if he'd driven to Atlantic City, Willy would have returned and slept in his own bed Sunday night. I wanted to call the police Sunday evening, but I didn't. God help me, I didn't. I felt foolish. What was I thinking? What if he was still alive Sunday? I'm old and foolish."

"You aren't old, George."

"No?" A few of the creases smoothed around his eyes. "We were sixty-seven on our last birthday. That's not exactly right . . ." He drew in a ragged breath. "I guess *I* was sixty-seven. Our birthday came after . . . after he disappeared. I suppose Willy . . ." His Adam's apple bobbed. "I suppose Willy was sixty-six when he passed."

"Sixty-seven isn't old, not today."

He exhaled slowly. "I suppose not, but it feels old. And looking at what years I have ahead . . . alone . . . without anybody but Sophie . . ."

"George . . ." She hesitated. "Did the police ask you about a notebook or journal Willy had? They found it . . . on him."

He nodded. "Always carried it in his pants pocket. Always scribbling in it. What he needed to do or buy . . . or collect on. If I owed him a cup of coffee, Willy would write it down. He kept phone numbers. Lists. You name it, Willy had it in that book."

"Do you know what 'A.T.B.R.' might mean? It was written in his notebook the day he disappeared."

George's gaze met hers. "I wish it had been me instead of him, Rachel. If I could go back and trade places, it would be me taken and my brother would still be alive."

Chapter 8

Stone Mill House was quiet when Rachel arrived home. She was tired, but it was still too early to go to bed, and her mind was in turmoil. Had it only been yesterday that Willy's body had been discovered? It seemed like days ago . . .

It gave her some satisfaction to know that Uncle Aaron was back with his family tonight, not sleeping in a police station cell. But she couldn't help wondering how long he would remain with them. Equally scary was the thought that a killer was walking free somewhere . . . a monster who held human life so cheaply that he could commit murder and then bury his victim with as little hesitation as a dog burying an old bone.

Rachel retrieved her laptop from the office and carried it and a tray with apple juice, a tangerine, and a ham biscuit up to her apartment. As she climbed the stairs, she saw that her remaining guest's door, off the second-floor hallway, was closed. There was a sliver of light seeping under the door, and she could hear the murmur of canned laughter from the television.

She continued up another flight of stairs to her apartment. She switched on the light and found Bishop already curled up in the middle of her bed on a folded quilt. As she entered the room, the cat raised his head, stared at her through slitted eyes, and yawned. "Just me," Rachel said. She carried her laptop and her supper tray to the end table that stood beside a comfy leather recliner.

Her retreat was on the third floor in the main section of the house, and her bedroom was en-suite, complete with a big soaking bathtub. She had plans for a separate sitting room and a small kitchen, but those would have to wait until her business began showing a healthy profit. For now, she made do with the recliner, a mini-fridge, and a microwave on a table pushed against the wall. In one corner of the room, she had a desk with a printer on top. Mounted on the wall, beside the desk, was a big white dry-erase board she used to keep track of tasks she needed to do.

Rachel wasn't complaining. The private bathroom, with its walk-in shower and marble-topped sink, was a treasure beyond counting. As a girl who'd grown up with eight brothers and sisters in a house without electricity and only a single bathroom, she appreciated the marvels of English plumbing. Sometimes, she was sure that she liked her bathroom even more than modern electric appliances.

She'd jump in the shower before bed, but for now, she wanted to check her email and then see if there were any new orders on the Stone Mill Heirloom Arts website. One of the things that she was most proud of, since her return to her hometown, was the crafts co-op she'd organized.

Her Amish community didn't know anything about the Internet, so they had had no idea that they could reach customers worldwide without leaving their workshops or kitchen tables. Like Mary Aaron with her quilts, others had found a market for rush-seat chairs, wooden toys, baskets, and other traditional crafts.

Tonight, she was pleased to find an order for one of Mattie Beiler's rag rugs, six jars of honey, and a willow egg basket fashioned by her oldest brother Paul's wife. Miriam would be delighted. She'd only finished the basket a few weeks ago, and the profit from her work would pay for the first goslings that she'd been wanting to buy to start her own flock. Best of all, a customer in Boston wanted additional information and photographs of another of Mary Aaron's quilts—the queen-size "Jacob's Ladder."

After Rachel sent the orders to the office printer downstairs, where Mary Aaron would collect and start filling them the next day, she toyed with the idea of trying to locate the missing waitress. There were a few questions she'd like to ask Dawn, wherever she was.

Of course, if Dawn were the murderer, no one would find her anytime soon. But Rachel doubted that the waitress had committed the crime. Not that a woman wasn't capable of killing, but she just couldn't picture the thin blonde burying a body in the dark of night in a cow pasture. No . . . Willy had been a tall man. This was definitely the work of a male.

Unless . . . Could Dawn have been involved in the murder as an accomplice? If so, with whom? Her boyfriend? What was his name? Floyd? Boyd? No, Roy. But he was probably innocent because he hadn't run away. Roy was still living in that run-down shack just outside of town. She'd seen him at Howdy's Garage and Tow two weeks ago, buying five dollars' worth of gas. And if Roy had robbed and murdered Willy, he would hardly still be driving an '84 lime-green pickup with the cracked windshield and expired tags.

Someone had told Rachel that Dawn had family in Florida. She went to a people-locator site on the Web and keyed in Dawn's name and the state. Immediately, five Dawns popped up . . . Palm Coast, Jacksonville, Orlando, and two towns that Rachel had never heard of. A few more minutes and she had a list of phone numbers. She glanced at the clock. It was eight thirty, a little late to call, but not outrageous.

The first two Dawns were strikeouts. The first was a nursing home, the second a disconnected number. She looked at the clock again: 8:42. Now it was probably too late to make the call . . . no sense in disturbing strangers or angering the real Dawn Clough, if she did find her tonight. She closed her laptop, placed it on the floor beside her chair, and reached for her supper tray. Tomorrow, she'd try again after breakfast. And if she couldn't find the waitress, there were some people right here in Stone Mill who could talk about her.

"What do you think, Bishop?" The cat switched his tail, but kept his eyes tightly closed. "Mouse-chasing dreams again?" she asked. Not that he would stoop to chasing mice. The Siamese was well aware of his exalted position in the household. Swatting at spiders was as plebian a pursuit as Bishop would stoop to.

Chuckling, Rachel reached for her tangerine. Maybe she would start taking notes on her investigation. Wasn't that the logical way to approach this? Then she thought of something else . . . another search she might make without leaving her recliner. Willy's rentals. If he had made his usual collections on the day he disappeared, maybe it would be smart to see what he owned. That way, she could retrace his steps; who knew what she might uncover?

Park Estates? Rachel had to laugh whenever she passed the mobile home park, which wasn't often as it was located at the end of a dead-end gravel road, a lane that could only be called a road in the most general sense. Willy's low-income housing venture was wedged into a narrow hollow between a ten-foot-high chain-link fence surrounding an abandoned gravel pit and a boulder-strewn hill that rose abruptly.

As Rachel geared the Jeep down into second and turned into the community, she saw that there had once been lots for a dozen mobile homes, with a single driveway between each trailer and a turnaround at the far end of the narrow street. Now the park held seven; one was a double-wide that took up two spaces. There were three burned-out hulks and a bare lot now partially occupied by an industrial-size Dumpster. Once off the access road and into the park proper, the gravel petered to nothing more than a few broken bricks, mud puddles, and sand.

"A veritable oasis," Rachel muttered. Her comment was lost in a cacophony of snarls, yips, and angry barking. Two mixed-blood pit bulls tied to the back step of the nearest trailer threw themselves against their chains, straining to attack the Jeep and, presumably, her. A German shepherd, caged beneath the mobile home across the driveway, bared his teeth, lunged, and added his vocal threats to her welcome. Other smaller dogs added to the din, peering out of windows, yelping from outside pens, or simply running loose.

Rachel parked and reached for a Ziploc bag on the passenger seat: cut-up carrots she'd grabbed for a snack. She threw two out the open window to the two hounds nipping at her tires. A black-and-white terrier darted in to grab a carrot and dove under the Jeep to gulp down his prize. "In for a penny, in for a pound." She tossed a few more carrot sticks out the driver's window, climbed over the stick shift, slid across the passenger seat, and cautiously got out of the vehicle.

Avoiding the mud puddle beside the door, she tried the first mobile home without a dog guarding the door. She went up a set of shaky metal steps and knocked. From inside came the shrill sound of cartoons and the cry of a baby. No one answered. Her gaze drifted to a rusty hasp: the hinged kind you used to secure a shed door. It seemed oddly out of place on a trailer door. She knocked louder.

The door opened a little, and an overweight young woman, barely out of her teens, peeked out. Her blond hair with dark roots was pulled back into an untidy ponytail. "Yeah?"

"Hi. I'm Rachel Mast. I was hoping you could answer a few questions about Willy O'Day. Your landlord," she added.

The young woman, dressed in gray sweatpants and a Justin Bieber tee, asked, "Who are you?"

"I'm a friend of George O'Day. He told me that his brother came here the day he disappeared last fall—to collect the rent."

"This is my grandmother's place," she said. "Blanche Willis. She paid Willy that night. She's got a receipt. Do you want to see it? She keeps all her receipts."

"Who is it?" someone asked from inside the residence.

An older woman's voice—Mrs. Willis, the resident, she presumed.

"Is it the police again?" the woman demanded.

"I'm just trying to get an idea of what happened," Rachel said. "Any help you or your grandmother could give me would be greatly appreciated."

The girl frowned and opened the door wider. "I thought they arrested Willy's killer. Some Amish guy."

"No," Rachel corrected. "No one has been arrested. It's important that we find out who really did kill Mr. O'Day, because the murderer might still be in the area." The baby screamed louder. A second child, a little boy, two maybe, pushed past the girl and stared at Rachel. He was wearing an undershirt and a diaper, and had a baby bottle in his hand. Through the open door, Rachel caught the odor of a dirty diaper. "Please, if I could just speak with—"

"What does she want?" the other person, out of Rachel's line of vision, demanded in a strident tone.

Justin Bieber's fan stepped aside, pushing the door open wider, and a heavyset woman steered her wheelchair to the entrance. "We pay our rent every month. I called Willy O'Day's house after he disappeared, and his brother said I could just put a check in the mail. He said he didn't need cash. So I do. I send a check every month. Somebody's cashing them. I've got my bank statements to prove it."

"I'm sure there's no problem with your rent. I didn't come to ask about that," Rachel said as she smiled. "I know you heard that Willy is—"

"Dead." The stout woman in the wheelchair scowled. "Serves him right, the old skinflint. Few around here will miss him, I can tell you that."

"If I could just come in," Rachel said. "I promise not to take up much of your time, Mrs. Willis."

"Oh, let her in." Mrs. Willis threw up her hand. "Nothing on television I want to see anyhow. They took off my show, you know. Twenty years I've watched that program. *As the Darkness Falls*. Did you watch it?"

"It's been off for more than a year, Gran." The girl opened the door and waved Rachel in.

The combined living room and eating area wasn't as bad as Rachel had imagined. There were toys scattered everywhere, and from the way the little boy's diaper sagged, she suspected he needed changing, but the house was messy and cluttered rather than dirty. The linoleum floor was worn through in spots, and the couch had seen better days, but the forty-some-inch TV looked new. "Thank you," Rachel said. "I'm Rachel."

"I'm Blanchette Willis. You can call me Blanche, everybody does. This is my granddaughter Chelsea and her Justin."

Rachel smiled and nodded. "Chelsea."

"Chelsea stays with me and helps me out," Blanche explained. "Chelsea pays me rent when she stays." She waved toward the sofa. "Sit down."

"Your personal affairs aren't any of my business," Rachel assured her as she took a seat. Her fingers brushed something sticky on the edge of the couch, and she quickly put her hand in her lap.

"Sorry about the place. It's all we can afford. If Aunt Millie hadn't been tricked by that tightwad, Gran would have gotten everything when she died," Chelsea put in. The little boy started whining, and his mother changed the channel on the TV. The child popped the bottle in his mouth and dropped onto an oversized pillow, shaped like a race car, to watch a cartoon cat chasing a squadron of mice across the screen.

"That Willy O'Day," Chelsea continued. "He scammed my aunt, Gran's daughter, into writing a new will and leaving her dry cleaner's to him instead of Gran."

"Millie was my daughter," Blanche explained. "She was a good girl, meant to take care of me. Always used to help out, pay my phone bill, pay something on the electric. She promised that I'd have her business if her heart gave out. Millie had a bad heart for years. Had four bypasses and more stents than you can count. It was too big, her heart."

"Uncle Steve—that was her husband," Chelsea explained. Still talking, she wandered into the kitchen and returned with a can of soda. "Third husband. Uncle Steve tried to sue the crook after Aunt Millie died, but you know, money talks. A judge threw it out of court; said it didn't matter if he was her husband, not if it was spelled out in the will. Not if his name wasn't on anything. Said she could do what she wanted with her estate. Said she could leave it to her cat, if she wanted to. She didn't even have a cat."

"But to give it to Willy and not her own mother? I still don't believe it," Blanche said.

Millie's romance with Willy O'Day had been common knowledge in Stone Mill, but no one had expected her to die in the middle of heart surgery. Afterward, public opinion had changed, elevating Millie, the newly deceased, as an innocent woman lured into a relationship by a Romeo.

"I guess you could call Steve a husband," Blanche went on. "But Millie knew he was two-timin' her. She never intended Steve to have any of her money. He took enough when she was alive. He wasn't worth the powder it would take . . . well, you know." She grimaced. "She never would have stayed with him if she'd lived. Lazy, he was. Always had big ideas. But at least he wasn't a thief."

"So your daughter left her estate to Willy?" Rachel asked. She had no idea. She didn't think anyone in town did. "I suppose Steve had reason to dislike Willy O'Day then?"

"Dislike him?" Chelsea laughed. "More like hated his guts."

Rachel nodded sympathetically. "Did you think about suing Willy?"

Blanche pulled a pack of cigarettes out of her bathrobe pocket. "Smoke?" she offered.

"No, thanks." Rachel shook her head.

"Thought about it."

"Gran was afraid that O'Day would evict her if she did," Chelsea said. "It's not so easy to find a place in this valley to put a double-wide."

Blanche lit her cigarette and took a long drag. "He warned me against trying, Willy did. Steve had asked me, but I never put much truck in lawsuits. And the judge had already told Steve that Millie could do what she pleased. All I've got is this place. It's not much, but it's mine. It puts a roof over my head, my granddaughter's, and my great-grandson's. I'm not messing with what I've got."

A pregnant tabby cat padded into the living room from the hallway leading to the bedrooms. It walked over and rubbed against Chelsea's ankle. "She's expecting kittens. Maybe you'd want one? The tom's longhaired. Her last kittens were pretty."

"No, thanks. Already have a cat. Did Willy seem worried?" Rachel asked. "The last time you saw him? Different in any way?"

"No," Blanche answered. "Same as always. Banging on the door, hand out for the cash money like every month. Always stood in my living room and counted out every dollar."

"And he collected from every home here in"—Rachel tried to keep a straight face—"Park Estates?"

"Every single trailer. You'd better be home when he came around, too."

"I'd like to speak to your neighbors. Do you think they'd talk to me?" Rachel asked as she rose to her feet.

"Some might," Blanche said. "Wonder what Willy did to that Amish man to cause him to kill him?"

"I heard he shot him," Chelsea said.

"I don't think the police have released the cause of death," Rachel replied. "But the Amish man didn't do it. The Amish are nonviolent."

"Supposed to be," Blanche said. "But I hear there's a lot of abuse in those families. The men are the head of the house, you know. The women don't dare say a word to them."

"A few," Rachel admitted, "but not nearly as many as Englishers—the *non*-Amish," she corrected. "The majority are really good people. God-fearing and gentle."

"That's what they'd like you to think," Blanche said. She puffed again on her cigarette and blew smoke at the cat. "Nasty-looking, if you ask me, all that face hair. I always liked a clean-shaven man. My Art shaved every day. You remember your grandfather?" she asked Chelsea. "A fine-looking man."

"Yeah," her granddaughter agreed. "He used to take me fishing when I was little."

Rachel moved toward the door, carefully avoiding the cat and the scattered toys. Justin rolled onto his back, and she got a strong whiff of the ripe diaper. "Thank you for your time," she said. "I appreciate it." She hesitated, her hand on the doorknob. "One more question. Do you know of anyone who disliked Willy enough to want him dead?"

Blanche snickered. "Who didn't? Half the folks in this valley, sweetie, and everybody in this sinkhole of a trailer park for certain."

Chapter 9

As she made her way down the muddy path from Blanche's trailer, Rachel heard her cell phone ring. She'd deliberately left it in her car. Now, she opened the door and retrieved it. The call was from Evan. She was tempted to answer, but she wanted to talk to more residents here in Park Estates. What if Evan asked where she was? She didn't want to lie to him . . . but she knew he would disapprove of her being here.

She placed the phone gingerly on the seat. If she didn't talk to him, he couldn't ask, and she wouldn't have to tell him she was snooping around. She ignored two dogs tailing her, in hopes of more snacks probably, and started for the next trailer.

If she found out anything important, naturally she'd tell the police. She didn't want to cause a problem. She wanted to right an impending wrong, and arresting Uncle Aaron for killing someone—even unlikeable Willy O'Day—would be as wrong as you could get.

Being raised Amish, she'd heard from the time she was a toddler that God has a plan, that everything that happens is meant to be. If Uncle Aaron was arrested, the conservative Amish would believe that that was part of God's mysterious plan.

She wasn't Amish anymore. She didn't know exactly what she believed, but she didn't believe God meant for her uncle to be charged with a murder he didn't commit. So on this matter, she and her family would have to agree to disagree.

That didn't mean that the Amish weren't still blood and bone of her body. She shared their history, their customs, and their language. And she loved her family and friends with every ounce of her being. Being rejected by some of the Plain folk hurt. Having her own mother refuse to speak directly to her caused her grief every time it happened. But it didn't lessen the ties she felt to her mother, and it didn't make her doubt her mother's deep love for her. If Esther Mast kept herself apart from her daughter, it wasn't for lack of caring. It was because she cared so much for Rachel's soul and wanted to bring her back to the faith. *Mam* and Uncle Aaron had always been close. Perhaps helping him would help breach the gap that had opened between them all.

With renewed vigor and determination, Rachel approached the next single-wide, a yellow Royal Crest model. The chrome *R* and *C* were missing, so that it actually read *oyal rest*. However, unlike the majority of the other homes, someone had made the effort to *spruce up* the tiny yard with crockery flowerpots full of early-blooming marigolds, seven brightly painted cement gnomes, and a collection of white wooden rabbits holding orange wooden carrots. There was also a four-foot-high blue plastic windmill with yellow blades that spun merrily in the breeze.

There was no vehicle in front of the trailer, but muddy tracks showed that there had been one there recently. Homemade cement stepping stones set with bits of colored glass led to a side door and a small stoop. This one bore a fresh coat of white paint. A plaque proclaimed, *The Blatts—Lil & Bill,* and just beneath it, a smaller sticker read, *Warning! House Guarded by Attack Cat!* Rachel knocked.

There was no answer. She knocked again, harder. Again, she was rewarded only by silence. "Hello!" she called. "Mrs. Blatt? Is anyone home?"

"They're not there!"

Rachel turned around to see Chelsea's face at one of the windows of Blanche's trailer. "They went to visit their daughter in Harrisburg! Home next week, I think!"

"Oh, thank you," Rachel answered, disappointed. She was curious to see what Bill and Lil were like. The gnomes intrigued her. And, of course, she wanted to see if they had any information about Willy's last day.

Rachel retreated past the row of rabbits and the round-eyed stares of the gnomes to the main and only street. The next space was empty, and the one after that contained one of the ruined trailers, but across the drive was a promising prospect, a green single-wide with a tiny bit of close-cropped grass and a five-inch-high picket fence. There were no flowerpots, gnomes, or windmills, but there didn't seem to be any dogs tied outside, either.

As she crossed the road, she could hear her cell ringing again. Evan was nothing if not persistent. The thought that he might have news about Uncle Aaron rose to worry her, but she was already approaching the mobile home. She'd try this one and then leave. She'd have to return later to question Bill and Lil. She could try the other residents then.

Here, at least, there was an older-model VW Bug parked in front, and the Bug had tags that were current. Maybe someone was home here.

A stack of concrete blocks formed the steps. Rachel took them gamely, opened the storm door, and knocked. There was silence within. "Hello?" she called. She rapped harder, waited a good two minutes, and then conceded defeat.

Retreating, head high, she returned to her Jeep, got in, and inserted the key in the ignition. Her trusty motor purred, and she drove to the far end of the drive and turned around in front of the Dumpster. As she steered the vehicle slowly through the ruts toward the access road, she glanced back at the trailer with the VW in the driveway. She saw the distinct movement of a curtain.

A prickling at the back of her neck seconded what her eyes

told her. The trailer wasn't empty. And someone was watching her, now, as she drove away . . . someone who didn't want to talk to her.

Rachel stopped at Wagler's Grocery for two gallons of organic milk and two pints of heavy whipping cream. Wagler's was an institution in Stone Mill, and although she ordered paper goods, cleaning supplies, and dish and laundry detergents online, she did as much of her day-to-day food shopping here as possible. Ed and Polly carried a full line of fresh and canned vegetables and fruits, cereals, baked goods, candy, bread, meat, and assorted sundries. The store was a little higher priced than the chain supermarkets in the larger towns, but most of Stone Mill, Amish and Englishers alike, preferred to support local businesses. Plus, Wagler's was only a few blocks from home.

Rachel added three pounds of butter and a dozen lemons to her cart and wheeled it into the checkout line. Naturally, she knew most of the customers in the store on a first name basis, including the teenage boy at the register. They all were buzzing about Willy's death and her uncle's questioning, and Rachel had to field questions, trying hard not to give away any information while not offending anyone. She waited until she was back at Stone Mill House and was pulling into the driveway before she called Evan back.

"Hi," she said when he picked up. "I thought you were on duty today." She drove to the carriage shed and parked the Jeep.

"Clearing up some old files at the station. Where have you been? I left two messages."

"Just got back from Wagler's," she said. Her mother was probably right. She *was* going to hell. She might not be lying, but this was *way* too close. "Have you heard anything about Uncle Aaron? Is he going to be arrested?" She scooped up her groceries and started for the back door.

"Haven't heard anything."

They were both quiet for a second.

"Anyway, the reason I was calling," Evan said, "was to see if you'd like to have dinner with me tonight. I thought maybe we could drive over to Huntingdon and eat at that Italian place you like, the one with the huge salads and the great antipasto."

She groaned. "Can't. High tea this afternoon and a meeting of the fund-raising committee for the Historical Preservation Society tonight."

"You can't skip the meeting?"

"Sorry. Wish I could, but it's here." She swung open the back door and blocked Bishop's escape with one foot. "Plus, I've got two couples coming in this evening after five. Can I take a rain check?"

"Sure." He sounded disappointed. "But I have to work through the weekend. How about Monday night?"

"Maybe. But I'm not sure they're open on Mondays. I'm really sorry. Why don't you go tonight anyway? Take your mom."

Now it was Evan who groaned. "I'm not *that* desperate. We'll try for next week, but don't say I didn't ask."

"Sorry. Our schedules don't seem to be in sync." She dropped the bags on the counter. Lemons rolled out of one, bounced, and rolled across the floor. Bishop yowled and flew out of the room, his tail fluffed into a bottlebrush.

Evan chuckled. "Sounds like you're trying to kill your cat."

"Tried. Failed. Again." They shared a laugh together, both knowing how absolutely devoted she was to the spoiled Siamese. "You're welcome to come to our meeting," she offered.

"Not *that* desperate, either. Dinner out with my mother sounds better."

She smiled. "Hey, any word on the notebook that was found on Willy's body?"

"Nope."

"The letters. They seem familiar. Like I've seen them before," she said. "But I can't think where."

"Well, let me know if you think of it. At this point, anything would be helpful."

"Right." She picked up one of the lemons and tossed it in the air and caught it again. "What else was in Willy's pockets?"

"His wallet with the credit cards. All accounted for. But no cash. George confirmed that he carried his cash in his front pocket with a rubber band around it."

"And nothing else, huh?"

"Nope. You're pretty nosy."

Rachel set the lemon on the counter. She thought about telling Evan what she'd been up to, but she decided not to. "That's me," she said. "Always nosing in other people's business."

"Well, I better go," he said.

"Sorry about dinner."

"Later."

Thursday night was so busy that Rachel didn't get a moment to herself until after nine, too late to try to find Dawn Clough in Florida. The committee meeting had gone all right. At least, Ada's sandwiches and cherry scones had been a hit.

It would have been better if the members had been able to agree on anything, anything at all, but they hadn't. Plans for a Christmas house tour were still in the works without any decisions made, since George, who was serving as president of the Society, was absent. The tour was his idea, and so far, George and Hulda were the only residents, besides herself, who'd agreed to open their houses to visitors.

George had also been writing a self-guided tour of the valley, with stops at various historical sites, including a Revolutionary War skirmish site and a farmhouse that had been on the Underground Railroad. He also wanted to include a cave that had been used by Native Americans for thousands of years and was now being excavated by state archeologists. George had said at the last meeting that the map and text were almost ready, but again, without his input, there wasn't much they could do. The one conclusion that the committee did reach was that Stone Mill House was the best place to hold the general meeting next month.

They also decided unanimously that Rachel should take over the bookkeeping for the committee. She didn't mind. With her business background and their small budget, it wouldn't be hard. She picked up the ledger she'd been given and set it on the table. The hardest thing was going to be reconciling years of—

She glanced at the ledger. Reconciling . . . She picked up her cell. Evan answered on the second ring. "Accounts to be reconciled," she said.

"What?"

"I'm sorry, were you asleep?"

"No," he said, but he sounded drowsy. "In bed, reading."

"The letters in Willy's notebook, 'A.T.B.R.' *Accounts to be reconciled*. That might be what it means."

"Accounts to be reconciled," he repeated. "Okay. Exactly what does that mean?"

"If you reconcile an account, you double-check numbers, make sure all the columns add up. That sort of thing. It's like a final accounting."

He was quiet on the other end.

"Does that make sense?" she asked. "I mean, what was under the heading?"

"I don't know. I didn't see inside the notebook. The detective just mentioned the letters. He was thinking out loud, I guess. Wondered if any of us knew what it meant."

"Well, I could be wrong. I just wanted to tell you because it came to me that that might be what it meant. You know, Willy being a money man."

"Well, thanks. I'll mention it to the detective."

"You have dinner with your mom?'

"I did."

They talked for another five minutes and then Rachel let him go.

Friday morning was hectic, but Mary Aaron arrived early, and breakfast went off smoothly. Mary Aaron packed new orders for the craft co-op, and she had everything ready to go when the parcel truck arrived for pickup. Together, Rachel and Mary Aaron cleared away the dining room things while Ada and Minnie took care of housekeeping.

By eleven, Rachel was done with her immediate chores and was able to slip into her office and make the call to Florida from her office. This time, a cheerful woman answered on the third ring. "Hello," Rachel said. "Is this Dawn Clough?" She was sure that it wasn't because the person on the other end of the line sounded much older.

"Yes, this is Dawn. I don't want another credit card."

"No, I'm not selling anything. My name is Rachel Mast. I'm from Stone Mill, Pennsylvania, and I'm looking for a woman who worked at a local restaurant here last fall."

"Is this a collection agency?" The voice took on a sharper tone. "Dawn is my daughter, but she doesn't live here, and I don't—"

"No, no," Rachel assured her. "I'm not calling about a credit issue. This is more . . . personal."

"You're a friend of my daughter's?"

"I just need to speak with her. It's important." Rachel went on quickly, afraid the woman might hang up. "How about if I give you my number and you ask her—if she should happen to contact you—to call me. I'd really appreciate it."

"Rachel Mast."

"Yes. Could you write down my number?" Rachel urged. "It would be a big favor if you would ask her to call me back."

"I suppose it wouldn't hurt. If she does contact me," the woman added. "We have the same name. Dawn took back her maiden name after the divorce. I guess that's how you got us mixed up."

Rachel thanked her again, gave her the number, and ended the call. She wondered if Dawn, the daughter, was there. If she wasn't, she guessed that she lived with her mother or nearby. That wasn't the response of a woman who didn't know where her daughter was. And she hadn't been unpleasant. Rachel could only hope that she would pass on the message, and that the waitress wouldn't ignore her request.

A half hour later, Rachel and Mary Aaron were able to slip away to continue retracing Willy O'Day's progress on the day he disappeared. They were going to see Alvin and Verna Herschberger, an Amish couple who rented a small hillside house and farm from Willy. Willy should have gone by their place to collect their rent that day, too.

Neither Alvin nor Verna had been particularly friendly with Rachel since she'd returned to Stone Mill. She knew they disapproved of her, but the couple often visited with Uncle Aaron and Aunt Hannah, so Mary Aaron knew them well. She'd offered to come along and try to smooth things over.

They pulled off the hard-top road onto a gravel one that led to several properties just below the edge of state game lands. "You aren't wearing makeup, are you?" Mary Aaron asked, glancing at Rachel. "Your cheeks are awfully red."

"No makeup," Rachel assured her. She rarely wore anything more than a dab of lipstick, but she hadn't even done that today.

The Amish had no television, and the majority had no radios or cell phones, but generally, they knew more of what was going on in the valley than their English neighbors. Rachel hoped that she'd learn something useful from the Herschbergers, something that would point suspicion away from Uncle Aaron and toward the real killer. She wasn't about to ruin her chances by doing anything to antagonize these people on sight.

"Verna is strict and Alvin stricter." Mary Aaron glanced out the window. "Not this mailbox. It's the next one, across from the ruins of that stone barn."

The road was bad, the gravel rutted by buggy and wagon wheels. "This ground is pretty poor," Rachel said. "I hope the rent isn't too high."

"Wait until you see the house; it's not much. And I've heard Willy's price was high, but it was the only place the Herschbergers could find to rent. It's not a great property, field-wise, either. Rocky. A garden and corn for the animals is all they can manage. Mostly, they make do by Alvin doing carpenter work when he can get it."

Rachel slowed and turned onto a long dirt driveway flanked by thick evergreens. Between the trees, Rachel caught sight of a single strand electric fence enclosing a pasture that looked like more rocks than grass. Grazing here and there were goats—a lot of goats.

"They milk them and make cheese."

"Is the cheese any good?" Rachel asked. "Maybe we could market it on the website." The goats were pretty, and she'd been around enough livestock in her life to know that the females, the milkers, didn't smell. The only stench came from the mature bucks, and farmers rarely kept more than one around because they fought each other.

"I didn't think so." Her cousin wrinkled her nose. "Tasted like old socks."

"Really?" Rachel chuckled. "I never tasted old socks."

Mary Aaron giggled. "I don't know if they know what they're doing or not."

"Maybe we could help, bring in some experts to give them pointers or something. Raising goats and making cheese is time-consuming and exact, but cheese can be extremely profitable if we can get it to the right customers."

"It would be good if you could find a way to help the Herschbergers. They have a young family, and I've heard that they're struggling." Mary Aaron pointed. "There's the house. Don't say I didn't warn you."

Willy O'Day had been known for his tightfisted ways, but Rachel couldn't believe that even he would have the nerve to charge rent for a house in such bad condition. The main two-story structure was stone, early nineteenth century, maybe even older. The roof had been patched so many times that it looked like a crazy quilt, the porch sagged, and two windows were boarded up. There were no electric lines, obviously, but there were no generators, either. Behind the house was what looked suspiciously like an outhouse. Beyond that was a tumbledown stone barn.

Rachel stopped the Jeep at a gate.

"Maybe it would be better if I went up and talked to them first," Mary Aaron said. "See if they're willing to speak to you. We'd hate to be run off—"

At that second, a scraggly-bearded man stepped out from behind the barn. He was barefoot and wearing Amish clothing. His expression was fierce, and in his hand, he was carrying an ax.

Rachel gasped. "That's Alvin, right?" she whispered to Mary Aaron.

Her cousin looked at her and nodded. "I'm afraid so."

Chapter 10

For a moment, Alvin Herschberger continued to glare at the two women. "Maybe we should leave," Mary Aaron said from the passenger's side.

"*Ne.*" Then, to Alvin, Rachel called in Deitsch, "We don't mean trouble for you or your family. I just wanted"—her gaze strayed to the field of goats—"to buy a goat," she said in a rush, looking at him again. "Two goats."

"Goats?" Mary Aaron said under her breath, cutting her eyes at Rachel. "You didn't say anything to me about buying a *goat*."

Alvin relaxed a little and lowered the ax to the ground. He squinted. "You want to buy goats?" he asked in the same dialect.

Verna appeared from behind the barn, carrying a toddler. "Mary Aaron?" Another child, a little girl about three, trailed after her. From the look of Verna's middle, there would be another little one before winter.

"Verna!" Mary Aaron smiled and climbed out of the Jeep. "My cousin Rachel wants to buy three of your goats."

"Three?" Rachel said to Mary Aaron as she got out of the vehicle.

"*Ya.*" Mary Aaron nodded, walking around the Jeep. "Maybe a doe and two kids? You have any for sale?"

Alvin walked back and leaned the ax against the building.

He picked up his daughter, and she clung to her father's neck and shyly buried her face in his shirt. "These aren't scrub goats," he said defensively. "They are purebred milking goats. We have Nubian and Toggenburg, and some crosses." He hesitated. "But some we might part with."

"Alvin was chopping wood," Verna volunteered. "He wasn't coming after you with the ax."

"Of course not." Rachel forced a chuckle. The notion had been silly, but for a moment there, when she first saw Alvin with his wild beard and the ax, she had to admit, he'd spooked her. She didn't watch much TV since returning to Stone Mill, but in her college days, she'd seen plenty of scary movies. *The Shining* came to mind.

"I have milk cooling in the springhouse," Verna said. "Would you like to try some?"

Rachel could see the eagerness in the woman's face. They needed the money a sale would bring. "I'd like that. It's a hot morning, eh?"

"Did your father send you here?" Alvin looked at Mary Aaron. "No need, because the bishop's already been."

"I don't understand. My father didn't send me," she answered. "I haven't seen the bishop."

Alvin studied her, his eyes narrowing. "The bishop thought maybe the police would come to talk to me. About your *dat*. He wanted to warn me."

The bishop was the leader of the church and responsible not only for church services but also for the moral behavior of his congregation. He was *not* responsible for interfering in a police investigation, not even one involving one of his parishioners.

"The police haven't come," Alvin went on. "I told the bishop, even if they did, I wouldn't say anything about what I saw. This is none of our business."

"Why was the bishop afraid you might speak to the police? Do you know something about my father . . . and Willy O'Day?"

Alvin glanced at his daughter, still in his arms, and murmured something to her. The little girl smiled, and he whispered again to her.

Though his response might have seemed odd to some, Rachel knew this was typical behavior among the Amish. If they didn't want to answer a question, they just pretended it hadn't been asked. Conversation could be painfully slow when trying to get information, particularly from Amish men. This kind of conversation bordered on an art.

Mary Aaron waited, then glanced at Verna. "I think I'd like some milk, too, if it isn't any trouble."

Rachel would have continued to prod Alvin, so she was glad she had Mary Aaron along. After living in the English world for so long, Rachel could be impatient with her Amish friends and neighbors. Not Mary Aaron.

Verna shrugged and jiggled the toddler on her hip. The child was in a long dress, but Rachel wasn't sure if it was a boy or a girl. The Amish often dressed male and female babies alike until their second birthday, at which point they would be clothed identical to their father or mother.

"Milk we have aplenty." Verna looked at her husband. "What about Thomasina? We could sell her."

Alvin set his daughter on the ground and straightened her white *kapp*. "Maybe."

The little girl stepped behind her father but then peered around his leg.

"A good doe, friendly to people," Alvin mused aloud. "She and Meta don't like each other. Meta is my best milker." He looked at Rachel. "Thomasina was never dehorned. You care about horns?" he asked, squinting.

"I don't mind horns." Rachel hesitated, then asked, "Did the bishop have reason to be concerned about what you might say if the police *did* come by?" They were still conversing in Deitsch.

His face flushed a dark red. He wasn't a good-looking man, Rachel thought, but when he wasn't scowling, he had a kind face. His hands were rough from hard work, and although his clothes were worn and patched, his hair was clean and freshly cut. Her earlier opinion of the Herschbergers softened. Life here was not easy for them, and maybe they had reason to be wary.

"We want no trouble." Verna shifted the baby from one hip to the other. "And we want to make none for your father."

Rachel was puzzled. What could Alvin know or have seen that the bishop didn't want him talking to the authorities about? "Look, I know that Uncle Aaron can be difficult at times, but he didn't kill Willy."

Verna and her husband exchanged guarded glances, and Rachel tried to read what was unspoken. What did they know?

"You still want that milk?" Verna asked.

Rachel nodded. "I'd like that." She looked back at Alvin. "And I'd like to see the goats you'd be willing to part with . . . the mother and two little ones."

Hope flared in Alvin's eyes. "*Ya,* let me go and catch her. She's in the pasture, but they'll all come in for grain."

"That's the last bag," Verna warned.

"And cheese," Rachel said. "I'd like to buy some of your cheese, as well."

"You would?" Verna looked surprised.

"*Ya*. My guests at the B&B like goat cheese." *Though maybe not yours,* she thought, thinking about what Mary Aaron had said about the taste of it. If the cheese was awful, though, Ada could always feed it to her chickens.

The young mother, still carrying the infant, led the way to an old stone springhouse built into the side of the hill. Inside, it was cool and dark, and Rachel heard the music of running water.

"We keep our milk here," Verna explained. "And anything else we need to refrigerate. Our propane ran out, and . . ." She shrugged.

All three women were quiet for a long moment while Verna poured a cup of milk from a covered stainless steel bucket. Several buckets sat on wooden shelves inside the springhouse.

"I saw your garden," Rachel finally said. "It looks good."

The garden lay on stony ground between the springhouse and a shed. Rows of lettuce, spinach, and kale ran straight as ranks of soldiers, while the first leafy tops of carrots pushed through the ground. Peas climbed the fence beside hills of potatoes. It was too early for corn or tomatoes here in the higher elevation, but Verna didn't have to tell them how much effort had gone into the vegetable patch that would go a long way toward feeding the family all winter.

"I just have one cup out here," Verna apologized. "But it's clean. Nobody used it."

"We don't mind sharing." Mary smiled and reached for the cup. They walked back out into the hot sunshine, and Mary Aaron and Rachel shared the cool milk.

The three women sat on a low stone wall outside the springhouse, and Rachel admired the blond-haired baby, which Verna proudly told them was a nine-month-old boy. Now, obviously more at ease with her visitors, she smiled in the same shy way as her daughter. She surveyed Rachel's shapeless skirt and blouse. "You still look Plain. Are you sure you wouldn't be more happy if you went back into the church?"

"I think about it sometimes," Rachel admitted truthfully, "but . . . I don't think so." Her throat tightened, and she couldn't say anything more.

How many nights had she lain awake and wondered the same thing? But she always came to the same conclusion. Her path lay somewhere between the English world and the Amish one, and she had to find her own happiness on that precarious ridge. She knew she had done the right thing, leaving the Amish all those years ago, but that didn't mean it hadn't been difficult. Or that it didn't hurt . . . even still.

"Thank you for the milk," she said, handing back the empty cup. "It's good."

"Some folks don't like goat milk," Verna said. "We like it fine, and it makes good cheese."

"I'd like to buy some of your cheese," Rachel said. "If you have any."

Verna stood and lifted the baby onto her hip. She motioned for them to follow her to the new shed. When she opened the door, Rachel saw a dairy and cheese-making area. There were cabinets, a propane stove, and a long table. Tall stainless pots, thermometers, ladles, and a cheese press were stored on open shelves. Everything was spotless and orderly.

"Alvin knows how to make cheese," Verna said. "He learned from his grandfather, and he has bought books and studied them. And he has even talked to the state people about getting a permit to sell it."

"Do you make different kinds?" Rachel asked.

"*Ya.*" Verna opened an insulated box stacked with neat, parchment-paper-wrapped squares and rectangles. "I don't know how much to ask . . ." She blushed. "If you buy some, it would be our first sale. So far, we've just been giving it away."

"I'll take five pounds," Rachel said, making a snap decision.

"For sure? You want so much?" Tears gathered in the corners of the Amish woman's eyes. Embarrassed, she shifted the baby from one shoulder to the other and rubbed her face against his blanket.

"Here," Mary Aaron offered. "Let me take Mosey while you pick out the cheese." And then, as Verna handed over the baby, she asked, "What is it that the bishop doesn't want your husband to tell about my *dat?*"

Verna didn't answer.

"Please," Rachel walked over to the cooler and looked into Verna's eyes. "It's important that we find out what happened so we can prove that Mary Aaron's father is innocent."

Still, Verna held her tongue. But she looked like she wanted to speak.

"Alvin doesn't think he did it, does he?" Mary Aaron asked. She looked at little Mosey in her arms, then at his mother. "He doesn't think my *dat* is guilty of this killing?"

Verna worked her jaw. "He wonders," she admitted. "You know—because of the argument at the auction. And because everyone knows that Aaron Hostetler has a temper. We saw his temper that day."

"What happened?" Rachel asked. "Exactly."

Verna sighed. She looked at the brimming ice chest and then at her bare feet. "We were there to sell some of our male goats. Alvin and me and the children were just walking through the pens to see how long before our goats would go into the ring when we heard shouting. It was Aaron and Willy O'Day. I heard Aaron say something about his dog, and Willy yelled back that he'd shot and killed it. But it wasn't just arguing like some said." She met Rachel's gaze. "Willy raised his fist and shook it at Aaron. That's when Aaron raised his hand against Willy."

"My father *hit* him?" Mary Aaron's eyes widened.

"*Ne*. Not exactly. He raised his hand, then dropped it." She demonstrated. "But then he pushed Willy hard against the wall."

"It was over our dog Bo," Mary Aaron explained. "We'd found him dead at the end of our driveway."

Rachel nodded. Bo had been their sheep and cattle dog. Not only had the family lost a valuable animal, but the children had been attached to him, too.

"He was a good dog," Mary Aaron continued. "Getting on in years, but he could still herd the animals. *Dat* would send him for the cows, and he'd bring them in."

Rachel remembered that Mary Aaron had said that the animal had been shot. But why would Willy O'Day shoot an

Amish herd dog? "So Willy admitted that he shot Uncle Aaron's dog?" she asked.

Verna nodded. "He did, and more than that. He cursed your uncle and threatened to start shooting his cows next. I don't know why."

"*Dat* and Willy had argued over the cows," Mary Aaron explained. The baby started fussing, and she bounced him. "*Dat*'s cows broke through the fence to get to the pond and Willy was angry about it."

"So, what happened after my uncle shoved Willy against the wall?" Rachel asked.

"Willy swung at Aaron, but Aaron jumped back out of the way. Then he said if Willy ever set foot on his farm, he'd be sorry. And Willy shouted that if the cows ever stepped over onto his property again, he'd be eating steak."

"Was that the end of it?" Rachel asked.

"*Ya*. About that time the deacon came and talked to Aaron and got him away. By then, some of the English people had called the security man, the man in the white shirt. We saw Willy talking to the security man and waving his arms. We couldn't hear all of what he said, but he was pointing in the direction Aaron had gone and he kept saying his name."

Rachel was shocked; she'd heard about the argument, but not about the physical altercation. Her uncle must have been furious when he learned that Willy really had killed Bo. She'd heard that Willy could be mean, but she couldn't imagine he could be cruel enough to shoot a dog. Still, for Uncle Aaron to shove Willy in front of witnesses—it would look bad to the police. It would look bad to anyone.

"Don't tell Alvin that I told," Verna begged. "He would be unhappy with me." She looked at Rachel timidly. "Do you still want the cheese?"

Later, as Rachel and Mary Aaron drove back to Stone Mill House, her cousin folded her arms over her chest and glanced at her. "Goats? And cheese? What are you going to do with goats? And all this cheese?"

Rachel could tell she was trying to make light of what they had learned about her father. "I'll think of something," she assured her. "And the cheese won't go to waste."

She was still going over and over again in her head what Verna had told them. If someone had told the police about the argument, which surely someone had, that would be enough reason for them to take Aaron in for questioning. But maybe the police didn't have anything else. Was that possible?

"I guess it's a good thing you didn't want to go to Sampson Miller's farm to ask questions. We would have come home with the Jeep full of pigs."

Rachel gestured. "We don't have goats in the Jeep."

"*Ne,* but they're coming tomorrow."

Rachel's cell rang just as she was getting out of the shower. It was ten twenty. She almost didn't pick up. She was dripping water all over her bathroom rug, and if it was Evan, she could call him back. But even as she was hesitating, she grabbed a bath towel, wrapped it around herself, and made a mad dash for the ringing phone.

It will stop ringing just as soon as I grab it, she thought. True to form, when she did manage a hello, there was a dead silence on the other end of the line. Water dripped onto her floorboards. "Hello?" she repeated.

And then a faint voice asked, "Is this Rachel Mast?"

"Yes, it is." She thought she recognized the sound of the caller's voice. The women had a slight southern accent. "Dawn? Dawn Clough? Yes, this is Rachel. Thank you so much for—"

"Did Roy put you up to this?"

Roy? Who was Roy? And then Rachel made the connection. Roy Thompson. The man that Dawn had lived with here in the valley. "No. I'm calling about something else."

"Do I know you, Rachel?" the woman asked.

"I have the B&B in Stone Mill, and I used to come in to Junior's. You waited on me a couple of times. I'm a redhead. I always sat in the corner booth. English breakfast tea?"

"Oh, yeah. You're the one with the cute cop boyfriend."

"That's me. He's not exactly my boyfriend . . . never mind. That's not important. Do you remember me now?"

"Yeah. You were a good tipper. I always remember the tightwads and the good tippers. So why are you tryin' to get up with me?"

Rachel sat on the edge of her bed. "You may not have heard, well, I don't suppose you could have . . ." She started again. "Did the police call you about Willy O'Day?"

"Cops? No. What'd Willy say I did?"

"No, nothing like that. Did you know that Willy was missing?"

"Missing? No. What's that got to do with me? I haven't seen him since . . . I don't know. Since I left Stone Mill in October."

"Yes," Rachel said eagerly. "I know. I was wondering why it was that you left town so suddenly."

"Why do you want to know?"

"It's . . . well . . ." She stopped and started again. "The thing is, Willy disappeared the same weekend that you did. Nobody knew where he went. Then, a few days ago, he turned up dead. Murdered."

"Murdered?"

Dawn would have had to be a good actress to fake her surprise. And Rachel suspected that she wasn't good at much, least of all acting. "My uncle has been accused of killing Willy. My uncle's Amish."

"An Amish man? How is that?"

"Long story," Rachel said. "Anyway, I'm just trying to talk to anyone who knew Willy. To help my uncle out. I understand the two of you were . . . going out."

"Going out? No way. I went on two dates with him, but we were never *dating*. Willy was a bigger jerk than Roy, if that's possible. He took me to dinner in Huntingdon and expected me to pay for my own meal. Can you believe that? *And* he shorted the waitress on her tip. You can tell a lot about people by the way they tip. Nice guys leave a good tip. But murdered and dead? That's awful. Willy didn't deserve that."

"No, he didn't."

Dawn was quiet for a second, then, "Why would you think that me and Willy were goin' out?"

"George. His brother. He said you two were really friendly at the restaurant. The day he disappeared. Joking around, acting as though . . . you know . . . you were . . . good friends."

"Honey, I'm a waitress. I get paid by tips. I flirt with *all* the guys because flirting gets you tips. I couldn't get Roy to understand that, either. Roy was jealous—besides being a mean drunk. I thought maybe him and me might have something . . . but I don't stand for being knocked around. Had that with my kids' father, and no more."

"So you left town to get away from Roy?"

"More or less. My mama tripped over my Tommy's fire truck and broke her wrist. My kids live with her, and with her arm in a cast she was having a hard time with them. She said she'd send me money to come home, and I took it. I'm sorry about Willy, and your uncle, but I don't know anything about it. Sorry. I gotta go."

"I don't suppose Willy ever said anything about being in trouble with anyone? Or owing a lot of money to anybody or—"

"Nope. Told you. I don't know nothin'. 'Course anything is possible with that one. He liked to gamble, you know. Wanted to take me to Atlantic City with him for a weekend, but I wasn't interested. If you ask me, somebody knocked him over the head for that cash he carried. Anyway, really, I gotta go," Dawn said. "Sorry about your uncle. Tell the cops to look for some mugger."

"Thanks." Bishop jumped up on the bed as Rachel disconnected. "Well, that was a dead end," she told the cat, tossing her cell on her pillow.

Then she remembered the open grave with Willy's body sprawled in it. And despite the warm May evening, she shivered.

The answer had to be out there. She just had to look harder.

Chapter 11

After breakfast, Rachel collected her market baskets and drove her golf cart to the town park. She went to the farmer's market every Saturday.

The commons, which covered most of an ordinary city block, was a grassy area, surrounded by trees, in the center of Stone Mill. Several giant oaks and a few poplars were scattered across the open space. What was significant about the plot was that when the streets were laid out early in the nineteenth century, the land had been designated to be communally owned by the town citizens.

Here, for hundreds of years, craftsmen and farmers had exchanged the fruits of their fields and workshops, children had played, neighbors had gossiped, and news had filtered through from the larger world beyond the mountains. These massive trees with interwoven branches had witnessed weddings and hangings, joyful laughter and more than their share of bitter tears.

During the French and Indian War, when hostile raiding parties of Indians had terrorized the valley, burning and slaughtering peaceful Amish and English settlers alike, a militia had been raised on this spot. A generation later, volunteers had assembled to fight the British in the War of Independence, and nearly a hundred years after that, the sons of farmers, gentlemen, and merchants alike had gathered to march south against Robert E. Lee and the Army of Northern Virginia. Over the centuries, as proclaimed by granite memorials, many of Stone Mill's volunteers hadn't survived to return to their valley home.

Still, the park evoked more pleasant memories for the residents of Stone Mill than sorrowful ones. As a child, Rachel had sneaked away from her father's farm to watch town parades and holiday celebrations here. And if the strict codes of the Amish faith had prevented their followers from actively participating in or even watching the festivities, there was no such prohibition against bringing crafts and produce—and even the occasional lamb, piglet, or chickens—here to sell to the English.

Sometime in the 1980s, the farmer's market had ceased to exist in Stone Mill, and it was Rachel's enthusiastic urging that had brought it back the previous year. At her suggestion, the town charged no fee for valley residents to sell goods. Instead, additional revenues were realized by increased traffic from tourists, shoppers who later might stop for a meal at Junior's or patronize George's bookstore, the pottery or quilt shops, or Russell's Hardware.

The market opened every Saturday, rain or shine, from March until December, closing only in the bitterest months, when snow piled high across the commons and black ice made the roads over the mountains dangerous. Emulating a colonial tradition, Stone Mill residents had joined together to erect sturdy wooden stalls, covered by a procession of canvas coverings. Here, amid a fluid mixture of Amish and English merchants, Rachel's sister Annie offered jars and crocks of her valley honey; Coyote Finch displayed hand-thrown mugs, bowls, and plates; and George operated a mini-bookstand. Members of Ada's family displayed whatever fruits, herbs, or vegetables were in season. And Hulda Schenfeld never failed to show up with an array of old-fashioned candy, soda pop, and inexpensive children's toys.

Rachel parked her golf cart near her Aunt Hannah's buggy

and scanned the market. The beautiful weather had brought out a lot of sellers. Every stall was buzzing, and a few merchants had set up their wares in the center, some on blankets or simply by arranging their goods on the grass. She caught sight of one of Eli Rust's daughters selling handmade shovels, rakes, and hoes out of an open barrel, and one of the waitresses from Junior's offering tuna and chicken salad sandwiches from an ice chest.

Elsie, her cousin, was at the Hostetler chicken-and-egg stall, but Rachel didn't see her aunt. She usually came to chaperone her daughter, but she never spoke to or waited on any of the English. Rachel was surprised that Elsie had come at all today, but maybe the family was doing its best to get back to normal in spite of the worry about Uncle Aaron. In any case, eggs from free-range chickens, raised without antibiotics, were always in high demand. Some customers came from as far away as Huntingdon and State College to buy them, and they brought a premium price.

Rachel knew almost everyone at the market, and a lot of them were her relatives. It would have been easy to spend the entire morning here, just visiting. She wore her normal clothing: jeans, a short-sleeve T-shirt, and flip-flops. In Amish homes, she wore a long skirt and a kerchief over her hair, but here, even the conservative Amish were used to dealing with outsiders. And oddly enough, at the farmer's market, they treated her as if she were one of the English. There was some logic to the reasoning, but it was difficult for most people to understand. After living two years in Stone Mill in this strange world of hers, being neither English, nor Amish, she simply went with the flow.

"Rachel!" Coyote Finch waved to her from her pottery table. She was a tall, slender blonde who could have graced a magazine cover. "Come and see my rainbow bowl. I'm really happy with the way it turned out."

As Rachel approached the stall, two little giggling, blue-eyed girls crawled out from under it. They were close in age, both with hair so pale that it seemed almost silver-white, nearly mirror images of their pretty mother. A third little girl, also blond and equally adorable, sat in a stroller inside the booth. Both chubby hands were smeared with honey, and she clutched a turkey feather that she passed back and forth from one set of sticky fingers to the other, all the while squealing happily.

"Mama! Mama! Can we have gingerbread? Please, please, please?" the older girls begged in unison.

"Please, Mama! Please!" The fourth little Finch, a boy with black hair and a round face the exact shade of peach honey, struggled to roll his wheelchair across the grass. "I want one!" Remi's hooded eyes were as black and shiny as ripe elderberries.

Coyote rolled her eyes and handed two dollars to her son. "You'll have to share. And Baby gets some, too."

"Yes, Mama, we'll share," Remi promised. Each sister ran to take a position on either side of the back of the wheelchair, and with great effort, the three progressed across the lawn toward the booth selling gingerbread men.

Coyote and her husband, Blade, and their four children were newcomers to Stone Mill—*refugees* from California, as Coyote put it. She was a potter, and they had happily set up a small business down the block from The George. And although the town folk often referred to the Finches as "the hippies," the family had fit into the community with the ease of an old leather slipper. Coyote's pottery was beautiful, as evidenced by the large bread bowl that she proudly displayed. The swirl of colors in red, yellow, orange, and violet made the piece seem old and new at the same time.

"It's gorgeous." Rachel ran her fingertips around the bowl. "I love it."

"It's so big, Blade was afraid it would crack in the kiln, but it didn't."

"I'm sure it will sell," Rachel assured her. "At your shop, if not here. When my birthday comes, I want to commission one just like it for myself."

Two English women stopped to admire Coyote's mugs, and Rachel moved on. She stopped for a moment to speak to George and give Sophie a dog biscuit she had remembered to tuck in her pocket. "You have anything really good this week?" she asked as she offered the little dog the treat.

George had brought an assortment of romances and Pennsylvania Dutch cookbooks, a new science fiction novel written by an author in Harrisburg, and several gardening books. As always, he had a box of used children's books that he gave away to interested kids or their parents.

He adjusted his ball cap. "The usual."

"You'll never make a profit that way," Rachel teased, pointing to the box.

"I might if I turn a few young ones into readers," he replied with a wry grin. It was a running joke, and one that George always enjoyed and seemed to look forward to. But today, his voice was hoarse and his eyes shadowed. Rachel suspected that the shock of his brother's death was still sinking in.

"Have you made any arrangements?" she asked. "For Willy's services?"

George looked even more distressed. "They haven't released the . . . his remains yet. Your Evan called me; he thinks we'll hear something today. I'm thinking midweek. I'll let you know, of course." He sank into his folding chair and steepled his hands. "I still wake up in the morning and think it's all a bad dream. I keep thinking . . ." George trailed off. "It shouldn't be this way," he said. "Twins belong together. It's just wrong."

"Morning, George." Bill Billingsly strode toward the bookstall. "Did that *Peterson Field Guide* come in yet? My son's birthday is . . ."

Rachel waved a hello to Bill, nodded to George, and returned to her shopping. She'd hoped to tell George about her visit to Park Estates, but Bill was one of the town's biggest gossips. She liked him well enough, but she didn't want to get into a discussion about her attempts to clear Uncle Aaron with him, and she didn't want the information published in the next edition of the *Stone Mill Gazette*.

Moving from stall to stall, Rachel purchased lettuce, scallions, and asparagus. A young English woman whom Rachel recognized from the next valley over had quarts of strawberries for sale as well as her usual flowers. It seemed early for berries, but when Rachel asked where they were from, Carol explained that her cousin had brought them up from Assateague in Maryland. "They were just picked yesterday," she added. Rachel took four quarts and two bouquets of flowers.

Her baskets overflowing, Rachel walked back to her golf cart and piled her goodies in open cardboard cartons in the back. As she was transferring them, she couldn't help overhearing an agitated male voice from the far side of her Aunt Hannah's buggy. Whoever it was was speaking in Deitsch.

Rachel didn't want to eavesdrop, especially on a disagreement, but as she turned to walk back to the market area, she heard another voice. The heated retort made her stop and turn back. *It was her Aunt Hannah.*

"If not here," the man said, "where?" Rachel recognized the voice but couldn't place it at once. "I told you—"

"*Ne.* You'll listen to me, Eli. You'll hold your tongue if you know what's—"

The rest was muffled, but Rachel had heard enough to be concerned for her aunt. *Was one of their own accusing Uncle Aaron?* Unable to stand there and allow Aunt Hannah to be confronted that way, Rachel hurried around the buggy.

A red-faced Aunt Hannah caught sight of her and gasped. "Rachel!"

"Hist!" Eli warned Hannah. "Say nothing." Slowly he turned his gaze to Rachel and nodded. "Hannah and I—"

"This is none of your affair, Niece." Aunt Hannah's face grew stern. "Best you get on about your own business."

Stunned, Rachel glanced from one to the other. Her aunt looked almost frightened. No, she decided, not frightened. *Guilty.* But of what? Why would she and her neighbor be having angry words in a place where anyone might hear them? And what could possibly make her aunt so cross with her when she knew that she was doing everything possible to help Uncle Aaron? "I'm sorry," she murmured. "I heard . . . I thought you . . ."

"*Ne.* It's nothing," her aunt said. But her words were stilted.

"Dat?"

Rachel turned to see Eli's daughter walk around the far end of Hannah's buggy and stop short.

Rachel thought that Barbara was about fifteen, old enough to have left school but not old enough to attend singings yet. She had light-brown hair, brown eyes, and a bad complexion. Her face was now flushed, as if she realized that she'd interrupted something that she shouldn't have.

"*Dat,* there's an Englisher," Barbara said hesitantly. "He wants to talk to you about an order for ten shovels to sell at his lawn and garden shop in Belleville."

Eli was known for the fine shovels he made by recycling sheet steel he bought cheaply and adding his own hand-hewn handles. The shovels were not only distinct but well made, too. Practically everyone in Stone Mill owned one; Rachel did.

"*Ya,*" he said. "I'm coming." He looked back at Aunt Hannah, started to say something else, but thought better of it and walked away. His daughter followed him without saying a word.

"How's Uncle Aaron?" Rachel asked her aunt, watching Eli and Barbara go. "Have you heard anything more from the police?"

"*Ne.* Nothing. Your uncle says they must know they made a mistake and are ashamed to admit it." Her features took on a vulnerable look. "Don't say anything to him about this," Aunt Hannah said. "With Eli." She averted her eyes and toyed with one of her *kapp* strings. "He has enough on his mind to worry about without troubling him further."

"No." Rachel shook her head. "I won't."

"*Gut.* I knew you would understand. You were always a sensible girl." She rubbed her forehead. "I think I'll go and help Elsie with the eggs."

Rachel watched as Aunt Hannah walked away. She wouldn't mention this incident to her uncle, but she sensed that something wasn't right. It was almost as though Aunt Hannah and Eli were keeping a secret.

On her way back to her golf cart, Rachel ran into Fred Wright and asked him about building a fence for her goats. He ran a small business out of his home building fences. Fred insisted she come to his table to get a pamphlet and price quotes. They chatted for fifteen minutes and agreed that he would start work Monday or Tuesday. She was headed back to her golf cart again when Carol walked toward her.

"I'm leaving early today," she said. "I had some daisies left over, and I wondered if you'd like them, free?"

"Are you sure?" Rachel asked. "That's so nice of you."

"You're my best regular customer." Carol handed over the bucket with the flowers. "I thought that you can always use them at your B&B. I wrapped them in wet newspaper."

A horse and buggy left the parking lot at a fast trot. As the vehicle passed, Rachel saw Eli Rust on the front seat, back straight, shoulders tense. He kept his eyes on the horse and either didn't see her or pretended not to.

"What's up with him and Hannah Hostetler?" Carol asked, watching the buggy go.

Rachel looked at her. "What do you mean?"

"The two of them. I saw them last week with their heads together. If they weren't Amish, I'd think there was a little hanky-panky going on."

Rachel choked back a reply. She doubted that Carol knew

that Hannah was her aunt or that she couldn't have offered a greater insult about an Old Order Amish man or woman. Amish marriage was sacred, and nothing would make her believe that Aunt Hannah would do anything to threaten her salvation. *A secret romance? Impossible.*

"You've got it wrong," Rachel said. "She's my aunt, and she's devoted to my uncle. Whatever you saw, it couldn't be anything like that."

"If you say so," Carol replied. "But under that bonnet, she's still a woman, and you know what they say. 'Where there's smoke, there's fire.'"

Rachel was still puzzling over Aunt Hannah's behavior a short while later when she stopped in front of Russell's Hardware and Emporium to buy some screws to fix some doorknobs. Sometimes she wondered if doorknobs got together in the middle of the night to plan mischief, because when one came loose, it seemed that two or three others followed suit in the next twenty-four hours.

Russell's was owned by the Schenfelds. When Meir Schenfeld bought the store from Dobry Russell back in the 1880s the Schenfelds were the only Jewish people in Stone Mill. Not wanting to rock any boats, according to Hulda, her husband's grandfather had left the old sign hanging outside the store. Over the years, there had been some family discussion about changing the name of the business, but no one had ever gotten around to it. And although the store had been enlarged and modernized many times over the decades, Russell's it remained.

The hardware store carried everything from Eli's shovels to fancy stainless steel dishwashers. You could find T-shirts, Amish straw hats, lightbulbs, and diapers. They didn't carry food other than candy and an array of chips, sodas, and snacks, but there was a good selection of tools, electrical parts, horse bits and bridles, and every size of screw, nut, and bolt that Rachel had ever needed for Stone Mill House.

She pulled the golf cart into the parking lot at the back of Russell's, and was surprised to see her father's buggy in a covered parking area reserved for the Amish. Rachel supposed that the English thought all black buggies looked alike, but she would have recognized this one anywhere—not to mention her *dat*'s favorite horse, now standing hipshot and content in the shade.

It had been Hulda who'd insisted that her husband provide shelter for the horses, along with a source of fresh water and clean troughs. It was a courtesy that the Amish community appreciated, and it gained their loyalty as customers. That, along with the custom of offering each child accompanied by an adult a treat from the old-fashioned glass candy case.

Rachel paused to pet her father's horse and offer him a carrot from her bags of groceries. His nose felt velvety soft against her palm. When he'd finished, she wiped her damp hand on the back of her jeans and turned, nearly bumping into her father. "*Dat.*" She smiled with surprise. "I didn't hear you coming."

"Daughter." He smiled back.

Rachel felt a little self-conscious. Her head wasn't covered, and she wasn't wearing a skirt. "Is *Mam* with you?"

He shook his head. "Just me. Your mother needed some canning jar lids, pectin, and some other stuff." They both smiled, knowing how her *dat* hated shopping, and how her mother asked him to pick up one thing and then handed him a long list. Then, his expression became serious. "I hear that you've been asking questions around the valley about your uncle. Do you think that's wise?"

"Someone has to help Uncle Aaron. It's pretty clear he's not going to do anything for himself."

"But poking your nose in where it doesn't belong . . . I'm not sure it's best." He looked away.

"You don't think he's guilty, do you?"

Her *dat* puffed out his cheeks and slowly exhaled. "I

wouldn't like to think so, him doing violence. Killing a man. Burying him in a hole in the ground like an animal." He shook his head. "I pray not, but . . ."

"But?" she pressed, taking one of the bags in his arms and putting it behind the driver's seat of his buggy.

"He has a terrible temper, your Uncle Aaron. Remember when he took an ax to his windmill? Chopped it into firewood." He sighed. "A terrible waste."

"Do you believe Willy killed his dog?" She turned to look into her father's eyes. "Someone told me he heard Willy brag about it."

He made a clicking sound with his tongue, a habit of his when he was troubled. "At the auction, you mean. When your uncle and Willy argued last fall? It was just before Willy disappeared."

"You were there?"

"At the auction, but not near enough to see what went on between them. I heard gossip. There's always talk when men lose their tempers. I do know that Aaron believed Willy killed his dog." His mouth tightened. "Aaron put great stock by the dog. He was getting on in dog years, but he was a smart animal." He went to the hitching rail and untied the horse. "If I could see my way to help Aaron, I would. For your mother's sake as well as Aaron's, but I can't . . ." He averted his eyes. "We are not of this world, Rachel."

"I know, *Dat*. I understand. Maybe that's why I feel like I have to try and do something."

He was silent for a moment. "You be careful."

"I will."

"And . . ." Her father walked slowly to the open doorway that led to the driver's seat. "Have patience with your mother. She worries for your soul."

"I know."

"And she has never stopped loving you."

"I know that, too, *Dat*."

He nodded and climbed up into the seat.

She came close to the buggy and put her hand on the dash. "Something else . . ."

"*Ya?*"

She debated whether or not to say what she was thinking . . . then barreled forward. "I saw Aunt Hannah at the farmer's market. She was with Eli Rust, and they were clearly having a disagreement. When I come upon them, she acted . . . strange, as if she was hiding something." She met her father's gaze. "Like *they* were hiding something." She hesitated. "And I saw something similar the day Willy's body was found. In Aunt Hannah's driveway."

"Let it go, daughter. Whatever went on, it was private. Your aunt's business, not yours. Hannah is not a woman to shame her family. Be sure that you do the same."

"*Ya,* I will," Rachel answered softly.

He made that clicking noise again. "Your mother likes you better in a dress, with your head decently covered. So do I."

"I know."

He nodded again, and his eyes shone. "Don't wait for someone to be dug up in a cow pasture to visit. We all miss you." With that, he flicked the lines over the horse's back, and the buggy clattered away, leaving Rachel staring after him and wondering if he knew more of her Aunt Hannah's secret than he was willing to tell.

Chapter 12

As predicted by George, Willy's body was soon released, and that Wednesday at 12:45, forty-five minutes later than scheduled, Rachel joined the stream of mourners pouring into the Methodist cemetery. Most were there because of their relationships with George, she mused, and in spite of their relationships with Willy.

Workmen had erected a canvas shelter over a new gravesite inside the prestigious O'Day family plot to block the wind, but the tent could hold only a portion of the mourners. A cool temperature only added to the discomfort.

The authorities had released Willy's body late Saturday afternoon, and Rachel had endured both Tuesday evening and Wednesday morning viewings at McCloud's Funeral Home. The viewings—in name only because the casket had been closed—had been bad enough, but the funeral had all the makings of a three-ring circus.

Because she was raised Amish, Rachel had a very different idea about how big a send-off the newly deceased should have. In her community of Plain people, the family and close friends of the deceased sat up all night in the home with the body. The following morning, the body—interred in a simple wooden coffin—was laid to rest in an Amish graveyard. Afterward, there was a shared meal, usually at the home of a relative, but following that, life went on. Death, even when it came suddenly, was as easily accepted as birth. And because, to the Amish, the hereafter was more important than this mortal existence, intense mourning was discouraged.

Not so among the English. There had been tears and wailing aplenty at the two viewings. George had been inconsolable both times, sobbing so hard that he'd barely been able to greet the hundreds of mourners, both Amish and English, who'd come to pay their respects. Rachel had counted two state senators and several representatives, as well as two TV crews and several newspaper reporters. She couldn't help thinking that many were there because Willy had been murdered rather than dying of natural circumstances.

The night before, Teresa Ridley, after an impressive display of hysterics, had fainted over the casket, and had to be revived by two of Stone Mill's volunteer firefighters. An hour later, Dawn Clough's no-account ex, Roy, had arrived at McCloud's Funeral Home intoxicated, in the mistaken understanding that a free meal was being offered after the viewing. Roy drove his pickup onto the sidewalk, and then overcompensated in trying to correct his mistake and backed into someone's new car in the process.

At the second viewing, early Wednesday, attendance had been so heavy that an extra state trooper had to be called in to direct traffic. An assistant DA, who was running for county office, had given an interview to one of the TV news crews on the front steps of McCloud's. In the ensuing confusion, one of the cameramen had filmed the arrival of an Amish bishop, whom the assistant DA incorrectly identified as Aaron Hostetler, *a person of interest*.

Inside the funeral home, someone tried to sneak a smoke in the restroom, setting off the smoke alarms and causing the evacuation of the funeral home. Then, someone opened the wrong door, thinking that it was the exit to the side parking lot, and accidently let George's Sophie out. The little dog escaped into the street, and Rachel had joined a search party that included Ell and half a dozen Amish teenagers. Twenty minutes passed before Ell discovered Sophie hiding under the staircase that led to her apartment on the O'Day property.

Rachel didn't know what else could go wrong today, but she kept an open mind. Stone Mill didn't lose a leading citizen to murder every day of the week. She'd had quite enough of Willy O'Day's funeral services, and she would rather have had a root canal than attend the burial and following reception at the Methodist church hall. But George was her friend. He needed her support.

Plus, she'd been so busy in the last few days, she'd not come up with any information that would help prove Uncle Aaron's innocence. She needed to be here today. Since almost everyone in the valley over the age of ten was here, other than her mother, it might give her a chance to speak to those people she hadn't been able to catch up with. She had a list of questions she wanted to ask, and this might be the only opportunity she'd have to do so without attracting attention.

The Amish, all in black clothing, were clustered together under the trees. She saw her father and several of her brothers and sisters as well as Aunt Hannah and Uncle Aaron and the elders of their church. She wanted to go over and speak to them, but dressed English as she was and here among so many strangers, she knew that it would be awkward for them. Her Amish relatives might even refuse to acknowledge her. Once again, she was acutely aware of being caught between worlds. Sometimes, she felt as though she was balancing on top of a fence post, poised to fall one way or the other.

She glanced around, hoping to see Evan. She'd met him for coffee Monday morning, but he hadn't been able to—or wasn't willing to—tell her anything more about the case against her uncle. She supposed he was on duty today. As far as she could tell, he wasn't here. She had the impression that he was still unhappy about her intrusion into the murder investigation. Evan was her best friend, but he hadn't grown up Amish; he didn't understand how responsible she felt for her family and the Amish community. She knew bad things sometimes happened to good people. She just couldn't let it happen to Uncle Aaron, not if she could prevent it.

George had phoned the previous night, after the viewing, to ask that she join him in the seats reserved for family inside the tent. She'd tried to refuse, but he'd insisted that while he had friends aplenty, he had no living relatives. He'd sounded so pitiful that she hadn't had the heart to say no.

Rachel had left her umbrella at home and had hoped that the rain would hold off long enough to get Willy in the ground. That wasn't to be. Before she was halfway to the gravesite, thunder rolled overhead, lightning cracked, and the skies opened up. Dripping wet, shoes sodden, Rachel threaded her way through the forest of flower arrangements to George's side. He caught her hand and squeezed it hard. Ell, garbed in her standard black tunic, black boots, and black tights, was standing on George's left. She looked like a scared child, despite the exaggerated dark makeup and the numerous piercings.

Between the thunder, the downpour, and Teresa's ragged sobbing from the row just behind her, Rachel could barely hear the minister. She knew there was no chance that those sheltered by the army of umbrellas or the Amish, standing even farther away, could follow the service. Mercifully, the minister kept the eulogy short. She thought it was just as well, for the Willy O'Day memorialized by his kind words bore little resemblance to the tough businessman she'd known.

When the clergyman finished and the funeral director motioned for anyone who wished to come forward and place a rose on the coffin, Ell's mother pushed forward past George. She fell to her knees, weeping as though her heart would break.

"Mom, please. Don't . . ." Ell, dressed head to toe in black, including silk gloves, dashed forward and caught her mother's arm. "Stop it. You're making a scene," she whispered loudly. Her face glowed red, and Rachel thought that the young woman looked so embarrassed by her mother's behavior that she might burst into tears herself.

"You don't understand!" Teresa wailed. "He . . . he . . ."

George stood up, seemed to lose all the strength in his legs, and sat back down, hard, in the folding chair. One of the McClouds offered him a rose, but he clutched it so hard that the stem snapped, and the man had to provide a second. "Please . . ." George managed, and Rachel helped him up and walked with him to the graveside.

Ell was still tugging on her mother's arm, trying desperately to get her away from the coffin. Then, Polly Wagler made her way to Teresa's side, put her arm around her, and murmured in her ear. Polly and Teresa had known each other since they were teenagers. Whatever Polly said seemed to console Teresa because she got up and allowed them to lead her away.

George straightened his shoulders, placed the single rose on top of the spray-laden casket, and said his final good-byes to Willy. Rachel was standing right beside him, and as he braced himself against the coffin, she saw that George was wearing Willy's ring—the one that Willy was never seen without, the one that had been on his body. Rachel shivered. She supposed that having his brother's ring meant a lot to George, but she still found it vaguely creepy. Then the minister shook George's hand, and she lost sight of him as mourners swarmed around them to offer condolences.

Rachel took the opportunity and hurried out into the rain. She couldn't avoid going to the reception in the church hall, but she could try and discover where Polly, Ell, and Teresa had gone. Rachel found it odd that Teresa, who rarely showed any emotion at all, seemed so broken up by Willy's death.

Rachel wondered what Polly Wagler had said to Teresa that had allowed the middle-aged woman to get her grief under control. Rachel doubted that she could get Teresa to confide in her, and Ell would naturally be protective of her mother. But Polly was a cat of a different color. Her grocery store was a natural gathering place, and Polly was rarely averse to discussing the affairs of her acquaintances.

Rachel had hoped to catch up with the three women before they returned to the church hall, provided, of course, that they were going there. But it seemed that everyone had made a dash for their vehicles at the same time. Although the rain had slackened somewhat, it was still coming down, and the cemetery was a maze of bobbing umbrellas and people holding coats over their heads. There was no sign of Ell, her mother, or Polly. Since Rachel was already soaked and not that far from Stone Mill House, she decided to stop at home and change into dry clothes before going on to the reception. The day already seemed to be long, but she had a bad feeling it was going to get even longer.

Half an hour later, Rachel found a parking place on a back street near the Methodist church and, umbrella now in hand, crossed the boxwood garden to the hall. As she approached the side entrance, a man called out to her.

"Rachel Mast? Wait up. I want to talk to you."

Rachel turned to see a short, stocky man wearing black shoes, tan corduroy slacks, and a navy-blue sports coat bearing down on her, a disagreeable expression on his face. She didn't know Steve Barber well, but she remembered what Chelsea and Blanche had said about him at the trailer park. Obviously, he was no friend of Willy O'Day's, so what was he doing at his after-funeral reception?

"I understand that you were at my mother-in-law's place asking questions about our family." Steve pushed his wire-rim glasses up on the ridge of his nose. Rachel guessed that he was somewhere in his late forties, but his hair and mustache were a suspiciously uniform black. Steve had a slight lisp; his tone was sharp and unpleasant. "I want to know why."

Rachel waited, expecting him to say more. And he did.

"What call do you have to be sticking your nose in our

business?" He advanced on her and shook his finger in her face. "Don't you know that Blanche is a sick old woman? How dare you badger her—"

"Wait." Rachel forced a smile and, at the same time, raised her hand, palm out, to keep him from intruding further into her personal space. "I wasn't *badgering* anyone, and Mrs. Willis invited me into her home." She drew herself up to her full height and fixed Steve with a firm gaze. "I'm surprised to see you here. It was my understanding that you didn't like Willy O'Day very much."

"Like him?" Steve muttered something under his breath that sounded like something Rachel would rather not hear on the back steps of a church. "Willy was a con artist and a thief. He took advantage of my late wife, and half the women in this town. I didn't dislike him. I *hated* him."

"Hard words on the day of a man's funeral."

"Not hard enough. If you ask me, he got what was coming to him." Steve's lips drew back into a sneer and his lisp thickened. "Whoever killed him did this town a favor. And if I'd known how he was going to twist my Millie around his little finger, I'd have killed him myself."

"Did you?" Rachel flung back, taking a step toward him. "Did you kill him, Mr. Barber?"

Steve's eyes widened in surprise. Then he grimaced, hawked, and spat on the ground near her feet. "Sorry. You can't pin this on me. Paper said he went into the ground the day he disappeared. I was in Williamsport that weekend. A family wedding."

Shouldn't be too hard to prove or disprove. "Fortunate for you," she said sweetly. "Weddings are always enjoyable."

"My cousin Trudy married a welder." He raised his chin. "I didn't get back until Tuesday, October fifth. Took off from work."

"You remember a lot of details for something that took place eight months ago."

He pointed his finger at her again. "We're talking about

you, not me. Why are you asking so many questions? That's what I want to know."

"I'm trying to help my uncle."

"The Amish guy? Hostetler? Didn't Willy shoot that guy's cow?"

"His dog. At least, that's what people are saying." She glanced over her shoulder toward the church. George would be wondering where she was. "It's been pleasant talking to you, but—"

"Yeah, pleasant," Steve scoffed. "Believe me, lady, there were a lot of people in this town who had good reason to want Willy O'Day dead. And you shouldn't be grilling a senile old lady in a wheelchair."

"She didn't seem senile to me," Rachel said. "On the contrary, Mrs. Willis was—"

"That's because you don't know the old bat like I do. The whole time Millie and I were married, Blanche tried to cause trouble. Millie was too good for that family. Blanche and that granddaughter of hers are nothing more than trailer-park trash."

Abruptly, Rachel heard running footfalls behind her, and she glanced back over her shoulder to see her sister Lettie running toward her. Her *kapp* had slid back off her head, and she was hanging on to it by one string.

"Rachel! Come quick!" Her face was pale, her eyes huge in her face. "It's Uncle Aaron!" She seized Rachel's hand. "Hurry!" She turned and raced back up the sidewalk. Together, they dashed into the side entrance of the church hall, down a short corridor lined with classrooms, up a short flight of stairs, and through swinging doors.

As they burst into the hall, Rachel saw a wall of people, their backs to the two of them.

Lettie whispered, under her breath, "The police."

Townspeople and Amish parted to let her through. Rachel's heart was pounding; she had a bad feeling about this. Directly ahead of her was a woman in a wheelchair, and as Rachel wiggled around it, she recognized Blanche Willis. "What's happening?" she asked the older woman.

Blanche, in sequined black harem pants with a shapeless black-and-white tunic blouse, pointed to the space in the center of the room. "They're reading him his rights," she said. "Can you imagine? The nerve of him. To come to the man's funeral after he ran a pitchfork through him and buried him in a pigpen?"

Rachel froze in her tracks. Directly in front of her, a hard-faced Evan Parks was placing handcuffs on her Uncle Aaron's wrists. Aunt Hannah was clinging to her husband's black coat and weeping.

". . . arrest for the murder of Willard O'Day," Evan said. "You have the right to remain silent . . ."

Rachel's knees went weak.

". . . If you cannot afford an attorney, one will be provided for you," Evan continued.

"Ne!" Aunt Hannah wailed in Deitsch. "You can't take my husband. He's a good man. He didn't hurt anyone. He didn't kill anyone."

Another trooper reached to grab her, but Rachel's *dat* and Mary Aaron's oldest brother, John Hannah, were suddenly there. They took Aunt Hannah gently by the arms and half dragged, half carried her into the arms of the other Amish women.

Uncle Aaron didn't say a word. His face might have been carved of stone. He didn't fight; he didn't protest. He simply stood there, features immobile, eyes fierce, and looking, for all the world, like a martyr being willingly led to the stake.

Rachel regained use of her muscles. She rushed forward. "Evan, what are you—"

"Stay out of this, Rachel," he said, not unkindly. "You can't interfere in this. This isn't the place."

"What am I supposed to do?"

Evan's face was stern. "I can't talk to you right now." He

motioned toward the front of the hall. "This way, Mr. Hostetler."

For a few seconds, Uncle Aaron didn't seem to hear, and then he nodded. "*Ya,*" he said. "I will come." He went without protest, a state trooper on either side holding his arms.

Rachel went to her aunt. Her father stepped aside to let her embrace Aunt Hannah. "We have to bail him out," Rachel said. "We can't let him remain in—"

"How much money will it be?" her aunt asked between sobs. "We don't have . . . My poor Aaron . . . my poor, poor Aaron." She covered her face with her hands and wept.

"If you can't afford it, I'll raise the bail myself," Rachel offered.

A warm hand settled on her shoulder. "This is a terrible mistake," George said.

She looked into his tear-swollen eyes. "George, I'm so sorry. It was wrong of the police to come here. I know Uncle Aaron didn't—"

"Of course, he didn't," George assured her. And then he motioned to the onlookers. "Please," he said. "There's food. Eat. We need to be together as a community now more than ever. Don't let this sully Willy's memory or our gathering." He caught Rachel's hand and led her to a quiet corner. "I believe in your uncle's innocence as much as you do," he said. "And if a judge sets bail for Aaron, I'll gladly put it up myself."

Rachel stared at him in disbelief. "You? But why would . . ."

George sighed. "Stone Mill is the only home I've ever known. The people here, my friends, Amish and English, are the only family I have. Especially now." He pulled a handkerchief from his pocket and wiped his damp forehead. "We can't let something like this destroy our community."

"But the money—"

"Money isn't an object. Not now," he said. "I have more than I need for the business and for Sophie and me to live quite comfortably. You know that I have a special place in my heart for you, Rachel, for what you've done for this town. And if I can help in any way, I will."

"It's wonderful of you to offer," she began, "but—"

"No buts, Rachel. I've decided." He looked down at her with teary eyes. "I want to do this." He hesitated. "I need to. Not just for Aaron but for the community." He looked away. "For all of us."

Chapter 13

Rachel kicked off her sandals and curled her legs up under her on the couch as Evan poured her a glass of pinot grigio. It was eight o'clock the next evening, and it had been a long, long day. The two of them were alone in the living room of Evan's ranch house. Rachel had just finished a plate of his famous spaghetti with marinara sauce, one of two entrées Evan had perfected and their usual fare when she dined at his place. She always brought salad and bread, and following their customary pattern, they finished off the meal with a single glass of wine.

Rachel wasn't much of a drinker, and she rarely had anything other than wine. Among the Old Order Amish in her community, partaking of any alcohol was a sin, and doing so always made her feel a bit daring. It was something that her mother would definitely not approve of.

"I think I might have put in too much garlic." Evan dropped into an easy chair across from her. He'd lit a small fire in the fireplace, even though it was May and the evening was warm.

"No, perfect," Rachel replied. She took a sip and then turned the wineglass thoughtfully between her fingers. "I still can't get over the judge . . . that he let Uncle Aaron out on such low bail." Her uncle had been held overnight and then brought before the judge the next day. Against the odds, he was home by milking time.

Evan nodded. "I think the assistant DA was surprised, too." He gazed down into his glass as if he might find the answer written there. "And then, come to find out, George O'Day put up the money. That's got everyone scratching their heads."

"George offered yesterday, right after you arrested Uncle Aaron. I appreciated the offer, but I didn't think he really meant it. I was afraid bail was going to be set high, and I was going to have to take a second mortgage on my place, but George insisted. He had me come by his house. He took a fat envelope with a rubber band around it from a kitchen drawer and gave it to me. Inside was a wad of cash. He obviously believes that Uncle Aaron is innocent."

"That's good, because if George believes in him, it will sway public opinion. In a trial—"

"A trial? You think they'll put Uncle Aaron on trial?"

Evan gave her a surprised look. "He's been arrested. There'll be a trial."

"Not if I—" She caught herself. "Not if the real murderer is discovered first."

He scowled. "I know what you've been doing, and it's time you take a step back. You're not qualified to do this."

"I can't do that."

Evan massaged the back of his neck, running his fingers over his close-cropped hair. He'd had it chopped short in a military style a few days ago, and Rachel still hadn't gotten used to the new look. "Honestly, Rache, the more I think about this, the more I'm beginning to believe you're right." He glanced up at her. "Mr. Hostetler's looking less guilty to me every day."

"I'm glad you think that." She hesitated and then said what she'd been holding back all through supper. "I was so angry when I saw you putting handcuffs on him. I know it's not fair, but I felt as if . . ." A burning log shifted, and she glanced into the fireplace.

"Rache, you have to—"

"No, it's all right. I understand that your job comes first." She searched for the right words. "Call me naïve, but I didn't think he'd actually be arrested. It never occurred to me that you'd be the one to—"

"I asked to be on the detail," he interrupted. He regarded her steadily. "I thought that since he knew me, it might be easier."

"But at the funeral, Evan? You couldn't have done it later, in the privacy of his home?" She was angry again, but her roots ran deep and she kept the anger out of her tone.

"It wasn't up to me *when* to arrest him. That decision came from way above me."

She looked away, and they were both quiet for a few moments. She waited until her anger subsided, knowing it would get her nowhere. "You said you were beginning to think Uncle Aaron didn't do it. What makes you say that?"

Evan exhaled slowly. "It was mostly the way he behaved. Not like a guilty man but like someone who's been falsely accused. He was different than most of the perps we have to bring in."

"Don't most people claim to be innocent?"

"Sure." Evan sipped his wine. "But all the while they're protesting, they're *acting* guilty. Little things you notice. How they don't look you in the eye, or how they can't tell an alibi the same way twice. Most of them never shut up. They just keep talking. But your uncle just gave me that *look*. Maybe it's a hunch, but I think we've got the wrong man, which means that our real killer—"

"Is still out there," she said. "Which is exactly what I've been saying." It was on the tip of her tongue to tell him that she'd gone out to the trailer park again today, trying to find some answers to the questions that were nagging at her. This time, either no one was at home, or no one was opening their door to her. She was beginning to think that she wasn't very good at this investigation stuff. But she said nothing about her activities today. Evan had made it clear he didn't approve. "Do you have any idea why the DA's office decided to bring charges against him now?" she asked.

This time it was Evan who glanced away. And he definitely had a guilty look on his face.

She waited. Silence stretched between them. The sweet odor of burning apple wood filled the room. Rachel closed her eyes, determined not to be the first to speak. She was learning that this was a game with hidden rules.

Evan blinked first.

"I don't suppose it's any big secret. Judge Thomas is appointing counsel for your uncle, whether he wants it or not. And as soon as they find someone, it will be common knowledge." He shrugged. "You know what they say. When more than one person knows something in Stone Mill—"

"Everyone knows it." She managed a half-smile.

That familiar muscle twitched along Evan's jaw. He was a nice-looking man, but was never able to quite pull it all together. There was something perpetually awkward and boyish about him, as if he'd wandered into a black-tie affair in gym shorts or something. She found it endearing and very human. "Don't keep me in suspense," she urged. "If you're going to tell me what everyone's going to be talking about, do it."

"All right, all right. The notebook they found in Willy's pocket . . ." He hesitated. "It had something incriminating in it. Incriminating enough to arrest him."

"But it was in code, right? That's what you said. So they might be wrong."

"I don't know. I'm not a detective."

"Did you actually get a look at the notebook?" Rachel sat up straighter in her chair.

"No, not since we took it off the body. It was just a pocket-size, cheap spiral notebook."

"This is silly. The police obviously misunderstood Willy's code. George verified that Willy would have had a large sum of cash on him. I know it wasn't found on the body." She thought for a moment. "I assume you searched my uncle's home. Checked his bank account. You didn't find a large sum of cash anywhere, did you?"

He didn't answer. She went on. "It's logical that whoever killed him took the money. How much are we talking about? Ten thousand dollars? More? If Uncle Aaron had taken the money, you'd have seen evidence of it somewhere in the last eight months. And you haven't. No one has. Because my uncle doesn't have it."

He still didn't respond.

"Can you let me see the notebook?"

He got up and went into the kitchen. She put her sandals back on and followed him.

"No can do, Rache." He turned on the water in the sink and began to rinse a plate. "It's already been logged into evidence. Chain of evidence can't be broken. I can't just walk out of the station carrying an evidence bag."

"So you won't help my uncle?" She stood in the kitchen, hands on her hips.

He slowly turned from the sink to meet her gaze. He looked miserable. "I can't."

"You can't or you won't?" she asked, her anger bubbling up out of nowhere.

He opened his arms beseechingly. "Does it matter?"

She spun on her heels and went out the back door.

"Rache?"

She headed for her Jeep. The May air was warm and soft. A chorus of spring peepers chirped from the low spot at the back of Evan's yard. The moon was a silver disk rising over the mountain. The air smelled of evergreens, fresh-cut grass, and home.

"Rache, please."

She got in her Jeep.

"You're not being—"

She slammed the door. She saw him standing in front of her vehicle. She turned the key and pushed the gearshift into reverse. She knew it was childish, but she couldn't help herself. She backed out of his driveway and drove away without looking back.

By eleven the following morning, Rachel had paid bills, checked out a guest, and spoken to the plumber about a leak in the bedroom she wanted ready for the wedding party whose reservations Hulda had taken. Mary Aaron was on duty in the gift shop, Ada was busy baking several Moravian hickory nut cakes for the Methodist bazaar, and the muted hum of the vacuum assured Rachel that Minnie was hard at work vacuuming the front staircase.

She was eager to get to her uncle's farm, but she'd wait until the late afternoon. Uncle Aaron had a dentist's appointment in State College, which he had seen no reason to cancel just because he'd been to jail. A driver had taken him this morning and he wouldn't be home until later.

Even though Uncle Aaron had been released on bail and was safely home on the farm, things were still looking bad for him. If he was tried for murder, even if he was found innocent, it would not only devastate the family; it would affect the entire valley. Lurid publicity could brand Stone Mill and the Amish community for decades, destroying the town's revival and the influx of struggling new businesses, including her own B&B.

Naturally, clearing Uncle Aaron of wrongdoing came first, before any financial considerations. He might be difficult at times, but he was her blood, and she loved and respected him. Beyond that, she desperately wanted Stone Mill to be synonymous with peaceful and picturesque farmland, history, clean air, and traditional values, not scandalous headlines. The Plain people found it difficult to accept change, which included welcoming strangers to their valley. They had made this valley their home for more than ten generations. The earth was stained with their blood and sweat. But given reason enough, whole church communities could vote to sell their farms and move west to someplace more isolated. And if the Amish left, Stone Mill would die as surely as had so many isolated coal belt towns.

No matter what Evan had said, Rachel knew that she couldn't sit and wait for the authorities to discover their mistake and free Uncle Aaron. She had to continue her own investigation and hope to stumble on something that the police had missed.

Because she couldn't go to the Hostetler farm until later, she decided to drive out to Park Estates again this morning. As she passed through her kitchen, she snagged a basket of orange-pecan muffins. If she couldn't talk her way into those trailors, maybe she could bribe her way in.

Fifteen minutes later, she pulled up in front of Blanche Willis's home. The neighborhood dogs must have been off chasing mailmen or rabbits; other than the two barking pit bulls, there wasn't a dog in sight. Taking a deep breath, Rachel grabbed the basket of muffins in one hand and her keys/pepper spray in the other. She marched up to Mrs. Willis's side door and knocked.

"Who is it?" A familiar face peered through a window to the right of the door.

"Mrs. Willis? It's Rachel Mast."

A metal crank squeaked, and the window cracked open. "What do you want?"

"I came by to drop off some muffins. You were so kind last time that I—"

The floor creaked, and the face vanished. Rachel heard the faint sound of a wheelchair moving across linoleum. A lock clicked, and Mrs. Willis opened the door a few inches. She didn't look particularly friendly, but she *had* opened the door. Rachel took heart.

"I don't want to bother you, but my Amish friend made these this morning, and I thought that you . . ."

The door swung open. "Come in. Wipe your feet. I don't want any dog doo on my clean floor. My great-grandson plays here." She closed the top of her bathrobe. "And I told you, everyone calls me Blanche."

Rachel stepped inside and closed the door behind her. The house was quiet. No crying babies, no TV. And no lights. It was almost noon, but the living room was shadowy. Rachel thought it strange that it was so still. The room was neater than the last time she'd been here. No smell of soiled diapers, no scattered toys.

"Muffins?" Blanche's expression softened. "Homemade, you say?"

"Completely from scratch."

"Ummp." The older woman turned her wheelchair and rolled toward the kitchen. "I've got coffee. Fresh. Not instant. I can't abide that powdery stuff. Want some?"

"Thank you." Rachel followed meekly. "I'd love a cup of coffee."

The table was covered with a faded flowered oilcloth, but it was spotless. A single cup and spoon lay on it. In the center, a lazy Susan held a matching sugar bowl and cream pitcher shaped like a pair of chickens. Blanche waved toward a chair. "Sit down." Her eyes lingered on the basket of muffins.

Rachel sat at the kitchen table. She couldn't help noticing a clock over the gas stove; the hands had stopped at 3:05. There were no lights on here in the kitchen, either, and the curtains had been pulled back to allow as much sunlight into the room as possible.

"Electric's off," Blanche conceded. "Check got lost in the mail, but it's all straightened out. The man at the electric company said they were sorry, and they'd have it back on by five. They better. Buddy brought me some ice to keep my perishables from spoiling, but the milk soured." She gave Rachel a sharp look. "If you want milk in your coffee, I've got canned."

"No, thank you." Rachel smiled at her. "Your granddaughter's not here today?"

"Moved back in with her baby's daddy." She sniffed. "Won't last any longer than the last time they tried to make it work. She's no better at picking men than my Millie was. I told her, find a man that can work when it rains. My Art, he was a good provider. We fussed with each other, but we were together thirty-seven years before he died." She motioned toward the stove, where a battered aluminum coffeepot stood. "You mind pouring the coffee? Gas stove," she said. "I just light it with a match. Works fine, with or without the electric. Heats good, too, in a pinch."

"It must be a change for you." Rachel rose to pick up the old-fashioned percolator coffeepot. "Being alone. And I know you miss the children." Without being told, she removed a second cup from a mug tree on the counter and poured each of them a cup.

Blanche sighed and ran a hand through her hair. Finding pink foam curlers, she began hastily pulling them out and tucking them in her bathrobe pocket. Blanche's hair was black, a distinct change from the former gray. Rachel thought she preferred the gray. The unnaturally dark hair did little for Blanche's pale complexion.

"Little Justin . . ." Blanche sighed. Tucking the last curler into her pocket, she rolled up to the table in front of her cup of coffee. "Cute as the dickens and bright as a button. Yes, I miss them both, but Justin most of all. 'Gram-Gram,' he calls me. 'I wove you, Gram-Gram,' he'll say when he gets into something he shouldn't. Never a peaceful moment in this house with those two, but . . ." She stirred sugar into her coffee. "Justin's my only great-grand."

"The baby?"

"Oh, no, she's not ours." She plucked a muffin from the basket that Rachel had set on the table and took a big bite from it. "Good." She chewed. Took another bite. "Chelsea watches her for a girlfriend. Sweet little girl, but colicky. I won't miss that crying all the time."

Something furry brushed up against Rachel's ankle. Surprised, she looked under the table. The tabby cat, no longer plump with kittens, rubbed and purred loudly.

"Danged cat. Had four kittens. Chelsea wants the black one for Justin. Lil, next door, she's taking one for herself and one for her sister." Blanche threw Rachel a meaningful look.

Rachel didn't bite.

"That's one left."

"I already have a cat."

"So you said . . . They're cute. Female. They're all females. Hard to find a good home for females. Buddy said he'd *take care* of any I couldn't get rid of."

Rachel stirred her black coffee.

"The mother's a good mouser. Maybe you could use a good mouser around those barns of yours. Don't imagine guests like mice in their rooms." Blanche sighed again and bit off another piece of muffin. "I'm having the mother fixed as soon as these are weaned. Can't afford more than one cat. A pity. Looks like it's going to have them big paws, you know, with an extra toe."

Rachel could feel herself caving. "Maybe I could find someone to take the kitten. I wouldn't want to see it . . ."

Blanche smiled, her teeth white and perfect. She pulled a pack of cigarettes out of her pocket. "Smoke?"

Rachel shook her head. "No, thank you."

"You can have the kitten any time after six weeks."

Rachel nodded dumbly. A kitten? She hadn't found a place for the goats yet, and they were coming next week. Any more animals and she'd have to build an ark.

"Another reason I had for coming by," Rachel said. "At the funeral, I spoke with your son-in-law, Steve."

"*Ex*-son-in-law," Blanche corrected.

Rachel nodded, eager to move on from cats and worthless men to the questions troubling her. "He seemed to think that I was taking advantage of you. If you felt that way, I wanted to apologize. I didn't want to make you uncomfortable. I'm only trying to help prove my uncle's innocence."

Blanche scoffed and spat a derogatory phrase that seemed to describe Steve Barber rather aptly. "Don't give anything that jerk says another minute's worry. I've still got all my senses about me. If I didn't want you in my house, you wouldn't be here. And if I didn't want to talk to you, nobody could make me."

Rachel leaned toward her. "I hoped you'd feel that way. I've been trying to talk to people who saw Willy that last day, but I haven't had much luck."

"Well, Steve hated him. That's for certain. Maybe you should look at him. If anyone had a reason to hate Willy O'Day, it was Steve Barber."

Rachel nodded. "I asked him if he'd seen Willy that day, but he told me that he was out of town. At a wedding in another state."

"There you go! He's a danged liar." She slurped her coffee. "Chelsea and I always do our grocery shopping on Fridays. I saw him that afternoon at Wagler's. Danged fool nearly backed into us in the parking lot."

Chapter 14

Rachel's muscles tensed. "You're certain? Steve told me he was in Williamsport when Willy disappeared." Excitement washed over her. If Steve had lied about being away, what else could he be lying about? What had he been up to that he didn't want anyone to know? Maybe he knew something about Willy's death. Or maybe . . . Rachel tucked her hands around the warm coffee mug. "Why do you suppose he'd say that?"

Blanche looked over her shoulder as if Steve were sneaking up on her at that instant, then back at Rachel. She reached for another muffin. "I always knew he was no good. He comes around here pretending to care whether I live or die, but I know he's just trying to see how long I've got to live and whether he'll inherit anything when I'm gone. He tried to take back the car Millie bought me, said it was only a loan. But she wanted me to have it. Chelsea's using it now. I don't drive much," she confided. "Could if I had to. Nothing wrong with my feet. It's my knees that don't work so well. But it's just easier to let Chelsea drive me where I need to go."

Blanche's expression pleaded for agreement, so Rachel nodded.

"Steve says Chelsea takes advantage of me, but she's between a rock and a hard place, that girl. Not so easy to raise a little one alone. And you can't count on that boy's daddy for any help. I expect to get a call any minute that she and little Justin are coming home."

Rachel nodded and finished her coffee; luckily she'd poured herself only half a cup. "Thank you for letting me come in and talk with you," she said, scooting her chair back. "I just didn't want there to be any hard feelings."

"Won't you have another cup?" Blanche talked through a mouthful of muffin. "I can make another pot. Coffee I don't run out of. My Art used to say, 'Blanche, honey, you drink so much coffee, you must have coffee in your veins instead of blood.' He didn't mean anything by it. Just his way of kidding. I was working full time back then. We had a nice little house. I could show you the pictures of the garden we had out back. Used to grow the biggest tomatoes. Would you like—"

"Another time, perhaps," Rachel smiled and sidestepped toward the door. "I've got to get back to my guests at Stone Mill House, but if you hear anything or think of anything that you haven't told me about that last day Willy came by for the rent, please give me a call." She took a business card out of her pocket and laid it on the table.

Blanche followed her to the door in her wheelchair, her faded eyes filling over with loneliness. Rachel couldn't help thinking about the Amish way. The Amish didn't leave their elderly to manage on their own. Grandparents, uncles, aunts, even cousins were welcome members of the community, assured of a loving place in the family circle. She'd never known of an Old Order Amish person with Alzheimer's or dementia who was placed in a nursing home.

Rachel didn't know Blanche Willis very well, suspected they didn't have much in common. She wasn't certain that she even liked the woman, but a part of her, deep inside, wanted to scoop Blanche up and carry her home with her. "I'll stop back another day for that coffee," she offered. "If it's no trouble."

"No trouble at all. When you come back for the kitten.

My Chelsea will be here then, I'm sure of it." She grimaced. "And the lights will be on. I don't have air, but I've got plenty of fans. You need 'em in the summer. It gets hot as blazes here without a couple of fans blowing on you."

Rachel reached for the doorknob, but Blanche caught her arm.

"Wait," the older woman said. "There is something else." Her face flushed. "I wouldn't want you to think I'm a gossip. Mind my own business, I do, but . . . Have you talked to Buddy? Over there?" She pointed across the street.

"The house with the VW parked outside?" It hadn't been there this morning, but Rachel had seen it there twice. She opened the door.

"No secret. Lil next door, she or Bill would have told you if you'd caught up with them. Everybody in the park heard it—probably everybody in this end of the valley. Buddy can be a loudmouth when he drinks, and a bully. And he usually stays drunk most weekends."

Rachel turned to face her. "Heard 'it'?"

Blanche rolled her eyes. "Buddy and Willy O'Day. They argued something fierce. Willy had come for rent, and from what I could gather—not that I'm an eavesdropper—"

"No, of course not. But, if they were loud, you couldn't help—"

"Exactly. They were shouting at each other about Buddy being behind on the rent once too often." She drew herself up in the wheelchair with a satisfied expression.

"And?" Rachel urged.

"Willy said he was putting him out then and there. And Buddy screamed right back at him that he wasn't going one step. He'd see Willy in hell first!"

"That's terrible." Rachel glanced out the open door in the direction of Buddy's trailer. If that was true, it added one more person to an ever-lengthening list of those who had reason to wish Willy ill. But if the argument between Willy and Buddy was common knowledge, why hadn't anyone said anything about it before? And how had that missed the Stone Mill gossip line? "But when I asked you before . . ." She waited, uncertain as to what to say.

The woman in the wheelchair seemed to shrink a little. Lines gathered at the corners of her mouth and eyes. Her chin sagged. "I didn't know you from Adam before," she admitted. "Now . . . now maybe we're . . . friends?"

Rachel nodded and smiled. "I think we are, Mrs. Willis."

"Blanche. Please call me Blanche." Her lips puckered and her eyes brightened. "Everybody here's a little scared of Buddy. You never know . . . what with the drinking and all. But if he did do something bad, he deserves to pay for it, doesn't he? Maybe you can get to the bottom of it. Because if that Amish farmer didn't kill Willy, who did?"

Rachel's thoughts were churning all the way home. She'd been looking for a suspect. Now she had two: Steve and Buddy. Should she go to the police with what she had found out?

Not yet. If they ignored her, thought she was interfering in the investigation, it might hurt Uncle Aaron more than help.

Her thoughts went back to the notebook. And to Evan. It had been unfair of her to pressure him. She hadn't meant to pick a fight with him, if that could even be called a fight. She knew it had been wrong of her to just take off like that. Childish.

She hit the speed dial on her cell for Evan's number. It rang four times and then his voicemail picked up. She ended the call. She wasn't the kind of person to leave an apology message.

At home, Minnie didn't seem any further along on vacuuming the guest rooms upstairs than she'd been when Rachel had left. The office phone was ringing, something was burning on the stove, and someone was knocking on the back door. Rachel shut off the burner under a pot of Swiss chard and hurried to answer the door. An Englisher in work clothes and a Nittany Lions ball cap stood there. Behind him were a black pickup and a stake trailer. A nanny goat and two half-grown kids thrust their inquisitive faces through the wooden bars and bleated.

"Delivery for Rachel Mast," the man said. She didn't know him, but new people had been moving into the valley lately. "Goats."

"I can see that," she said. "But I wasn't expecting them until next week. I'm not sure where—"

"Hauled a billy goat for Jakob Peachey. Alvin Herschberger said you bought these three off him. I don't know anything about next week, but if you're Rachel Mast, these are your goats, and I've got other stops to make. Where do you want them?"

The phone stopped ringing behind her. Then she heard Minnie's voice and Ada's over it. "Burned my nice chard!"

"Just a moment, please," Rachel said to the Englisher. "If you'd just give me a second, I'll be right with you." She turned back to find her housekeeper admonishing Minnie in no uncertain words.

"She let a pot burn. Again," Ada said. "I just stepped out to the herb garden. All she had to do was lower the flame under . . ."

"Ya, ya," Rachel agreed. She needed to see if someone had answered the office phone or if whoever was on the other end had left a message. Ada and Minnie's problems would have to get in line behind reservations and goat housing. She hurried out of the kitchen and down the hall to find Hulda manning the desk again.

"Thank you. We'll be expecting you," her elderly neighbor said to the caller. Hulda Schenfeld beamed when she saw Rachel. "Not to worry. Another reservation. Next weekend. One couple. Saturday and Sunday."

"You are a lifesaver, Hulda," Rachel said, and meant it. "I've got to put you on the payroll."

"I'd be worth every penny." Hulda's rouge was particularly bright today, but Rachel didn't care. She could have kissed her.

"There, that should do it." Rachel swung the gate closed in a large stall in the stone barn behind the main house. "You girls will be fine here," she assured the goats, "until we can get some pasture fenced off for you."

The dam, Thomasina, stuck her nose through a crack in the gate and bleated. Rachel reached over the gate and scratched between her ears. "You've got food, you've got water, and I'll leave the barn door open so you'll have plenty of fresh air and sunlight."

The goat had a doubtful expression on her face.

Rachel stepped back and studied the interior of the huge barn. There were stacks of junk everywhere: furniture, tires, wooden chicken crates, an old dishwasher. Some of the stuff had been hauled from the house to the barn during the renovations; other items had been here when she moved in. And dust and cobwebs . . . and heaven knows what else. But the building was sound and it didn't leak when it rained—at least not in this corner.

Maybe cleaning the barn would be her next big project. She walked out of the barn and into the sunlight. Minnie had agreed to milk Thomasina tonight and tomorrow morning. That would give her time to set up a schedule with some of her brothers, maybe cousins.

"I'll be back to check on you later," she called to the goats as she walked out of the barn. "And I'll check about the fencing. I promise."

Hulda met Rachel at the back door of the kitchen with a glass of iced tea for her.

"It has mint leaves in it," her neighbor said. "And honey. I always make it with honey instead of sugar. That commercial stuff will give you wrinkles."

Rachel accepted the drink gladly. "I haven't eaten lunch,"

she said. "I'm sure there's something good in the refrigerator. Will you join me?"

"No, no, you go ahead. I already had a salad. Have to watch my figure. Never know when I might meet an interesting gentleman."

They laughed together. It was Hulda's ongoing joke that she was going to find a new husband. And they both knew that she was only teasing. It was Rachel that she was always trying to marry off.

Rachel grabbed some of the Herschbergers' cheese from the refrigerator, which had turned out to be delicious after aging a few days. She also gathered crackers and cookies from the counter, and she and Hulda carried their tea out to the seating by the grape arbor.

From the backyard, Rachel could hear the steady bleats of the kid goats in the barn. Apparently, they were unhappy or homesick, because they hadn't stopped making that sound since she'd left them.

"Goats," Hulda said. "Whatever will you do with goats, Rachel?"

"I'm not sure. I didn't exactly plan to buy them." She didn't mention the kitten, although Hulda had several cats. She might be a possibility . . .

The older woman chattered on, moving from one subject to another. Rachel smiled, made comments at the pauses and nodded her head. She didn't want to be rude, but she kept mulling over the conversation she'd had with Blanche about Buddy being evicted.

Obviously, if he was still living in Park Estates, which he was, he hadn't been evicted. Why not? Had he caught up on his rent? George hadn't mentioned anything about there being a problem with Buddy. And if Buddy hadn't had the money the night Willy came for it and if he was behind on his payments, how had he suddenly come up with enough to . . .

"You aren't listening to a word I say, are you?" Hulda asked.

"I'm sorry," Rachel said quickly.

"No problem. No one in my house listens, either. I talk too much. It's what Mr. Schenfeld always said. 'Hulda, you never stop long enough to draw breath.'" She patted Rachel's arm with a soft hand. "I'm not offended, child. Really. I was talking about the funeral. That will be one for Stone Mill people to gossip about for the next fifty years."

"I suppose," Rachel said. "It was pretty awful." The picture of Teresa being hustled away from the graveside surfaced in her mind. She never had caught up with Teresa that day. She'd been meaning to look for her at the church hall, but then Evan had arrested her uncle, and everything else had gone out of her head. "I had no idea that Teresa was so fond of Willy," she said. "Carrying on so at the grave."

Hulda chuckled. "Well, you know why."

Rachel shook her head.

"Why, those two were an item for a few months, once upon a time. You didn't know?"

"Willy and Ell's mom?"

"None other. Opposites attract and all that." Hulda lowered her voice. "Of course, it wasn't common knowledge. Her being a teacher and a single lady, and Willy being, well, Willy. People used to expect teachers to behave in a certain way. It would have caused talk, so they kept it quiet."

"But you knew about it?"

Hulda's lips curved into the hint of a smile. "If I ever told all I know about this town, the earth would open up and swallow it." She gave a wave. "And that's old, old news about Teresa and Willy. He threw her over for a lawyer's wife, and Teresa quit her job at the high school and ran off to South Carolina. She didn't come back for five or six years, and when she did, she had Ell with her. She told everyone she'd adopted the baby, but no one believed it. Of course, there was a lot of counting going on, but Ell couldn't have been Willy's child because she wasn't born for a year and a half after Teresa left Stone Mill."

She tilted her head and peered over the rim of her gold-rimmed glasses. "Whoever the daddy was, he must have soured Teresa on men. She's been a good enough mother to Ell, but so far as I know, she's never been so much as out to dinner with another man."

Rachel glanced away, thinking.

"I see that look in your eyes. You don't think all that could have anything to do with Willy and his private grave, do you?"

Rachel cut her eyes at Hulda but didn't say anything.

"You needn't do that with me. Don't think I don't know you're playing amateur detective—trying to clear your uncle's name." She reached for a butter cookie. "If I were your age, I'd probably be doing the same thing."

"He's innocent."

"I hope so, for your sake. And for your family's. That's what's important in this world, you know, family . . . and friends. You've been like a daughter to me since you came back to Stone Mill. And I'd hate to see anything or anyone break your heart."

Unable to stay away any longer, Rachel decided it was time to head to the Hostetler farm; if her uncle wasn't home yet, he soon would be. She hadn't seen him since he was arrested, except for a brief moment when he'd been released. And they hadn't spoken then; Uncle Aaron had only nodded to her and she back.

When Rachel and George had gone to bail him out, George had offered to give Aaron a ride back to the farm. Neither her parents nor any of her aunts or uncles had ever ridden in her Jeep. Apparently, the red color had offended the bishop of their church, and although he hadn't forbidden any of his flock to set foot in it, most would not. Thankfully, Mary Aaron had no such compunction.

Rachel parked the offending vehicle on a logging road at the foot of Uncle Aaron's driveway, covered her pinned-up hair with her kerchief, and stepped into the calf-length denim skirt. She didn't know if her uncle would talk with her, but if he wouldn't, she had some questions for Aunt Hannah. Her strange behavior at the farmer's market on Saturday bothered Rachel. What had she and Eli Rust been arguing about? Did Eli believe that Uncle Aaron was guilty, or was it something else?

There were few secrets in an Amish farming community. Everyone knew that there was no love lost between Uncle Aaron and his closest Amish neighbor. He and Eli grated on each other's nerves and bumped along, sharing a church community yet clearly disliking each other. Most people, including her own father, believed that the fault was Uncle Aaron's, and that he resented Eli because Eli had courted Aunt Hannah first.

The fact that one of the two, either Aunt Hannah or Eli, had broken off the romance didn't seem to matter. So many years had passed, and yet her *dat* said that Uncle Aaron was still jealous. He hadn't said it in front of the children, but Rachel had heard her parents discussing an incident. And she'd distinctly heard her *dat* tell her *mam* that Uncle Aaron's heart was still full of jealousy, and that it sometimes made for awkward moments for others in the church. *Mam* had told him that he'd best tend to the log in his own eye rather than the speck of dust in someone else's, but she hadn't denied it. And as quick as *Mam* was to defend her own family, her absence of argument spoke louder than words.

It was hard to picture either Eli Rust or Aunt Hannah as a young couple walking out together. No one had ever hinted at what had caused the breakup between them or why Aunt Hannah would choose the rigid and sometimes morose Aaron Hostetler instead. It was as much a mystery as what Rachel had just learned from Hulda about Willy O'Day and Ell's mother.

Rachel took a moment to try and reach Evan on the phone, but again, all she got was voicemail. Was he avoiding her? Or was he just busy? She really needed to apologize to him, but after that she wasn't sure what she was going to say because . . . the thing was, she *really* needed to know what was in that notebook.

"Hey, Rachel!"

Rachel looked up to see her cousin Jesse coming out of the woods with a fishing pole over one shoulder. Two trout hung from a string at his waist, and he was grinning from ear to ear. "See my fish?" he said.

Rachel switched her cell phone to vibrate and thrust it into her skirt pocket. "Only two," she teased. Jesse was nine, towheaded, bucktoothed, and one of her favorites of Uncle Aaron's children. "Not enough for supper. Maybe you should sell them to me."

"Ne." He laughed. "John Hannah already promised me a dollar for every trout I catch. He's going to have a bonfire tonight, him and some of his pals. I'm saving for a scooter-bike."

Rachel fell in step alongside Jesse. "Is your *dat* at home?"

He shrugged. "Don't know, maybe. They let him out of the jail. But I think he went to State College today. Appointment."

"I know." She rested a hand on Jesse's shoulder. "You know, it's all going to be all right," she promised. "They'll find out who did it, and everyone will know that your *dat* is innocent."

"Ya," he agreed. "That's what Mary Aaron says."

They walked up the lane in silence, past the field where John Hannah was plowing with a four-horse team and past the sheep pen where Elsie, John Hannah's twin sister, was combing the burrs out of a ewe's fleece. Both waved, and Rachel waved back. A wave of nostalgia made her throat constrict. Sometimes, the smells and colors of the farm swept her back to her childhood, and for just a minute or two . . . she wished that things could have been different . . . that she could be different.

You can take the Amish girl off the farm, she thought, *but can you ever get the farm out of*... Rachel sighed. She'd made her choice, and as far as she was concerned, there was no going back. The trouble was, she seemed to have a rough time going forward.

A flock of geese honked and spread their wings and made small rushes at her as Rachel entered the farmyard. Knowing it was all bluff, she paid them no mind.

"Get!" Jesse waved his fish at the gander, then laughed.

"See you. And don't forget. Next time, *I* want your fish." Rachel went to the back door. With family, there was no such thing as knocking, so she pushed open the screen door and walked into the kitchen.

"Rachel!" Her aunt turned toward her with a surprised look on her face.

It was all Rachel could do not to stare. The man sitting in her uncle's high-backed chair at the head of the table and drinking coffee wasn't Uncle Aaron. It was his neighbor Eli Rust.

Chapter 15

Eli's face darkened. His gaze met Hannah's, then Rachel's. "It's better if I go," he said.

The air inside the kitchen felt charged with electricity.

"Finish your coffee, at least," Hannah murmured.

"I should go anyway. He'll be home shortly. It's best if I not be here." He looked down at his mug. "I shouldn't have come."

"*Ne,* I'm glad you did." Her aunt's eyes grew misty. "Don't worry, Eli. She won't say anything to Aaron." But her brow furrowed with worry. "Rachel's a good girl. She wouldn't want to make trouble for us."

Looking at Rachel, he raised a thick finger. "Hold your tongue, Rachel Mast. If harm comes to my family or Hannah because of this, it will be on your conscience."

"Eli, please," Hannah said softly. "Say no more."

"I'm not afraid. You know that. What I did . . . I had to do."

"But the *Ordnung*, Eli. I worry for your soul."

Eli shook his head. "*Ne*. I do not." He drained the last of the coffee. "I'd do it again."

Aunt Hannah brought her finger to her lips, then pointed in the direction of an open window. "Do you want the children to hear—"

"Hear what?" Uncle Aaron threw open the screen door on the back porch so hard that wood splintered. "What business do you have here in my house alone with my wife?" he demanded, walking into the kitchen. "When I'm away from the farm?"

"Aaron, please . . ." Aunt Hannah began, but Uncle Aaron was not to be silenced.

He eyed Eli. "What did you not understand when I told you not to set foot on this farm again unless you've come for Sunday worship?" Uncle Aaron looked back at the sagging door. "Forgive me, Hannah. I was careless. I will fix it as soon as our . . . *guest* leaves."

Rachel moved back against the blue cupboard, wishing that she could shrink to the size of a mouse and hide. Raised voices were rarely heard on Amish farms in the valley. First Eli, and now her uncle. What was going on between Aunt Hannah and her neighbor when she walked in? What had Eli done? What did he and Aunt Hannah know that they were fearful of Rachel or Aaron finding out?

Rachel felt her cell phone vibrate in her pocket. She ignored it, not wanting to draw attention to herself. But Uncle Aaron must have heard the sound. He turned toward her.

"Rachel?" He looked startled. Then embarrassed. "I didn't know you were here. I thought . . ." He tugged at his beard, clearly aware of how rudely he'd spoken to his neighbor in front of her. "I was hasty. I—" Red-faced, he turned and stalked out of the kitchen.

"I'm sorry." Eli started for the door, ignoring Rachel, still directing his words to Hannah. "I didn't want to make trouble for you."

"Trouble follows you, Eli," she said. "It always has." She grabbed a broom from where it stood in a corner and began sweeping the dirt Aaron had tracked in. She swept furiously, as if, with a broom, she could clear her kitchen of the harsh words still hanging in the air.

Eli hurried out the back door. He made an effort to pull the broken screen door shut behind him, but it wouldn't close.

"Leave it," her aunt called after him. "I will pray for you and yours."

The cell phone vibrated again in Rachel's pocket. Rachel turned her back to her aunt and pulled the phone out. She saw that it was Evan and shut it off. She'd have to call him back.

"Best you go, as well." Aunt Hannah clutched her broom against her bosom. "I am not angry with you, but this is a bad time for visiting." Her lower lip quivered and moisture flooded her eyes.

Rachel nodded. She wanted to say something to comfort her aunt, but sensed it would be better if she just left her alone right now. She walked out of the house and into the barnyard.

She looked around. The Dutch door on the barn, which should have been closed, stood open. Not a cousin or even a goose was in sight. Even the dogs had made themselves scarce. She knew that she should do the same, but against her better judgment, she entered the barn. It smelled of hay and livestock. At the far end, she spotted her uncle, standing at a tool bench.

"Uncle Aaron?" she ventured. "Are you all right?"

"Rachel?" He squinted; bright light poured into the barn from behind her.

"*Ya.*"

"Come in. I need to speak with you." The anger had drained from his voice, making him sound weary and older than his years.

Cautiously, she approached. This corner of the barn was shadowy, but she could see that Uncle Aaron held a screwdriver in his hand.

"Why can a man never find the right size screws when he needs them?"

"*Dat* has the same trouble. No matter how many he buys, the ones he wants . . ." She trailed off. Her uncle hadn't invited her in to talk about screws.

"I have to fix the screen door." He held out the screwdriver. "I'm a wooden head, but . . . I must fix the door before the children see. People will say I have lost my mind—that maybe I *am* a man who could take the life of another through my willful temper."

"I know that's not true." She took a step closer. Her eyes were adjusting to the dim interior of the barn.

He nodded. "Always, you have believed in me." He didn't look at her. "I would have sat there. In that jail, but . . . it was good of you to make them let me out. The money."

"I told you at the courthouse. It wasn't mine. George, Willy's brother, put up your bail."

"Still," he said thoughtfully. "It was you. I know you did the arranging. For all your English ways, you're like your mother. Loyal to your family."

Rachel got the feeling he just needed to talk for a moment, so she let him go on.

"She was always my favorite sister. Did you know that? My father said that we shouldn't have favorites, that we should love all of our brothers and sisters equally, as the Lord God loves us. But Esther is special. She was always patient with me, and she knew what to say to lift my spirits."

Rachel pressed her lips together, feeling a little uncomfortable. Amish, especially Amish men, didn't talk about such things. She was touched by his candor. "I know she has a high regard of you. She says your heart is good."

"I've made a fool of myself in front of Eli." He touched his hand to his forehead. "Always, he brings out the worst in me." He exhaled loudly. "Your Aunt Hannah was supposed to marry him. Did you know that? The first of their banns had already been read." He dropped to one knee and began to dig through a big cardboard box full of small, plastic boxes. "Why they broke up, she never said, and I never asked her. I thought, in time, she would tell me, but . . ." He shook one of the boxes and the contents rattled. "These are too long. I need shorter ones."

"But she *did* pick you. She loves you, Uncle Aaron."

"First comes marriage. Then respect. Love follows sometimes, but men and women . . ." He shrugged. "I always wonder, am I second-best? Will I always be?"

"You're not." Rachel sat down on a bale of hay near him. "She married because she wanted to marry you. She loves you, Uncle Aaron."

His cheeks colored at the mention of love. It wasn't a subject often spoken of in the Hostetler family, but Rachel knew that didn't mean it wasn't felt.

"She is impatient with me these days. More than usual," he mused.

"Your arrest has been hard on you both. But they'll find out who did this, Uncle." She hesitated "I know you don't want to, but it would be better if you'd work with the court-appointed counsel—the lawyer."

Uncle Aaron didn't look up. "An honest man—especially an Amish man—should have no need of a lawyer."

Rachel sat there quietly for a moment. She knew he had said repeatedly that he wouldn't talk about the case, but she had to try. "Uncle Aaron, they found a journal on Willy. Did you know that? A notebook he jotted things in. He kept records."

He didn't answer.

"Apparently, before he died, he wrote something about you," she went on. "Did you see him that day?"

"I did not."

She thought about the initials A.T.B.R. "Did . . . did you owe him money?" she dared.

He looked up at her then began to rummage in the box. "I did not. I would not. 'The borrower is the slave of the lender,'" he quoted from Proverbs.

"Well, whatever he wrote, it made the police decide to arrest you. Do you have any idea what it could be?"

"*Ne*. I know nothing. What does it say, this notebook that tells the English that I am the one who killed him?"

"I don't know. I do know that Willy wrote in code."

"'Code'? What is that?"

"It means that he didn't spell out the words, that he used abbreviations, or letters that only he would understand."

"Why would the police think they know what it says, then?" Uncle Aaron snorted. "Crazy."

"Was Willy meeting with you that day?"

He exhaled slowly, as if debating what to say . . . or how to say it. "I have told you, Rachel," he said finally. "I have nothing to say on this matter."

"But you have to. You've got to help us prove your innocence."

"*Ne,* that is up to the Lord. His will be done."

She was the one who sighed this time; she should have known better than to think she could persuade him. Aaron Hostetler was one stubborn man. "Promise me that you'll at least tell them that you didn't do it."

"I cannot do that. The bishop tells me that the judge will ask me to swear in his court . . . to put my hand on the Holy Book and swear an oath. You know we are not permitted to do that. On my life, I could never do such a thing."

"You won't have to swear. If you explain to your lawyer . . . I'll tell them that it's against our—against *your* religion to swear an oath. You can just affirm that you'll tell the truth."

"It's wrong that they try to force their worldly ways on me. Unjust."

"And it's unjust that Willy O'Day ended up dead in your pasture."

"He was a mean man. Greedy. He killed my sheepdog. Willy wanted a piece of my land. He tried to buy it. Our true disagreement was about land, not cows. I don't sell my land. I've worked too hard for this farm." He stood and set two little plastic boxes on his workbench. "But what you say is true. No man should be left that way."

He dumped one of the boxes of screws out on the workbench, taking his time before he spoke again. "I know you mean well," he said. "And you know that I do not approve of what you have done. You abandoned your family and your faith." When he spoke again, his voice was rough with emotion. "But you have taught me a lesson, Niece. You did not abandon *me*. When I needed help most, you were there. I've given you nothing but grief when I owe you thanks."

"You don't owe me anything," she said, putting her hands together on her lap.

He turned to her, his gaze meeting hers. "Come back, Rachel. To the church. Turn your back on the English world and return to us. It would bring your mother joy."

"You know I can't," she said, fighting tears that suddenly burned behind her eyelids.

"And you know I cannot stop asking." He turned away from her again. "Ah, there. I have them." He held the screws out for her to see.

"Good." She forced a smile.

"*Ya,* good. Hannah hates flies in her kitchen." He took the screws and the screwdriver and headed for the yard. Clearly, he had said all he intended to about Willy and his arrest.

Rachel followed him out into the barnyard. He went to the house, and she stood in the driveway for a moment, debating whether or not to go back inside to try to talk to her aunt.

Out of the corner of her eye, at the sheep shed, she saw Jesse crouching against the side of the building. He waved to her.

"Why are you hiding back there?" she asked when he approached her.

"Where's *Dat?*"

"He just went into the house."

"I don't want him to see me."

"Why not?" she asked. "Have you done something wrong?"

"*Ne.*" Jesse shook his head. "But you know how he is. After he got home from the dentist, John Hannah told him about the shovel and he got really mad."

"What shovel?" Goose bumps rose on the back of her neck.

"*Dat*'s shovel. The police came this morning and took it." Jesse wrinkled his nose. "John Hannah said the shovel had cow manure on it. What would the police want with a dirty shovel?"

Instead of heading back to her Jeep as she'd intended, Rachel found herself wandering over to sit on the wooden bench next to the well pump in the yard. She turned her back to the house, pulled out her cell, and tried to reach Evan again. It was foolish to feel guilty for using a telephone. She knew for a fact that her cousin John Hannah had his own cell phone. The community didn't approve of it, but because he hadn't been baptized into the church yet, some irregularities were permitted. Common belief was that young people, especially the boys, had to *sow their wild oats* before settling into the responsibilities of adulthood. So why did she, who was no longer of the faith, go to such lengths to pretend that she wasn't outside the bounds of the Amish community? She'd make an appointment with a good therapist if she weren't so certain that it would be a waste of time and money. She might be crazy, but it was *her* crazy, and she doubted that any sage advice from a stranger would help.

Come on, Evan, pick up. Again, the call went to his voicemail. They were playing phone tag. She needed to talk to him, to have him verify what she thought—that the whole shovel thing was silly. Every household in the valley owned at least one shovel. She had three at Stone Mill House. What would possess the police to go into Uncle Aaron's barn and confiscate one of his shovels?

While she was still sitting there, Uncle Aaron came back out of the house, muttering to himself, and went back into the barn. He didn't seem to notice her, so she didn't speak to him. On a hunch, she hurried to the house. Maybe now that she'd had time to settle down, her aunt would give her some idea of what all the fuss with Eli had been about.

"Aunt Hannah?" Rachel peered through the opening where the screen door usually hung. The door lay flat on the porch, Uncle Aaron's screwdriver and screws beside it.

Her aunt stood at the stove, stirring the contents of a large aluminum pot. From the smell, Rachel thought it was soup, probably vegetable. One of her younger cousins was setting the table. She looked up at Rachel and smiled shyly. Rachel smiled back.

"Go fetch me a clean apron," Aunt Hannah said to the child. "There's one hanging on the back of my bedroom door." And when the girl had hurried off to do as her mother had asked, Aunt Hannah glanced over. "I thought you'd left."

Rachel hesitated. "I know it really isn't any of my business . . ." she began, "but something . . . Why was Eli Rust here? And what don't you want me to tell anyone?"

Aunt Hannah's chin quivered. "Not now," she said. "Not here. Your uncle will be back any minute. I cannot talk about this now." She fluttered her hands. "This is not what you think. If I've done wrong . . ." A man's heavy tread made the porch step creak. "Go, please."

"All right," Rachel answered. "But you know that you can trust me."

The smell of burning soup rose from the pot. "*Ach,* my soup." Her aunt turned back to the stove and turned off the flame under the kettle. Picking up a wooden spoon, she began to stir it again.

Wrong, Rachel thought. *Mam* always said that if you burned the soup, you should pour off the good into another pot, not stir the charred bits into the mix. That would ruin the whole batch for sure. But Aunt Hannah had her own ways, and it wasn't for Rachel to try and change them. "I'll come back and visit another day," she said.

"*Ya,* another day, Rachel . . . when I have more time to sit and talk."

Rachel didn't drive straight home. She had the feeling that her efforts to prove Uncle Aaron's innocence were not only proving futile, but might even be doing more harm than good. But there was no way she could just give up and leave him to his fate. She decided to go back to Park Estates and see if she could catch up with Buddy. If Buddy had threatened Willy, as Blanche had said, why weren't the police searching his trailer and confiscating *his* shovel?

Stripping off her denim skirt and kerchief, she rolled them into a bundle and threw them on the floor behind the driver's seat. She pulled the pins out of her hair and let it fall down her back in a single braid. She almost put on lipstick, but thought better of it. If she did find Buddy and started asking questions about his last confrontation with his landlord, he probably wouldn't be all that friendly. And if he was Willy's killer and things started to get really nasty, a dab of cotton-candy pink wouldn't matter one way or the other.

This time the VW was gone and a pickup truck was parked in the spot. Rachel drove slowly past Buddy's mobile home, turned around, and eased the Jeep into a narrow spot in front of it. *Just in case I need to make a quick getaway,* she thought wryly. Evan would not be pleased with her if he found out, but she wouldn't have to tell him that she'd talked to Buddy—unless she found out something that needed police attention. And then, Evan would have to admit that she'd only furthered the cause of justice.

As she got out of the Jeep, she noticed someone watching her from the window of Blanche's home. *All the better.* At least, if she went in and didn't come out, Blanche or her granddaughter would know it. Nervously, she walked up to Buddy's door and knocked.

Inside, a large dog barked, and a man shouted for the animal to shut up. Rachel knocked again. The metal door was dented, as if someone had given it a hard whack, and she noticed that, just like on Blanche's trailer, there was a hasp on it.

"Who is it?" came the male voice.

"It's Rachel Mast," she answered, with more confidence than she felt. "I'm looking for Buddy."

"Yeah?" The door opened.

Rachel hadn't been able to place the man before, but now that he was standing inches in front of her, she recognized him as someone she'd seen occasionally around town. Buddy was tall, with a wrestler's stocky shoulders and muscular arms. He was shirtless and barefoot, wearing only a pair of jeans. The hand holding the door was covered in reddish hair and bore tattoos on each knuckle. The tattoos spelled out his name.

His face was round, his eyes small and bloodshot; he needed a shave. He was waiting for her to tell him what she wanted.

"I'm trying to get a linear timeline of Willy O'Day's contacts on the day he disappeared," she said, attempting to sound official without actually representing herself as a member of the investigation. "I understand that you and Mr. O'Day had a misunderstanding—"

"You're not a cop. You're the Amish woman who ran away, then came back."

She forced a smile. "I'm acting on behalf of my uncle, Aaron Hostetler."

"The guy they arrested for Willy's murder."

"Yes." She stepped closer, close enough to smell the beer on Buddy's breath. "If you could just answer a few questions—"

"If you ain't a cop, I don't have to talk to you." He started to close the door.

"Please, it will take just a minute." She thrust her sandaled foot into the crack between the door and doorjamb. "I understand that you were in the process of being evicted when Willy disappeared."

"Who said that?"

She didn't answer.

"I'm here, right? If I was evicted, I wouldn't still be here."

Rachel looked up into his eyes. "Did you threaten him that day? When he came to collect the rent and you didn't have it?"

Buddy glanced in the direction of Blanche's trailer.

"Did you threaten Willy in the heat of an argument or not?" she pressed. "It's a simple question."

"And I'll give you a simple answer, lady." His face reddened as he glared at her. "Whoever killed Willy O'Day did me and this town a big favor." He looked down. "You should probably step back before I break your foot."

Rachel took his advice. The door slammed, and she made a quick but dignified retreat to her Jeep. Again, she was left with more questions than answers.

Chapter 16

Early Saturday morning, Rachel was on her knees, planting marigolds and dianthuses in a flower bed on the front lawn, when Hulda drove out of her driveway in her electric golf cart. She spied Rachel, applied the brakes, and backed up.

"Rachel, dear," she called from the street, waving. "I really need to talk to you."

"Sure." Rachel stood up and dusted the dirt off her hands.

She'd put in about half of the flowers and wanted to finish before jumping in the shower and making herself presentable. Evan had texted sometime after she'd gone to bed last night. He'd asked her to come over for breakfast at ten thirty. His text said that he was sorry that he hadn't been able to call earlier, but that he had worked late.

As much as Rachel liked Hulda, she hoped that she wouldn't get tied up with her this morning. She needed to talk to Evan in person. She wanted to apologize to him for getting angry with him Thursday night. She couldn't expect him to do anything unethical, not even for her or her uncle. She knew what kind of person Evan was; it had been wrong of her to even ask him to show her Willy's journal.

She walked over to the street and Hulda's golf cart. Her neighbor was looking especially well put together this morning in a blue-and-white-striped henley, white slacks, and a *Life Is Good* ball cap. Friday afternoons, Mrs. Schenfeld had a standing appointment at Shirley's Kwik Kurl for her styling, pedicure, and manicure, so Saturdays, she was always at her best.

"Can't talk now, though. How about if I come over as soon as I get back from the store?" Hulda bubbled. "They can't get the safe open again, and I've got to go down and do it for them. A fine fettle we'd be in if I wasn't available. The busiest day of the week, customers standing outside waiting to get in, and no cash in the registers."

Rachel nodded sympathetically. The fifty-year-old safe at the store was the size of a dishwasher and as solid as Fort Knox. If Hulda couldn't open it, it would take a team of locksmiths a week to pry it open. At least twice a month she had to go down and fiddle with it until the combination suddenly worked. Considering her neighbor's age, Rachel wondered if replacing the old safe might not be a better solution, but no one had asked her.

"Wait until you hear." Hulda lowered her voice to a whisper. "It may help your uncle's case."

"I have to run out myself, but I should be home for tea this afternoon." She had two couples checking out today whom she'd invited to stay for tea before they left, and she was expecting another couple to check in around the same time.

"I'll catch you later, then," Hulda said. "You are not going to believe what I found out."

Rachel nodded. This was pure Hulda Schenfeld. When she had a bit of gossip, she wouldn't simply spill it. She liked to dangle the tidbit like bait on a fishing line for a while. "Absolutely," Rachel agreed. "I can't wait. Please feel free to join us for tea."

The cell phone on the seat rang, and Hulda rolled her eyes. "I'm coming." She sighed. "You see, retired isn't retired. The store would run better if I went down there every day, but if I do, my grandchildren will never get the hang of it." She laughed. "Besides, I like having my free time. If I can't play a little now, when can I?"

Hulda put her foot to the pedal and zipped off down the street toward Russell's. Rachel looked back at the remaining flats of unplanted seedlings and decided they could wait until tomorrow. She piled the flowers, trowel, and watering can into her gardening wagon and pulled it around to the shed near the back of the house. As she was leaving the building, Mary Aaron ducked in.

"Rachel, I need to talk to you."

You, too? Rachel thought.

Mary Aaron pulled the shed door closed. "I met one of our neighbors this morning on my way here," her cousin said as she folded her arms over her chest. "I won't say who, but he stopped to tell me that he had a loose yearling colt the Friday night that Willy was last seen. He and his brothers were out looking for the horse, and he saw Eli going down the road in his wagon, not far from our farm. It was late, way too late for Eli to be out on the roads."

"Did your neighbor speak to Eli?"

Mary Aaron shook her head. "*Ne.* He doesn't think Eli even saw him. Eli's usually in bed by nine, but this was after midnight." She looked up. "What do you suppose Eli was doing?"

Rachel faintly heard her goats bleating in the barn. She'd already made sure they had food and water this morning, and her brother, Levi, had milked Thomasina, but maybe she needed to toss them another block of hay. She glanced at Mary Aaron. "Why do you think your neighbor told you this *now*?"

"He wanted to know if I knew anything . . . if I'd heard *Dat* mention it."

"You think your neighbor thinks Eli could be a suspect?" He'd certainly been behaving as if he had something to hide, but she hadn't had time to tell Mary Aaron about the conversation she'd overheard between him and Aunt Hannah at the house.

Mary Aaron shook her head. "I don't know what to think. All along, I've assumed the killer was a stranger, maybe a drug addict or somebody who'd just escaped from prison. I know it wasn't *Dat*. But Eli Rust? What reason would Eli have for wanting Willy dead?"

"I don't know . . ." She didn't want to think Willy's killer could be one of the members of her family's church community. It was difficult enough for her to sort through the people who *did* have reason to hate Willy, let alone adding those who didn't.

"I just thought you should know," Mary Aaron said. "I promised that I'd help you. Not that I've done much, but—"

"You *are* helping me," Rachel assured her, grabbing her hand and giving it a squeeze. "I'm glad you told me. It may not mean anything, but who knows? It could be a missing piece of the puzzle."

"I'd better get back inside," her cousin said, "and check on breakfast."

"And I'd better throw some hay to those goats and get a shower. I'm meeting Evan for breakfast this morning, and I wouldn't want to show up at his house looking like I've been—"

"Planting flowers?" Mary Aaron smiled. "He likes you, Rae-Rae, a lot. I don't think he'd care if you showed up after wrestling in the mud with an alligator."

"Luckily, we don't have too many of those in the valley."

An hour and a half later, Rachel finished off her second blueberry pancake and nodded *yes* to another cup of Earl Grey tea. "I can get it," she offered. "You don't have to wait on me."

"Sure I do." Evan rose to go to the stove. "At my table, I'll do the honors. When I come to Stone Mill House, I'll let you be nice to *me*."

She accepted the refill he brought to her, stirred in a spoonful of honey, and smiled at him. They were sitting at his kitchen table, and for once neither of their cells had rung and no one was close enough to overhear their conversation.

"Well, I owe you one because I haven't been very nice to you lately," Rachel admitted. "I'm sorry about the other night. I was wrong. I should never have asked you to let me see what was in Willy's journal."

Evan's expression turned serious. "You don't have to apologize, Rache. I understand your motives. And I'm sorry for being such a hardnose about my job." He reached across the table and covered her hand with his. "I know you're under a lot of stress. If it were one of my uncles . . ."

He left the rest unsaid, but Rachel knew how close he and his family were . . . at least on his father's side. "No," she said. "I was wrong, and I'm sorry. Forgive me?"

"Absolutely." He squeezed her hand. "You know how I hate it when we argue."

"Me, too." She smiled at him. "You really are a good guy, Evan."

He grinned. "Isn't that what I've been telling you all along?" He withdrew his hand, picked up his fork, and captured the last bite of pancake on his plate. "You know that the judge appointed counsel for your uncle. Her name is Monica Cortez. She's young, but she's smart. She'll work hard for your uncle. He could do a lot worse, believe me."

Rachel grimaced. "A woman? I can hear Uncle Aaron now. I doubt he'll talk to her."

"Right," he agreed. "Anyway, apparently, an entry on the day Willy disappeared strongly suggests that Willy was meeting with your uncle that day and that there was an issue to be settled between them."

"That's why they arrested him?" She tried to control her tone of voice; she and Evan had just made up. And he was trying to help her. There was no reason for her to be angry with him. "That doesn't mean Aaron killed him. Willy met lots of people that day. Like his renters."

Evan sat back in his chair. "I got the distinct impression from the detective that rent collection wasn't mentioned. They think it was like a . . . to-do list that went beyond his normal activities. Collecting rent on the first of the month was a normal activity. They liked your idea that the page was a list of accounts to be settled that day," he added sheepishly.

"That was just a guess," she argued. "The letters might not mean that at all."

"I don't know, Rache."

She thought for a minute. "Did the detective say if Willy indicated *why* he was going to talk to Uncle Aaron?"

"No. He didn't say. Maybe the journal didn't say."

She opened her hands. "So my uncle was arrested based on a journal entry that no one can figure out?"

"It's about all the evidence collected." Evan moved his hands as if building an invisible snowball. "There's other evidence. You heard about the shovel they confiscated at the Hostetler farm yesterday morning. They sent it to the lab. I imagine they were looking for traces of blood or strands of hair."

The thought was gruesome. "So the coroner believes that Willy was killed with a shovel?"

Evan nodded. "They weren't looking for just any shovel, though; they were looking for one with a special maker's mark on the back of the blade. A mark exactly like those on the shovels that your uncle's neighbor Eli Rust makes. The shovel confiscated was one Eli made."

"And they can tell Willy was killed by one of Eli's shovels how?"

"Whoever killed Willy hit him hard enough to leave an impression on his skull. Fortunately or unfortunately, Mr. Rust's shovels are distinct. I think that evidence is sound."

Rachel suddenly felt as if she'd swallowed lead pellets instead of blueberry pancakes. "Eli's shovel? Uncle Aaron *would* have one, but so do most of the Amish in this valley. I have one. And so do you; I gave it to you." She took a moment. "Willy may have died from a blow from one of Eli's shovels, but that doesn't mean that it was Uncle Aaron's shovel or that he was the one who committed the murder."

"No," Evan agreed. "No, it doesn't."

She pushed her plate away, unable to finish the last bite. She wondered if she should tell Evan what she'd learned from Mary Aaron about a neighbor seeing Eli on the road that night near the place where the body was found. But if she told Evan, he'd have to report the information to the district attorney's office, and she didn't want to drag Eli into this mess if she didn't have to. He could have had a perfectly good reason for being out on the road that late at night, and her instinct was to not tell the English any more than she had to about the Amish.

She got up and carried her plate to the sink. "I'll wash if you dry," she offered. She set the plate in the sink. "I need to know exactly what that journal entry said. Do you think you could find out?" She raised her gaze to meet his. "Without doing anything . . . unscrupulous?"

He exhaled. "I know you're trying to help your uncle, but don't you think you're crossing the line? Maybe, at this point, you just need to let us—"

"Please, Evan?" When he didn't respond, she went on quickly. "The way I see it, Uncle Aaron's lawyer is going to learn exactly what the journal says, and she'd tell him, if he'd talk to her. So I'd find out anyway . . ."

He narrowed his gaze. "Did anyone ever tell you that you should be selling refrigerators at the North Pole?"

"You."

"All right, so I've used that one before. Seriously, I wouldn't be telling you anything if I didn't think your uncle was innocent. I know the Amish don't do things like this. They do some strange things, though. The worst thing I've ever heard of one Amish doing to another was setting fire to his chicken house—and that was down in Lancaster."

She nodded. "I heard about that. It was a religious squabble. One brother thought the other's chicken house was too fancy, so he set fire to it. In retaliation, the younger brother burned down his brother's empty chicken house. They were both thrown out of their church over the issue and had to move out of state with their families. Violence simply isn't accepted in the faith."

"Murder is a lot more serious than destruction of property."

"It is," Rachel agreed, "and that's why I'm certain Uncle Aaron didn't do it."

"So if he didn't, who did?"

"I don't know," she answered honestly. "Hopefully, we'll find out, before the justice system makes a huge mistake, and a lot of innocent people suffer."

This time Rachel's departure from Evan's house was on much better terms. On the way home, she stopped at the farmer's market and picked up a few things. Walking to her golf cart, she spotted Eli Rust getting out of his buggy. Summoning her courage, she approached him. "Eli?"

"*Ya?*" His horse tossed its head and shied at the sound of a motorbike pulling into the parking area. Eli went to the horse's head and spoke to the animal, stroking its head and calming it.

Rachel followed him. "Eli, I need to know . . . what's between you and my aunt—does it have anything to do with Willy's death?"

He kept his attention on the nervous horse that was now pawing at the pavement. "You should not pry. It's not our way."

"But my Aunt Hannah was obviously upset."

Still, he wouldn't look at her. "It has nothing to do with you."

"You were out late the night Willy vanished, weren't you? Very late. Someone saw you near the Hostetler farm, near the spot where the body was found."

He turned on her. "I had nothing to do with that man's death. You think I would—" He cut himself off.

"Then why all the secrecy?" Rachel pressed. "What did you mean by what you said in Aunt Hannah's kitchen? What are you afraid for my uncle to—"

"Enough!" His glare was so fierce that Rachel found herself taking a step backward. "It's true that I was there on the road that night. I was on my way home."

"So late?"

"*Ya,* late it was. But where I go is not for you to question."

"But my Aunt Hannah—"

"If you don't leave it alone, Rachel Mast, you'll be sorry," he insisted. "People close to you will be hurt."

"Eli? Rachel? What is this?" Rachel's Aunt Hannah hurried toward them.

"Please," Eli said under his breath. "Do not put your aunt in this position. Don't force her to speak of . . . what should not be spoken of."

Rachel glanced at her aunt, now even more confused. Was this about her uncle? Or was it more of a personal nature? She thought about what her uncle had said about Hannah and Eli. Surely he had no reason to—

"I told you, this is not what it appears." Aunt Hannah spoke as if she knew what Rachel was thinking about. "This . . . it's not a matter for you or your uncle to concern yourself with."

Chapter 17

Rachel was still thinking about what Eli had said—or hadn't said—when she returned home with her purchases from the outdoor market, including two more flats of flowers. She wasn't sure why she'd bought more when she hadn't finished setting out the flowers she already had. But Verna Herschberger had been selling them. Her baby had been wailing, her little girl was pulling at her apron and begging for a cookie, and the crowd of shoppers had been thinning out. Verna's gaze had been so full of hopeful expectation that Rachel couldn't bear to walk away empty-handed.

At least she hadn't been selling goats, Rachel thought as she carried her basket into the kitchen. No one seemed to be around; the house was quiet, and there were no messages on the phone and no emails that weren't spam. She gathered her plants and tools, hoping to get some flowers into the ground before she had to get ready for afternoon tea. She'd no sooner planted the first petunia than Hulda came through the gate in the hedge between the two properties.

"Ah, Rachel, there you are. I got the safe open, but then that new girl called in sick. Saturday, always Saturday, they fall ill. She'll come back Monday with a tan, looking fit as a fiddle, mark my word. That one won't last long. Anyway, someone had to take her register, so I stayed until the boys finished checking in the new shipment." She paused to catch her breath.

Still on her knees, Rachel sat back. "Could you hand me another plant, please?" Hulda settled in the grass, and they worked in pleasant silence for ten minutes while Rachel planted petunias. "You said you had something to tell me?" she finally asked as she got to her feet.

"Oh, yes, I did. I nearly forgot." Hulda accepted the hand Rachel offered and got to her feet. "I love flowers, but I never had the green thumb my mother did. Flowers give us so much pleasure, and they don't ask for much in return. Decent soil, sunlight, and water." She looked around as if to reassure herself that they were alone. "This is confidential, you understand. But a reliable source—you know that one of my grandnieces works at the bank—anyway, I won't say who, but this person told me that Willy O'Day had been secretly making monthly deposits into Teresa's account for years."

"To Teresa's bank account?"

"Yes." Mrs. Schenfeld nodded firmly. "Unethical to mention it, of course, but what is even stranger is that the deposits ended abruptly the month before Willy's disappearance."

"Do the police know about this?"

Hulda shrugged. "Just about his balance, right after he went missing. They never requested details of withdrawals. An oversight, if you ask me. Of course, Willy O'Day's account was a substantial pillar of our local bank. No one would want Willy moving his business to one of those larger banks elsewhere."

"Why would he be giving money to Teresa? You don't suppose they were still . . . friendly, do you?" Rachel glanced at the remaining bed. One of Ada's grandsons had worked it up for her, and the ground was ready for the flowers to be set out, but they'd have to wait until tomorrow. "I can't imagine Teresa and Willy were still . . . together."

"No. Absolutely not. Teresa is long over sowing her wild oats. She's much too involved in her volunteer activities at church and the library to have time for running with Willy O'Day or anyone else, for that matter. Their fling was more than twenty years ago, when she left Stone Mill."

"More than twenty years ago," Rachel repeated. "And she came back when Ell was, what? Four or five?"

"Like I said, we all did the math. Teresa was gone almost seven years. The little girl was only five when her mother brought her to Stone Mill."

"Teresa returned to Stone Mill about the time I left," Rachel mused. She looked at Hulda. "So what possible reason could Willy have had for giving Teresa money?"

"For *years,*" Hulda interjected. She crossed her arms over her tiny chest. "Suspicious, isn't it?"

"Not blackmail? I can't imagine . . ." Rachel's voice trailed off. She was becoming frustrated. It had been almost two weeks since Willy's body had been found. Two weeks she'd been investigating and she felt as if she'd come no closer to solving the crime.

"We couldn't imagine Willy being robbed and murdered in Stone Mill, either, could we?"

Rachel nodded. "You're right. Thank you for telling me." She hesitated. ". . . Do you think we should report this to someone?"

"What? Hearsay? The first thing the policeman would want to know is who told me. I couldn't hardly lie, and that would put my—my *confidant's* position in jeopardy. It wasn't a professional thing to do—telling tales out of school, as it were. But . . . it's certainly nothing like blackmail or murder. And someone committed a terrible crime right here in our town, and your dear uncle is being blamed for it. It's a travesty of justice."

"I agree, but . . . Well," Rachel hedged, "I suppose I'll simply have to find out if your *confidant's* statement is accurate. You think I could talk to her?"

Hulda grimaced. "Then she'd know I shared."

Rachel thought for a moment. "Well, if it *was* blackmail,

what could Teresa have known about Willy that he didn't want anyone to know about? I mean, he may not have been a likeable man, but he never hid who he was." She paused. "Maybe it wasn't blackmail. Maybe Teresa loaned him money or—"

"Not possible." Hulda stooped to pick up a fallen petunia head from the lawn. "Teresa was struggling financially when she left, and she certainly doesn't make a large salary now. The O'Days have always been well off, gas and oil money—even railroad money, some say. I have heard that the great-great-grandfather came here from Ireland during one of the potato famines, and that their first money came from marrying into a wealthy Quaker family. Hearsay only, of course."

"Of course."

"My husband's family predates them. The Schenfelds emigrated from Austria to Philadelphia in the late seventeenth century."

Rachel smiled. "So what you're saying is that the O'Days are *new* money?"

"Exactly."

"And the Schenfelds have had the common sense not to offend anyone enough to end up buried in an Amish cow pasture."

The couple who had reservations for that night changed their plans and rescheduled for the following weekend, so Rachel had a bowl of cereal for supper and enjoyed the quiet of the house. After her delicious meal, she decided to take a walk and headed for The George. She wasn't satisfied with Buddy's explanation of what had taken place between him and Willy the night that Blanche said Buddy had been evicted. She wanted to ask George if he knew anything about it. And, of course, she wanted to see how he was doing. When you lost someone close to you, as George had, shock often got you through the funeral, but once life went back to *normal*, that, she knew, was when you realized nothing would ever be *normal* again.

Ell was at the checkout desk. The bookstore seemed empty of customers, and Rachel's footsteps echoed on the granite floor as she entered what had been the old lobby. Although she knew it wasn't possible, Rachel never came into The George without sensing that dozens of theatergoers were laughing, talking, and walking around her. "Hi," she called to Ell. She would have loved to ask the young woman about the details of her mother's association with Willy, but of course that would have been wrong. What if Ell knew nothing about it? It wasn't Rachel's place to cause trouble between a mother and daughter.

"Hi." Ell gave her a shy smile. "Rachel. It's been as quiet as a tomb here tonight. I'm glad to see you."

"Unusual for a Saturday evening, isn't it?" Rachel remarked. The theater had been boarded up for many years, and when George bought it, most of the original features remained intact, including the six-foot-long glass refreshment cases, filled now with displays of children's books.

"Not so many people want to come out at night since Willy's body was found," Ell said. "I guess they see murderers behind every bush." She tugged at a lock of straight, dark hair that had fallen forward. "It was busy today, but after supper . . ." She motioned toward the empty aisles between the bookcases in the main room. "George is here, though, upstairs. He had a delivery from London, and he's unpacking it."

"How's he doing?"

"Not so good. He can't stop thinking about Willy, talking about him. You know how the two of them were. Twins are supposed to have a psychic bond stronger than other brothers and sisters." A faint smile tugged at the corners of her mouth. "I've always thought that it would be neat to be a twin . . . or even to have a brother or sister."

Ell was particularly talkative tonight. While her Goth persona, the piercings, and the impossible hairdo were all a little unsettling, Rachel liked the young woman. She was smart and sweet, but seemed to be struggling to figure out who she was. Rachel had rarely seen her with other girls, and as far as she knew, Ell didn't have a boyfriend.

"How's your mother?" Rachel asked. "She seemed so upset the day of Willy's funeral." *That certainly wasn't crossing the line.*

"Mom can be very emotional. Most people don't know that about her. She doesn't do death well. It's a natural part of the circle of life, you know. It's what I like about you, Rachel. You never freak out when I talk about that stuff."

A dog's bark echoed in the lobby. Rachel glanced toward the curving staircase, with its ornate brass railing. The brass shone, and the wide steps were rose granite like the lobby. "Sophie?"

Ell nodded. "George won't let Sophie out of his sight since she ran away at the funeral home. I don't know what he'd do if anything happened to her." She lowered her voice. "George doesn't think of her as a dog. He knows she's a dog, but he treats her as more human than animal."

Rachel picked up a flyer off the front desk advertising an Amish breakfast being held to raise money to help pay the medical bills for a baby who needed heart surgery. The Old Order Amish didn't believe in insurance because they felt that it showed a lack of belief in God's plan, but whenever someone needed help, the communities would pitch in to assist in easing the financial burden. Giving breakfasts or holding auctions were popular fundraisers, and most of the valley's residents, Amish and English alike, could be counted on to offer support. When there was a sick child or someone in need of lifesaving care in the valley, the differences between Amish and English residents seemed insignificant.

"I was wondering," Rachel said, glancing at the information in the flyer. "Do you remember when the last time was you saw Willy before he disappeared? Did he happen to come to the bookstore that day? I know that sometimes he picked up a paper here."

"I don't know." Ell paused from putting price stickers on a box of assorted best sellers that had just come in. "I was out sick. Worst day of my life. Either a stomach bug or the pad Thai I had the night before. The place I got it in State College was kind of shady. I was barfing nonstop."

"So you were at the house all day and the evening, too?"

"Yup. Mindy covered for me. I only got out of bed to let the cat in or out or to run to the toilet. She was my third cat last year. I didn't seem to be having much luck with them. They kept disappearing. Anyway, Paws turned out to be a winner. I still have her. Anyway . . ." She waved. "I didn't set foot out of my apartment until Sunday afternoon. I wasn't scheduled to work that Saturday. It was my day off."

"So I guess you were asleep early that night. Friday night," Rachel said.

"Nah. I stayed up pretty late watching *Interview with the Vampire* on TV. I couldn't sleep because I slept a lot of the day. Great movie. Not as good as the book, but still prime. One of my top five faves. Have you seen it?"

"No, but if you recommend it, maybe I will."

"You won't be sorry." Ell went back to her stickers. "Pretty much anything Anne Rice writes is heavy. A shame they didn't make all of her novels into movies."

Rachel returned the flyer to the pile on the counter. "And you never heard Willy come home that night? Never heard his truck come up the drive?"

Ell rented a small apartment over Willy and George's barn, or what had once been a barn and was now a garage and storage area. Rachel had never been in the apartment, but George had told her about it. Hulda said the O'Days had done a nice job on the remodeling. All the appliances had come from Russell's Hardware. Willy might have been known for his tight grasp on his wallet, but that had been one time he'd apparently loosened his grip.

Ell glanced up. "You know, I thought I heard the truck pull in about nine thirty, ten o'clock, but obviously I was mistaken. I was in the bathroom, upchucking again, and the vampires were stalking somebody."

"Did the police ask you about it?"

She nodded. "I told them I wasn't sure, because I wasn't. But George said that he was waiting for Willy and he never came home. George would know." She gave Rachel another hesitant smile. "Sorry, I've got to put these best sellers out. George asked me to be sure I did it before we close."

"No problem." Rachel returned her smile. A pity this bright young woman hadn't gone on to college. Working in the bookstore might be fine for now, but it couldn't provide much of a future for Ell. "I'll just go up and find George and Sophie."

"Up in his office. He'll be glad to see you." She picked up the heavy box of books. "It's always nice to talk to you."

"You, too." Rachel turned toward the stairs leading to the second floor.

There was still so much stuff whirling around in her head that nothing was making any sense anymore. Why would Ell think she had heard Willy that night when, in reality, he never made it home? Had he pulled in, then left without George knowing it? Had Willy encountered someone in the yard? Was that how his truck ended up parked in town and him in a grave?

"George?" Rachel reached the top hallway and saw that George's office door stood slightly open. "It's Rachel."

Sophie put up a furious racket, running into the hallway, yapping. She curled her lip, giving a little growl. Then the bichon frise began leaping up on Rachel's legs.

"Down, Sophie," Rachel ordered. "Good dog." But she never was. Sophie kept on jumping, spinning, and scratching until George came to Rachel's rescue and scooped the dog up into his arms.

"Bad doggy," George crooned. "Naughty girl. No jumping. That isn't polite." He slipped a piece of dog biscuit out of his shirt pocket and offered it to Sophie. She took it politely, daintily chewed, swallowed, and looked for more.

"No more treats," George said. "You'll get fat." His eyes twinkled as he looked at Rachel. "As my vet says, there are fat doggies and old doggies, but few fat, old doggies."

George set Sophie on the floor, and Rachel greeted him with a hug and a kiss on the cheek. "What a nice surprise," he said, leading the way back into his office.

"Just wondering how you were making out." George waved toward an overstuffed chair, and Rachel sat down. "Hoping you'd like to come by for supper tomorrow. If it's nice, we could eat out on the terrace."

"You cooking?" George chuckled at his own joke and adjusted his ball cap.

"I thought we could all pitch in. I can make a salad. Hulda's coming, and Coyote."

"Not spending Sunday with your family?"

"Church Sunday. I ran into our bishop at the farmer's market, and he invited me to services, but . . ."

George's eyes held understanding. "Not ready for that yet?"

Rachel shook her head. "Anyway, you probably know that I've been asking a few questions around town . . . just trying to sort some things out."

"For your uncle's defense."

"Exactly. I was out to Park Estates. Do you know Blanche?"

"I've known Blanche for years. We had a nice conversation at Willy's . . . after the funeral. Blanche is a little rough around the edges, but she's a good soul. I've been thinking about lowering her rent. I can't imagine that her husband's pension stretches very far in these times." He sighed. "I was reluctant to make any changes to Willy's business affairs until . . . Well, I'll do my best by his tenants now. Not his way, maybe. Willy was a much better businessman than I'll ever be. But it never hurts to do a good turn when you can. Good karma, as Ell would say."

"Exactly. But Blanche told me something that has me a little confused. She said that her neighbor Buddy had a disagreement with Willy that Friday night—that Willy was attempting to evict him for not paying his rent."

"Really?" George looked puzzled. "I wasn't aware of that. I know Buddy had gotten a little behind, but he came by that Saturday after Willy . . . after his disappearance. Of course I didn't know Willy was missing," he added thoughtfully, looking away. "Anyway," he continued after a moment, "Buddy paid up in full, and he's paid regular ever since." George glanced toward a mahogany Victorian end table where a Keurig coffee maker, a creamer, and a sugar bowl stood. "I was just going to make a cup. Would you like—"

"No, thanks, George." Willy's money had been missing when his body was found. Wasn't it a little suspicious that Buddy didn't have the money to pay his rent Friday, but he did Saturday?

"Maybe a cookie? I've got some lovely Scottish shortbread. I order it directly from Glasgow. It's to die for."

"No, thanks." She smiled at him. "Really. Another time." Cookies were her weakness, and she'd had George's shortbread before. Tons of butter. Delicious, but a pound a bite. If she ate one, she wouldn't be able to stop herself from eating a dozen.

"Look at this." He slipped on a pair of white gloves and carefully lifted a small leather-bound volume out of a box. "*Gulliver's Travels*. Isn't it exquisite? Not a stain. No mildew. Beautiful."

"It is. And I suppose you have a buyer waiting."

"I do. No auctions for this little treasure. It's going straight to a good home and a temperature-controlled library. Tucson. Lovely for books there."

"George . . . Ell and I were talking about that Friday night," Rachel said. "You're certain Willy never came home?

Maybe pulled into the yard and then left again? Because Ell thought she might have heard the truck . . . around nine thirty."

"No, he never came home." He carefully replaced the precious volume in the box. "Maybe Ell heard the boy next door. He has one of those souped-up cars, and I think he's taken his muffler completely off. To make it louder." He shook his head. "No, I'm sure of it. The last time I saw him was after lunch."

"After lunch?"

George looked up. Frowned. "I guess it was breakfast that day, wasn't it?" He closed his eyes for a moment, plucking off the white gloves. "I'm sorry. I suppose I'm becoming forgetful." He sighed. "Willy never arrived home that night . . . He was probably already gone."

George seemed so sad that Rachel ended up sitting down for a cup of decaf coffee with him and not one but two pieces of shortbread. Forty-five minutes later, she was walking home when her cell phone beeped in her pocket. She pulled it out.

There was a text from Evan.

Working late.

Attached was a photo of the cover of a small spiral notebook. Willy's elusive journal. The phone beeped again. Another photo text. She knew what it was the moment it flashed on the screen.

A screenshot of the last page of Willy O'Day's journal.

Chapter 18

Rachel stood on the cobblestone sidewalk and stared at the iPhone in her hand. A street lamp shone over her shoulder; it was almost dark and the town was quiet. At the top of the screen, in masculine printing, was the date, October 1, and the letters *A.T.B.R.*

Accounts to be reconciled—that's what she'd told Evan it meant . . . or might mean. She stared at the list written by Willy, probably hours before his death, and she shivered, despite the warmth of the May evening.

The words on the list made no sense. Evan had said they were in code. This wasn't exactly *code,* not like the kind spies used or anything, but the list certainly needed to be deciphered. Rachel ran her fingertips over the screen to expand it, making the words bigger, then scrolled down. She read through the list written in Willy's handwriting again:

Stamp Collecting
Fencing Fred
Bearded A
Sophia Loren

It made no sense. The police arrested and charged her uncle with murder because of *this?* It was practically gibberish. She tucked the phone into her pocket and headed for home, but twice, on the way, she read the list again. Obviously her suggestion that "A.T.B.R." meant "accounts to be reconciled" was wrong. What account would Willy O'Day have been settling with an Italian actress from the '50s and 60s? Rachel wasn't even sure if the film star was still alive.

Rachel reached home and crossed the wide, grassy lawn in the dark. The square fieldstone house loomed in front of her; light glowed from both sides of the door. She was glad she had thought to leave the front porch lights on. She salvaged those carriage-style lamps from a box of junk she'd bought at a yard sale. No light shone from any of the windows. Because of the cancellation, she'd be alone tonight, something that happened less and less often as her B&B became more popular.

The May air had turned chilly on the walk home, and she hurried the last few steps. She plucked a house key from under an iron boot scrape to the right of the door—another yard sale find—and let herself in. Inside the door, she looked at her phone again. *Bearded A . . .* Did that refer to Aaron? Did the police arrest him on the basis of *that?*

She took the time to return the key to its place, then checked the other doors in the house to be sure they were locked and headed upstairs. Some people might have felt uncomfortable, even afraid, alone in such a big house, but not Rachel. Tonight she was almost glad she had no guests to check on. She was eager to have a good look at Willy's journal page. And have time to think. She might even print it out if she could remember how to use the printer app on her phone.

As Rachel headed up the stairs to the third floor, she didn't bother with any lights; electricity was money, and though she was beginning to turn a profit, there was no cash to be wasted. She could navigate the entire house, cellar to attic, with her eyes shut. When she'd first taken possession of the property, there had been no electricity. She'd climbed the stairs plenty of times in the dark in those early days without so much as a flashlight.

At the top of the second flight, she turned toward her door and bumped into something on the floor with the toe of her sneaker. Something soft and unexpected. She gave a startled squeak at the same time that Bishop howled and raced down the hall.

"Bishop! I'm sorry. You okay?" she called after him, her hand on her pounding heart. "What are you doing, standing in the dark like that?"

Inside her room, she flipped on the light switch. "Come on, if you're coming," she called to the cat. "I'm closing the door." No matter that she'd insulated the house, it still seemed drafty at night.

She removed her cell phone from her jacket pocket, tossed the jacket over a chair, and sat down on her bed. She held the phone, poised to text Evan.

Should she ask him questions? For one thing, she was curious as to how he had been able to take the photographs. She knew he was working tonight, but wasn't evidence locked up? Did he have a key to evidence storage? As happy as she was to have the photos, she hoped Evan hadn't done anything that could cost him his job.

Besides wanting to know the particulars of how he had been able to take pictures of the journal with his iPhone, she had questions about the actual journal. Did the other pages make as little sense as this one? Had George been asked to translate the list? Were they even sure the journal was Willy's? She glanced up to watch the Siamese stroll into the room and rub up against one leg of her desk.

After a moment of uncertainty, she decided that it was better to not ask Evan any questions. At least not yet. She knew this had to be a big deal to him, to take these photos of the journal and send them to her.

Got it. Thanks, she texted him back.

She opened the list again: Stamp Collecting, Sophia Loren, Bearded A, Fencing Fred. What did they mean? Could something on this list be a reference to someone other than Uncle Aaron? Maybe one of the people she'd been looking into? Could "Bearded A" mean something other than Bearded *Aaron?*

She closed her eyes and opened them again. Stared at the white dry-erase board in the corner of the room. She needed to pay her gas bill and order a new hinge for one of the bathroom doors.

She looked at the phone in her hand again and jumped up off the bed. Tucking the phone into the back pocket of her jeans, she grabbed the eraser off her desk and wiped the board clean. Then she took a teal dry-erase marker, drew a rectangle right in the center of the board, and copied the text from Willy's notebook, letter for letter.

She stepped back. Stared at the board. Then, on impulse, she wrote *Willy O'Day* across the top in the same teal marker. Next, she grabbed a blue marker and began to make a list, on the left-hand side of the board, of the people she knew Willy had seen the day of his disappearance: George, of course; Dawn, the waitress from the diner; Blanche; Alvin and Verna; Buddy. Those, she knew of. Then, she took a green marker and added Steve's name, Eli Rust's, and . . . Teresa's.

She stood back to study her handiwork.

Dawn had gone back to Florida to be with her children and mother, and the conversation Rachel had with her by phone convinced her of the waitress's innocence. Rachel crossed her name off with a red marker.

She stared at Steve's name. He said he'd been at a wedding in Williamsport the weekend Willy disappeared. She studied the board for another minute, then went to her computer and searched for *Weddings in Williamsport, October 1*.

She got lots of hits. None helpful. She sat back in her chair. Bishop jumped up on the desk and rubbed against the laptop, moving the screen back and forth. She stroked his head. "Knock it off." She adjusted the screen.

Next, she typed in Steve Barber's name. Again, several hits, but after two false tries, she found a social network page with Steve's grinning face plastered across the top.

Rachel scowled and clicked on a bar giving details of his life, where he was born, where he graduated high school. She read that he liked to collect model trains. She clicked on his photo album and flipped through it. They were all photos of him: Steve, in a ball cap, pointing at a daffodil; Steve wearing a colorful knit cap and shoveling snow; Steve wearing a red-and-white Santa's hat; Steve in a tux, wearing a bride's tiara with a veil. There seemed to be a theme. Next, Steve in an engineer's hat, holding up a model engine. It was dated a week previous.

She scrolled back and stared at Steve in the tux. He looked inebriated. She checked the time and place tag: *Williamsport, PA, October 1, 9:05 p.m.* The wedding.

She sighed and closed her laptop. At the whiteboard, she took the marker and ran it through the middle of his name. Steve Barber didn't kill Willy.

Who was she kidding? None of these people had killed Willy.

She stared at the list in the middle of the board again. Her gaze crossed *Fencing Fred,* then went back.

Fred . . . Fred Wright . . . He was putting the fencing for the goats in for her. Was Fred Wright "Fencing Fred"? Had Willy settled business with Fred the day he disappeared?

And what was the deal with the money Willy had been depositing in Teresa's account? The fact that the deposits had stopped and then Willy disappeared was suspicious, wasn't it?

After getting into her PJs, Rachel lay in bed for a long time, staring at the dry-erase board, going over and over in her mind all the possibilities each name or phrase in Willy's ledger could mean. When she slept that night, she dreamed of Sophia Loren and Teresa Ridley sunbathing on an Italian beach.

The next morning, Rachel had the house to herself. After breakfast, she made herself busy emptying the trash and recycling bins, replacing lightbulbs, and doing other menial tasks. She kept an eye on the clock, and when eleven thirty finally came, she went into the kitchen.

Taking a wicker basket from a tall shelf, she spread a blue-and-white-checkered cloth over the bottom and helped herself to several banana muffins Ada had made the previous day. She added two blueberry scones and a wrapped slice of Dutch apple cake to the basket. She snipped several blossoms from a flower arrangement on the table and tucked them around the goodies, covering the basket with a second square of the checked material.

It was such a nice day that Rachel considered walking to Teresa's, but she decided that the baked goods would fare better if she took the golf cart. The streets were quiet, but a few cars passed. Church services were letting out; people waved to her as she drove by.

Ell's mother lived on a quiet street four blocks away. Hers was a modest beige ranch with dark-brown shutters, surrounded by a neatly trimmed lawn. A small sign in the picture window read *Piano Lessons*. A heart-shaped grapevine wreath hung on the front door with the word *Welcome* spelled out in artificial red grapes.

Rachel rang the doorbell, which played "Amazing Grace" inside the house. She waited a few seconds and then pushed the button again. This time she heard footsteps.

"Coming." Teresa opened the door. An expression of surprise was quickly replaced with pleasure. "Rachel Mast? Whatever . . . why . . ." she stammered, and then said, "Please, come in. I just walked in the door from church."

Rachel held out the basket and whisked away the top

cloth. "I hope you don't mind me stopping by unannounced, but I've been worried about you. You seemed so upset at the funeral. So I brought you some snacks."

"You brought those for me?" Teresa backed away and held the door open. "How nice of you. I so rarely . . . I couldn't imagine who it was. I have a student coming for a lesson at one, but . . ." She still seemed surprised, but also pleased.

Rachel followed her into a living room dominated by a piano. The floors were hardwood, which Rachel loved, but the fussy faux-country furnishings and hanging baskets of artificial flowers were definitely not her thing. Studio portraits of Ell lined three of the four walls. One wall was completely covered with baby pictures progressing from newborn to toddler stage. In every photo, Ell was buttoned, sashed, and wrapped in an overabundance of ruffled bonnets, lacy dresses, and shoes more suited to a boutique display case than a baby's feet.

On the next wall was a row of school-age portraits, and in every one, Ell was garbed in ruffled frocks, frilly lace-edged socks, and Mary Janes, white or black patent leather, depending on the season. Her light-brown hair was tortured into long corkscrew curls, à la Shirley Temple. On the third wall were high school portraits, including four versions of what could only have been Ell's senior portraits. Rachel studied the photographs, finding it hard to imagine that this child was the Ell she knew.

Rachel smiled reassuringly at Teresa but couldn't help thinking that, at least in this case, there really could be too much of a good thing. Maybe the Amish custom of not allowing photographs of people wasn't such a bad idea.

"I'll put on some coffee," Teresa said. "If you'd like to stay a few minutes."

"As long as I'm not intruding."

"Not at all. It was sweet of you to think of me. I know that I must have looked . . . I've known, or rather I *had* known Willy since I was a child. It was very hard to see him taken from us in such a violent manner." She kept walking and Rachel followed her into a small kitchen with a table against one wall. The table was so small that there was only room for two chairs, and the surface was nearly taken up by a fifteen-inch glass cookie jar shaped like a red rooster with a bright blue comb.

Rachel slid into one of the chairs. "I'll be honest. The treats weren't the only reason I stopped by. I was wondering if you could help me," she said. "I've been attempting to help Uncle Aaron. You know, because of his arrest."

"You don't have to convince me." Teresa filled a teakettle with water from the tap. "Aaron Hostetler couldn't have done such a thing. I know people say he has a temper, but he's never been anything but nice to me." She took down two matching cups and saucers. The china was red and white, decorated with red hens and baby chicks. "I hope you don't mind instant. I have those little coffee pouches that make one cup at a time. I try to limit myself to one cup a day. Milk?"

"Just black, please." Rachel forced another smile, wondering what her mother would think of all the poultry décor. "The court has appointed a lawyer for Uncle Aaron, but I'm talking to everyone who saw Willy that last Friday. Just looking for anyone who might have noticed him talking to a stranger or seen anything out of the usual."

"I see." Teresa's mouth tightened. "Of course, if I could be of any assistance, I'd be happy to see justice prevail."

"Did you see Willy that day?"

"Me?" She looked uncomfortable. "I don't think so. No, I'm sure I didn't—"

"You're certain? Maybe at the restaurant or the grocery—"

"I said I didn't." Teresa's face paled. "Why are you asking me these questions?" Her hand tightened on the back of the other chair. "I'm suddenly feeling a little light-headed. This might not be the best time for us to visit." She seemed to sag. "I think it's best if you go and come back another day."

"You want me to leave?"

"It would be best."

And as swiftly as Rachel had talked her way into Teresa's home, she found herself gently ejected and standing on the walk outside the closed front door. "Interesting," Rachel muttered to herself. What was Teresa hiding?

Rachel's next stop was Wagler's Grocery. She didn't really need anything, but she took a cart, threw in some staples, and wheeled it up and down the aisles until she found Buddy stocking cans of tuna fish on an end cap. She waited until two women that she knew passed by and there was a lull in the flow of shoppers before approaching him.

He'd obviously already seen her because his face had taken on the same shade red as the Wagler's apron he wore over his khaki pants and blue shirt. He glanced over his shoulder, looking for an escape route, but Rachel was too quick for him. She shoved her cart forward, pinning Buddy between a five-foot-tall dancing tuna fish and the towering display of cans.

"I know that you didn't tell me the truth about the night Willy disappeared," she said in a low but determined voice. "I'm giving you one more chance before I go to the authorities with what I suspect."

"Please." Buddy groaned. "I'm working." He glanced around. "I can't talk here."

"We couldn't talk at your place, and you made it clear that you didn't want to see me there again. So it'll have to be here."

"You'll make me lose my job."

A loaded cart nosed around the end of the aisle, manned by a young couple. "Rachel," the woman said. "How are you?"

"Good." Rachel gave her a big smile. "And you? How are the sheep?"

"Good, good," the husband said.

"And your mother?" Rachel asked. "Her sprained wrist is better?"

"Praise be to God," the woman answered. "And your parents?"

"Well, well," Rachel said, ignoring Buddy. The three exchanged a few more pleasantries before the couple moved on.

When they were out of earshot, Rachel returned her attention to Buddy, only to find that his eyes were welling up with tears.

"Are you *crying?*" she asked, staring at him. "Why are you crying?"

"I'm not . . . crying." Buddy trembled and a large tear slid down a five-o'clock-shadowed cheek. "Just . . . just something in my eye." He rubbed at his face with the back of a big, hairy, tattooed hand.

Rachel put her hand on his arm. Suddenly she felt terrible. She hadn't meant to make him cry. Apparently, he wasn't the tough guy he pretended to be at his house the other day. "It's all right, Buddy. Just tell me the truth now."

"If I get fired, I'll lose my new truck. And my new girlfriend. There's no way she'll stay with me if I don't have a car and I have to borrow her Bug again to get to work."

"I don't want you to be fired," she said, keeping her voice down. "But I want to know what happened that night with Willy. I already know you argued about your rent."

"Yeah," Buddy admitted. "I lied to you. Please don't say anything to my girlfriend. She's real religious. I had a little too much to drink, and I lost my temper with Willy. I didn't want you to know that I'd said some bad stuff to him, but I didn't mean it. I've just got a big mouth when I drink."

She patted his shoulder. "Tell me what did happen."

"I got mad because Willy locked me out of my house. Put a padlock right on the door. There's hasps on all the doors—even Blanche's and she owns her own trailer." He hung his head. "It was my own fault. I'd already been late twice. Three times and you're out. That was Willy's rule. I can understand why he'd have to be tough. Nobody would pay their rent if he let you slide too many times."

George hadn't said anything about Willy locking Buddy out, only that Buddy brought him the rent the next day. "So," Rachel said gently, "what happened after Willy put the padlock on your door?"

"Put one on the back door, too. He actually carries padlocks with him. *Carried,*" he corrected.

She waited a moment, then went on. "Did you kill Willy, Buddy? Did he make you so mad that you followed him and—"

"Did I *kill* him? Heck, no. I did what any guy would do. I bought another six-pack and went to a friend's to crash on his couch. The next morning I went to the bank as soon as it opened and cashed a check. See, I had the money to pay my rent because I sold my *old* truck to a buddy. But he said I couldn't cash the check till the second."

"So that's the money you used to pay your rent to George?" she asked. *And not money from Willy's pocket?* she wondered.

"How'd you know I gave George the money?" He wiped his eyes. When she didn't answer, he went on. "I took it right over to Willy's house, but his brother said he wasn't there, so I gave it to him. George was real nice. He followed me back to the park and used Willy's keys to take off the padlocks. It was decent of him. He didn't have to do that. He could have told me to wait until Willy got home." He pulled a rumpled handkerchief out of his pocket and blew his nose. "I haven't been late once since then. I pay George every month on the dot. You can ask him."

"If you lied to me before, Buddy, how can I be certain that you're telling the truth now?"

"I am. I swear it. I didn't hurt Willy. I never saw him again after he left the trailer park." He blew his nose again.

"So," she said, thinking out loud, "you went to a friend's house that night?"

"Ricky's. Ricky Truder's. He and some guys play *Call of*

Duty every Friday. I was there all night, killing Nazi zombies."

"So if I asked Ricky, he'd tell me that you were with him all night?"

"Sure. I whipped his butt at *Call of Duty*. I had a real good night."

She arched a brow. "I hope so," she said quietly, "because I will find Ricky and ask him if you were there."

"That's okay," Buddy said, nodding. "If you don't believe me, you can ask Evan."

"Evan?" she said.

"Evan Parks. I know you know him." He smiled. "I've also heard he's sweet on you. But I'm probably not supposed to tell you that," he added quickly.

"You were playing video games with Evan Parks the night Willy O'Day disappeared?" The minute he said it, she knew his alibi was solid. Evan *did* play video games on Friday nights, once in a while, with some guys he had known from high school. Ricky was one of those guys.

Rachel went home, went straight upstairs to her bedroom, and crossed Buddy's name off on the dry-erase board.

Chapter 19

Rachel put a clay pot of blue and violet pansies in the center of the wrought-iron table and stood back to admire them. The day had been warm, and since George had insisted on bringing steaks to cook on the grill, she had decided to have supper outside on the porch. Hulda was throwing together her fantastic organic salad with wild greens and tiny tomatoes that she grew in her orangery, and Coyote had promised a cherry torte. Rachel's contribution was green beans sautéed with olive oil, pecans, and garlic. She didn't call herself a cook, but she could make decent green beans. And, of course, yesterday Ada had whipped up yeast rolls so light that they practically floated up out of the breadbasket.

Rachel centered a plate at one of the place settings. She was looking forward to an evening with friends, when she could forget about her worries for a few hours. Satisfied with the table, Rachel went back to the house for a pitcher of lemonade. As she came out onto the back porch with it, Hulda appeared, carrying a bowl of salad large enough to feed half of Stone Mill. Rachel greeted her warmly, and the two of them finished setting the table. They chatted about the weather and the price of gas until George arrived in his golf cart with Coyote sitting beside him. George was wearing his usual ball cap and a red apron that proclaimed *CHEF* in white lettering.

"Where's the baby?" Mrs. Schenfeld asked. "I was hoping to get to see that sweet baby of yours."

"Home with Daddy and the rest of them." Coyote's infectious smile lit up her pretty face. Her white-blond hair hung loose around her shoulders, and beaded deerskin moccasins peeped out from beneath her long gypsy skirt. Coyote was such a free spirit that it was hard for Rachel to remember she was the mother of four children. "It's only fair he gets *daddy time* with all of them." Coyote put her cherry torte on the table beside Hulda's salad. "It was so nice of you to invite me, Rachel. I love my kids, but sometimes it's a treat to get out of the house and the pottery shed and just talk to grown-ups."

George kissed cheeks all around and then set about getting the steaks on. Hulda and Coyote quickly discovered their mutual love of Florence, Italian art, and growing their own herbs. Although the two hadn't known each other well before this evening, Rachel was delighted to see how well they got along. She genuinely liked Coyote, and it pleased her to see how easily she and her family had fit into life in Stone Mill.

"I forgot the pepper," George called over his shoulder. "Rachel, could you—"

"Sure thing. I have to get my green beans anyway."

Coyote was pouring lemonade in the tall glasses as Rachel dashed back into the house for a pepper mill and her beans, which she had kept warm in the oven. She hurried back to George with them and watched as he seasoned the sizzling T-bones. There were only three. Coyote was an easygoing vegetarian. She didn't eat meat, but she jokingly said she never minded watching barbarians enjoy it.

"Stand back," George warned. "I wouldn't want you to

get burned." He used a long-handled fork to turn the steaks. "Should be ready in the flick of a lamb's tail."

Rachel hesitated. She didn't want to do anything to spoil their relaxed evening, but Buddy's statement about George unlocking the mobile home for him the day after Willy's disappearance kept nagging at her. "George," she said, too quietly for Hulda and Coyote to hear. They were too busy discussing the best way to grow basil. "There's something I'd like to ask you."

"Sure, anything." He smiled at her.

"You know that I've been talking to people who saw Willy that last day."

He nodded.

"Well, I'm a little confused." Butterflies fluttered in the pit of her stomach. She didn't want to offend George or suggest that he wasn't telling the truth when it was probably Buddy who was being less than forthcoming, but . . . "You said that you didn't know anything about Willy evicting Buddy," she said quietly. "But Buddy told me that Willy locked him out of his trailer that night, and that he came by your house the following morning with the money he owed Willy. He said Willy wasn't there, so he paid you what he owed your brother."

"Really?" George rubbed his chin. "Buddy said that?" His face flushed, either from embarrassment or from the heat of the grill.

Rachel nodded. "Buddy also said that you followed him out to his place and took the padlocks off for him so that he could get in."

George rubbed his hands on his apron. "Gosh, Rachel. Maybe I *did* let Buddy in." George hesitated, obviously trying to recall. "The truth is, I've been becoming more forgetful lately. Ell says I'd forget my head if it wasn't attached." He grimaced. "I guess I just didn't remember."

Rachel didn't know what to say. She was certainly forgetful at times. Everyone was. But this was a big thing to forget.

"You know," George mused, "my aunt had memory problems. Of course, she was in her eighties, but it got so bad that Willy and I had to hire someone to stay with her around the clock." His brow wrinkled. "Do you think I should make an appointment with my doctor?"

"It probably wouldn't hurt," Rachel said. "This has been a stressful time. I'm sure it's just that, but best to get checked out."

"I'll do it," he agreed. "I'll call tomorrow morning."

"How long does it take you to grill three steaks?" Hulda called. "We're starving over here."

"They're done!" George slid the T-bones onto a serving plate, tented them with foil, and carried them to the table.

"I didn't think to put steak knives out," Rachel said.

"No problem." George grinned. "I brought my own." He walked back to where his cart stood at the edge of the lawn. "I stuck them in the picnic basket with the . . . pepper!" he called, holding up a silver pepper mill. "I did remember it." He chuckled. "I've got steak sauce, too. But, apparently, I forgot the steak knives."

"I'll get some out of the house," Rachel offered. "Be right back."

George followed her across the lawn and into the kitchen. "Just a quick visit to the boys' room," he said.

She waited, and when he returned, she touched his arm lightly. "There's something else," Rachel said.

"Yes?"

Rachel took a deep breath. "I learned that . . ." She swallowed. This was personal, and definitely not her business. "George, did you know that your brother was paying Teresa a regular sum of money every month—deposits that went on for years and years?"

The lines around George's mouth tightened. "How did you find that out?" he asked quietly.

"Does it matter?"

His features hardened. "I suspect someone at the bank has a loose tongue. Not very professional."

"No," she agreed. "But considering that those deposits stopped a month before Willy's disappearance and death, it might be something that the police should know about."

"No, they shouldn't." George shook his head. "I'm stunned. I never thought . . ." His Adam's apple bobbed, and he looked away.

"You knew?" Rachel asked with genuine surprise.

"I knew. Willy and I were always very close. There wasn't much about him I didn't know. I didn't always approve of how he did things, but we never kept secrets."

Rachel's grip tightened on George's arm. "Was Willy loaning Teresa money?" She wanted to ask if he thought his brother was being blackmailed, but that sounded too dramatic.

"No." George sighed. "It was a private matter." He removed his glasses and wiped his eyes with the back of his hand. "This isn't the time or the place. If you just give me some time . . . to think." He replaced his glasses; his eyes were teary. "I can assure you that there's no need for the authorities to become involved. It had nothing to do with Willy's death. I can promise you."

Rachel felt her cheeks grow warm. "I didn't mean to cause you more upset. It's just that—"

"I understand." He forced a wan smile. "And it will be all right." His smile grew warmer. "Now, enough of all this fuss. Let's get to that dinner before the steaks get cold."

Monday morning, Rachel chatted with Fred Wright for a few minutes, exchanging pleasantries. He'd brought three men with him and promised to have the half acre fenced in maybe by the end of the day, the following day at the latest.

He gave her his business card, and she headed out. She was riding out to Alvin Herschberger's farm. This time, she went alone. He might answer her questions or he might not, but she had an idea that if she took Mary Aaron with her, they'd learn no more than they had the first time.

As she was pulling onto Alvin's road, her cell rang. She reached for it, saw that it was George, and braked the Jeep to a stop. There was no one else in sight, not even an Amish buggy, and there were potholes in the blacktop deep enough to swallow her vehicle. Better to take the time to see what George had to say and not risk popping a tire or breaking an axle as she had last winter, taking a logging road over Stone Mountain.

"George. Hi!"

"Hi . . . dinner was lovely last night. I really enjoyed myself. Hulda is a card, and that young lady, Coyote, is certainly a wonderful addition to our town."

"She is, isn't she? I had a good time, too. It's always wonderful to spend time together."

George rattled on about the food and the conversation, then said, "Where are you?"

"On my way out to Alvin Herschberger's farm."

"Buying more goats?" George chuckled at his own joke.

"Hardly." The goats had bleated and baaed all through Sunday evening's supper. Coyote had insisted on seeing them and thought they were adorable. Rachel, not so much. She hoped she wasn't making a mistake, having thought she could keep them.

"Listen, I'm holding you up, running on as I always do. But I did want to talk to you . . . about Willy and Teresa."

"Okay."

"Not on the phone, though. Could you stop by my house on your way back through town?"

"Of course," she said.

"I need to come clean with you," he said. "I need to do that, I realized. No more secrets between us."

"I imagine I can be there in an hour. Would that be okay?"

"That would be fine, I just . . . I'd ask that you not mention this to anyone. Coming to talk to me about . . . you know, a delicate subject."

She agreed, and they disconnected. As she drove, she wondered what the big secret was. It was just like George to drag out the suspense and make her wait for what might be a simple explanation. He and Hulda both. She pushed George and his secret to the back of her mind. For now, she had to concentrate on the best way to approach Alvin; she didn't know exactly why she thought she needed to see him. It was just a feeling she had. The police thought the "Bearded A" of Willy's journal meant Bearded Aaron. But what if it meant Bearded *Alvin?* If that was what it meant, would Alvin be willing to admit it?

Her dealings with the Amish were a delicate dance, and sometimes she didn't remember all the steps. Or, maybe, she decided, she'd never known the steps in the first place.

To her pleasant surprise, Alvin was repairing a fence near the end of his driveway. His wife and children were nowhere in sight. She parked the Jeep, got out, and approached him. "Good morning," she called cheerfully.

"Morning."

He used English, not Deitsch, and she wondered if it was because she was wearing a flowered skirt, not her usual plain denim one. But her arms weren't bare and she did have on her head covering. Gallantly, she charged ahead.

"How is Verna? And the children?" She wanted to get right to business, but she knew better. Good manners meant a lot among the Amish, and they hated to be rushed.

"*Gut.* All *gut.*" He concentrated on hammering an oversized staple into a fence post, securing a section of stock fencing. "Thomasina and the kids getting on all right?"

"They are. They're in a stall in my barn right now, but I've got fencing going in today."

"You need a good fence for goats." He continued to hammer. "Otherwise, they go under or over."

"That's what Fred said. Fred Wright. He's putting a fence in for me today: stockade and wire."

"Fred builds a sound fence." Alvin took another staple from his pocket and began to bang it in.

Rachel hesitated. "I need to talk to you, Alvin."

"*Ya?*" He turned to look at her, and she saw an uneasiness in his eyes. "What about?"

She folded her arms, taking care to stand a proper distance from him. Amish women were not nearly as dominated by men as the English liked to believe, but there were standards to uphold. "It's about Willy," she said. "Did you know that the police found a journal on his body?"

"*Ya,* I heard something like that."

His expression was clearly that of distress. He looked as though he'd turn and run at any second. Rachel didn't bother wondering how the Amish knew about Willy's book. Sooner or later, they knew everything, and news could fly up and down the valley in a flash.

"Willy kept a list of all the people he meant to meet with that last day he was alive."

Alvin's mouth quivered.

"I think your name was in that book," she said. She didn't tell him it just said "Bearded A." She was taking a chance . . . following her gut feeling. "Can you think of any reason why Willy would—"

The hammer slipped through his fingers and fell onto the ground, nearly hitting the toe of his black leatherwork shoe. "I told you I paid him the rent that day. He came and I gave him the money and he left."

"This wasn't about rent, Alvin. Plenty of people paid their rent that day, and their names didn't end up in that notebook." She watched him pick up the hammer. "Do you know why he would have written down your name?"

"*Ya,*" he admitted. "I do."

"You do?"

"Money," he said from between clenched teeth. He gripped the hammer in his hand. "I borrowed money from Willy. For the doctor bills. They threatened to take me to court if I didn't pay, so I went to Willy. He gave me the money. Verna didn't know. She would be ashamed. She already feels bad about us owing so much to people."

"You really did meet him that Friday night about the borrowed money?" She couldn't hide her surprise. It had just been a hunch.

Alvin nodded. "But I paid him the last of it. That night. He gave me a receipt." He set the hammer on the fence post, fumbled a wallet out of his back pocket with a stack of neatly folded little pieces of paper. From the pile he extracted one. It was on a piece of lined notebook paper identical to the paper in Willy's notebook.

He handed it to Rachel. "See. 'Paid,' it says. 'Paid in full, with interest.' " A muscle twitched in his cheek. "Twenty-four percent. High, but just a handshake I give him. And . . ." He trailed off. "I wish you would say nothing of this to my wife . . . or my neighbors."

"I won't," Rachel promised.

Finally, he lifted his gaze to meet hers. "It proves that I had no part in his death, doesn't it?" he said quietly.

"*Ya,*" Rachel agreed, switching to their common dialect. "It proves that you are an honest man who thinks only of his family."

Back in her Jeep, headed into town, Rachel thought about Willy's journal. After speaking with Alvin, she was convinced that the reference to "Bearded A" meant Willy intended to collect the money Alvin had borrowed from him. Her first impulse was to go right to Evan and tell him what she'd learned from Alvin. But that would mean violating Alvin's trust. If he didn't want his wife to know he owed Willy money, he certainly didn't want Evan or the police or anyone else to know. So even though she was convinced this was proof that Aaron wasn't the man the police were looking for, she couldn't provide the evidence to the police. She still had to figure out who had killed Willy.

The smartest thing for her to do was to track down the other entries in Willy's journal. Maybe one of them would lead her to the killer. "Fencing Fred" was the next entry to check on; she was almost sure it referred to Fred Wright. There was an easy way to find out.

She pulled over and fished his business card out of her bag. He answered on the third ring.

"Hi, it's Rachel Mast."

"Hey, Rachel. Hope you didn't change your mind because this baby's going up fast. Got a new auger that digs a heck of a deep hole fast."

"No, no, it's fine, Fred." A horse and buggy approached her from the opposite direction. "I was calling because I have a crazy question to ask you."

"Okay. Shoot."

"Did you see Willy O'Day that Friday that he disappeared? It would have been October first."

"Nope."

A sense of disappointment and frustration washed over her. "You didn't?" She frowned. Waved to the family that passed her in the buggy. "You're sure?"

"Positive."

She groaned inwardly. So much for her clever guess. "Well, thanks for—"

"I'm positive," he interrupted, "because we were supposed to meet. Out on his property next to Aaron Hostetler's. His real estate guy suggested he'd have a better chance selling the place if he fenced in the pond."

"Okay . . ." she said drawing out the word. "But you didn't meet with him?"

"Nope. My mom fell and broke her hip. Got the call in the middle of the night. Flew out of Harrisburg at six. My wife called and cancelled the appointment. Willy rescheduled for the following Wednesday." He paused. "But of course, by then, he'd gone missing."

"Thank you," Rachel said excitedly. "Thanks so much. You've been a huge help."

"I have?"

"You have."

Disconnecting, she dropped the phone into her lap, feeling very satisfied. She started the Jeep and pulled back onto the road. There were two entries left: "stamp collecting" and "Sophia Loren." Neither made any sense. A hobby and a silver screen star . . . Willy had been no stamp collector. She knew that for a fact because they'd once had a conversation about hobbies, and he'd made a point of telling her how ridiculous hobbies were.

Stamp collecting . . .

Stamps . . .

For a few minutes she drove along, enjoying the sunshine and warm air. It came to her out of nowhere.

Stamp collecting . . . postage stamps . . . post office? she mused.

She was almost back to town. She wondered if she should stop at the post office. But George was expecting her. Instead, she ignored the law and used her phone while driving. She activated the voice commands on her iPhone and called directory assistance. She was quickly connected with the Stone

Mill post office. The postmistress, who had been postmistress since Rachel was a little girl, answered the phone.

Rachel moved quickly through the pleasantries and then said, “Cora, do you happen to remember if Willy O’Day came into the post office the day he disappeared?”

“Sure do,” she answered pleasantly.

Rachel hesitated. “So . . . he did or he didn’t?”

“Came in that morning.”

“He came to the post office that morning?” she echoed. She couldn’t believe her luck. Or believe that she’d been clever enough to figure it out.

“Sure did. Bought two books of American flag stamps. I remember because it was the last time I ever saw Willy. He complained about tripping on the doormat as he came in. Bought his stamps and left.”

Stamp collecting . . . he was *collecting* his stamps.

“Thanks so much, Cora!”

Rachel was still smiling to herself when she parked on George’s cobblestone drive a few minutes later. Getting out of her Jeep, she walked past the stairs that led up to Ell’s apartment and rang the bell at the back door. Inside, Sophie began to bark. George and Willy’s gray stone house was of the same era as her own, a tribute to early settlers of wealth and vision. And next to Stone Mill House, it was her favorite structure in the valley.

“Rachel, come in,” George called.

She opened the screen door and stepped into the cool, shadowy kitchen. “Good morning.”

Sophie bounced into the kitchen, barking so loudly that George had to repeat himself for Rachel to hear him.

“In here.” George’s voice echoed over the flagstone floor and the heavy oak beams. “In the great room.”

She passed through the dining room, with its massive, antique German furniture and worn but still lush Kerman carpet. Sophie followed, keeping up her steady barking. “George?”

George stepped through the archway and took her hands. Sophie danced between them, then around them, bark, bark, barking.

"Thank you for coming. I'm sorry I was so . . . last night. I should have . . ."

He held her hands between his and looked into her eyes. "I can't stand it anymore, Rachel." He let go of her hands and looked away. "I have to confess."

Chapter 20

Goose bumps rose on Rachel's arms, and her mouth went suddenly dry. She wasn't sure what to say. *Confess?* What could George possibly have to confess? Why was he acting so odd? A thought rose in the back of her mind, a thought so impossible to consider that she shook her head. *No. Not George.*

"Sophie!" he ordered sharply. "Enough."

The dog sat down and was immediately silent.

"Please," George said to Rachel. "Come into the library. Teresa and Ell are already here."

Teresa? Here? Immediately, Rachel felt a rush of guilt and embarrassment about her vague suspicion.

George scooped up the little white bichon. Sophie responded with her usual whimpers of joy as she wiggled and licked his face and neck. "What can I say? She's spoiled rotten, and I've got no one to blame for it but myself. Doggy school, that's what you need, Sophie. That's what Ell says," he told the dog with mock severity. "Doggy boot camp."

Rachel followed George across the wide center hall and into a large room with a baby grand piano. A pair of tall sterling-silver candlesticks rested on top. She had been in this room many times, but today she wasn't entranced by the floor-to-ceiling bookshelves filled with leather-bound volumes, the

American Primitive oil paintings, or the antique furniture. Instead, she focused all of her attention on Ell and her mother, Teresa, who were seated side by side on a brown leather couch.

"Hi," Rachel said. She hadn't expected them to be here. "Who's minding the store, Ell?" There were several other employees who worked at The George, but George rarely left the business unless Ell was in charge.

"Megan. She can hold down the fort for a little while. For something this important. Whatever it is." She glanced at Teresa. "Finding Mom here was already a surprise."

"Yes," George agreed, waving Rachel to a Sheraton chair. "You'll find this house to be full of surprises."

Rachel glanced at Teresa, who, along with George, seemed to know exactly why they'd been invited here. A flush colored her throat and cheeks, and she looked as though she might have been crying. Rachel looked at Ell. "Maybe I shouldn't be here," she said hesitantly.

"No. You should be. Teresa and I agreed." George raised an open palm. "Bear with me. This isn't the way this should have been done, but Willy's tragic death has thrown more than *our* lives out of kilter. We've asked you here, Teresa and I, because you discovered our secret while hunting for my brother's murderer."

"I did?" Rachel asked.

"We couldn't have you continuing to ask questions," Teresa said quietly. "Not and risk Ell finding out from someone else."

Rachel's and Ell's gazes met.

Rachel thought the young woman looked particularly vulnerable today. She wore a modest black-lace dress that fell to her calves over high laced-up boots fashioned of black leather. Her long, black hair was pulled back and secured with a silver clip in the shape of a crescent moon, and her lovely eyes were lined in black kohl. Ell's lipstick was a deep purple, matching the intricate henna tattoos on her wrists and the backs of her graceful hands. Some might have thought that Ell's nose ring and pierced lip made her appear freakish, but Rachel had never seen anything but a quiet desperation under her Goth exterior. *A kindred spirit,* she'd thought, trying to find somewhere to belong and never quite succeeding.

"This is where the creepy music rises and Mom tells me that I'm not really human. Aliens from another galaxy left me on her doorstep when I was a baby," Ell said in a strained attempt at humor. "They're going to tell me I should never handle kryptonite." She looked from her mother to George. "No?"

George shook his head.

"Eleanor," Teresa said. "This is serious."

Ell made a face. "Do I win a prize if I guess what you're going to tell me?"

Teresa drew in a ragged breath. "All I ever wanted was to protect you—to do what was best."

"Wait." Ell rose, folded her arms, and fixed her mother with an *I knew it* look. "Let's cut to the chase. My last name should really be O'Day, shouldn't it?"

Teresa's face blanched.

"I knew it!" Ell pronounced. Laughing, she darted across the room and threw her arms around George. "I've got your eyes, don't I?"

"No," George protested, but he tightened his arms around the girl and hugged her against him. "No, Ell. Not me. I wish . . ."

Rachel looked at Ell and George wrapped in each other's arms, then at Teresa, then back at Ell and George.

His voice cracked and then steadied. "Willy. Willy was your father."

"Willy?" Ell stepped back and stared at him. "Really? *Willy?*"

George nodded dumbly. He threw Teresa a desperate look.

"It's true." Teresa rose and crossed the room to her daughter.

Ell seemed reluctant to let go of George, and he made no effort to pull away. "So you're really my uncle, not my father?" He murmured something, and she hugged him again. "Bummer, but I'll settle for Uncle George."

"I wish . . ." he said. "I've always wished you were *my* daughter."

Rachel felt as though she was intruding on what should have been a private moment, but getting up to leave would have made the situation more awkward.

She wondered why Willy and Teresa had felt the need to keep their relationship secret, and how George could have allowed himself to be dragged into it. It was Ell who'd suffered, not from being born out of wedlock but because she'd been robbed of her identity and that sense of belonging she would have felt if she'd known who her father was.

George seemed to have read her thoughts. He glanced over Ell's shoulder. "You understand now, Rachel, what those payments to Teresa were?"

"Child support."

"Yes." Teresa sighed. "Not telling anyone, that was my idea. I was afraid I'd be ostracized when I returned to Stone Mill. For being an unwed mother."

"Sounds like the dark ages." Ell said. She left George's embrace but continued to cling to his hand. "I'm glad people are more accepting now."

Teresa nodded. "Even fifteen years ago, things were different here. But I want you to know, that it wasn't just a fling. I truly cared for your father. Foolish, I know, but he had many good qualities. But . . . being content with only one woman just wasn't one of them. He wasn't interested in marriage until after you were born. And by that time, I didn't want to marry him. I simply came back to Stone Mill because this seemed the best place to raise a child. I had roots here, and since we were alone, I thought that you needed a sense of community."

Rachel wanted to ask why Willy had continued child support until a short time before his death. According to what Hulda had told her, Teresa had moved away almost two years before Ell was born. Under normal circumstances, Willy should have paid until Ell was eighteen. Could Teresa and Willy have agreed privately on twenty-one? But that still didn't make sense. "Ell," she asked. "How old are you?"

"Twenty-one this year."

"That's another misunderstanding," George said.

Ell looked at him and then back to her mother.

"Forgive me." Teresa burst into tears and covered her face with her hands.

"You were actually twenty-one on your *last* birthday," George explained.

"But I have a copy of my birth certificate." Ell released his hand.

George shook his head. "Willy had it altered somehow. But it wasn't his idea. Your mother wanted everyone in Stone Mill to think you had been born well after she left."

"So they wouldn't suspect I was an O'Day," Ell said.

To Rachel's surprise, there were no tears from the young girl. She didn't even appear to be angry. In fact, she seemed . . . relieved.

"It could have been worse, I suppose. Something bad could have happened to *you*." Ell went to her mother and slipped an arm around her trembling shoulders. "Don't cry. You know how I hate it when you cry."

Rachel got to her feet, thinking, *Well, I can cross Teresa off my list.* Mystery deposits solved. "I really should go."

"Sure," George said. "I just thought you needed to know. I didn't want you to think that Teresa had anything to do with my brother's death. As I said, his passing had nothing to do with her or the money he put in her account every month."

"There was never any court involvement," Teresa explained to Ell. "But Willy was most certainly your father, Eleanor. I never . . . had . . ." She sniffed and blew her nose on the tissue that George handed her. "There was never any other man."

"Oh, you're Willy's daughter, all right," George said. "He insisted on a paternity test."

"So everything you two did for me . . . renting me the apartment over the garage, hiring me to work at The George, it was *all* because he was my father?"

"Yes and no," George explained. "My brother was a shrewd businessman. He thought you had great potential as an employee. You were ambitious and bright. Everything you have, you earned on your own." He paused. "But there is something else you should know . . . something more."

"More?" Ell looked at him. "How could there be more?"

"My brother named you in his will as his sole heir. And he left you—"

"Willy left me some money?" Ell's mouth dropped open.

"He left you *everything*." George smiled at her. "I certainly don't need more than I already have. But other than this house and a couple of other properties he and I owned jointly, you are his sole beneficiary." His eyes twinkled.

"Wow. That's enough to mess with my head. He left me some money."

"A lot of money. And land. And businesses. And stocks in . . . Well, our attorney will explain it all to you in detail. I'll be seeing him this week to start the process." He hesitated. "There's just one stipulation."

"Yes?" the young woman said suspiciously.

"He wanted you to assume the O'Day name."

"That's it?" Ell glanced at Teresa. "Mom? What do you think? Should I do it? If I did, we could probably manage that vacation to Italy you've always talked about."

Teresa turned her tear-streaked face toward Ell. "You don't hate me?"

"No, I don't hate you. I'm furious with you for not telling me sooner. But I don't hate you."

"And me?" George asked.

"Neither of you," Ell said. "I love you both. And you, *Uncle George,* I've fantasized that you were my father since I was ten years old. You've always been so good to me, there when I needed a friend." She looked up at Rachel. "What do you think? Should I take the money?"

"You'd be a fool if you didn't," Rachel answered. "And I've always known that you're no one's fool."

"Ell O'Day." Ell laughed. "That should give the town something to talk about."

"Welcome to the family, darling," George said. "I only wish Willy were here to be part of it."

The following morning, Rachel drove over the mountain toward State College, with Aunt Hannah clutching the edges of her seat beside her. Rachel didn't know why they were going to State College or why her aunt was being so mysterious. She only knew that Mary Aaron had arrived before breakfast and asked Rachel to pick her mother up at the site of an old springhouse on the edge of Eli's farm. And to say nothing to Ada or anyone else of what she was doing.

Aunt Hannah had never ridden in Rachel's Jeep before, and she had the frozen expression of someone going to the headsman's block. "Thank you, Niece," she'd said in Deitsch. "It's good of you to drop your plans on such short notice to take me."

"You know that I'll do anything I can for you and Uncle Aaron," Rachel shifted into second gear as the road climbed steeply. On her right, an unsubstantial-looking guardrail was all that was between them and the sheer drop to the valley below. The road had been cut out of solid rock . . . almost solid. In winter, when freezing temperatures and heavy snowfall made the route iffy, chunks of stone as large as watermelons often fell onto the blacktop. Once, when Rachel had been younger and a little more daring, she'd tried to come over the pass in a snowstorm, and four-foot drifts had blocked the way. She'd had to abandon her car and walk back down the mountain.

Today, there were no such problems . . . if you didn't count lumber trucks and tourists who didn't regard the speed limit as gospel. The solid line that ran down the middle of the road meant what it said, and any attempts at passing a slower vehicle were often disastrous for all concerned.

"So fast, you drive," Aunt Hannah said. She tried to smile. Her freckles stood out on her face like raindrops on a dusty windshield. "But good, you drive good."

"We'll be fine," Rachel soothed. The speedometer hovered at thirty, faster than a horse and buggy, but nothing compared to what they'd be doing on the way down the far side of Stone Mountain. "The road is clear." Ice was the worst, worse even than snow, but they didn't have to worry about either in May.

"How is Uncle Aaron?" she asked in an attempt to take her aunt's attention off the abyss on her right. The rusty tops of vehicles that hadn't made it were bound to give Aunt Hannah a case of nerves. Once a car or truck went over the side, there was no retrieving it. And getting the passengers out was always dicey, provided it wasn't already a case for the coroner. "Did the public defender find your house all right yesterday?" Rachel had heard from Evan that she was going to the Hostetler farm, but nothing more.

"A nice young lady. I gave her coffee and raisin pie. She liked my pie. I gave her a second piece to take home for her supper." A FedEx truck came around the bend toward them, and Aunt Hannah gasped.

"It's all right," Rachel soothed. The truck passed them with two feet to spare. "See, no problem. What kind of questions did she ask Uncle Aaron?"

"Nothing. She asked him nothing. But she wanted the recipe for my raisin pie. For her mother. Such a nice girl. And she spoke good English."

"She's an American, Aunt Hannah, just like you and me."

"*Ya.*" Aunt Hannah nodded. "But maybe I think she is one of those immigrants who come here from Brazil or Cuba or—"

"Or Pittsburgh?"

"Maybe. But she was nice, anyway, not like most Englishers. Good manners. She did not stare at my children or look under the table as if I kept chickens or pigs in my kitchen. She sat right down and drank three cups of my coffee and took plenty of cream with it. A pleasant girl, pretty. Too bad she isn't Amish. My Alan would like her."

Rachel concentrated on the road. This was the steepest stretch. There was a pull-over at the top where she often stopped to admire the valley scenery, but she doubted Aunt Hannah would want to do that. Her aunt didn't like heights, not even ladders. Her bedroom was on the first floor. "If the good Lord wanted me up in the air, He would have given me wings," she always said.

"But . . . I don't understand why Ms. . . ." What was her name? Cortez? "Why didn't the woman ask Uncle Aaron anything about Willy? Did she ask where Uncle Aaron was that Friday evening?"

"*Ne*. Nothing. She couldn't." Her aunt caught her breath as the lookout came into sight. "Now we go down, right?" Aunt Hannah's black leather Sunday worship shoe was planted solidly against the floorboards as if she was ready to brake the Jeep herself, if need be.

"Now we go down. Not so bad." There were a few hairpin turns—several, in fact—but there was a special lane for trucks. If anything went wrong with their brakes, they could pull over into that lane. "If it bothers you, don't look, Aunt Hannah."

"*Ya,* better if I don't look." She pulled a clean handkerchief from her black pocketbook and mopped her brow. "You should have come to the school picnic. Jesse won the spelling bee. The teacher gave him a Bible with his name in it." She chuckled proudly. "And a box of fishing bobbers and hooks. I think Jesse liked those best."

"I'm sorry I missed it." Her aunt was definitely dodging the question about the public defender, and Rachel had a sneaking suspicion that things hadn't gone as well as she'd hoped, or as well as Hannah was pretending. On impulse, she turned into the overlook and stopped the Jeep. "What is it you don't want to tell me about Uncle Aaron and the lawyer?" She exhaled in frustration. "He didn't talk to her, did he?"

Chapter 21

"*Ne.*" Aunt Hannah sighed, folding her hands in her lap. She glanced away, then turned back to Rachel. "He didn't talk to her. He is a good man, your uncle. A good husband, a good member of the church, and a good father. But he is stubborn. Nobody is as stubborn as the Hostetlers when they set against a thing. The lawyer lady came in the kitchen door, and Aaron, he went out the front. He went into the fields and didn't come back until she drove away. I think she was disappointed. She said she would come again on Thursday, but I don't know if it will do any good. He told me that it is a waste of her time. He trusts in God to see him through this."

Rachel shut her eyes for a moment and rubbed her temples. She felt a headache coming on. She reached behind her seat into the cooler and brought out two cans of Coke. She tried to avoid sugary drinks, but she had a feeling that a dose of sugar and caffeine was exactly what she needed. And she knew that Aunt Hannah had a secret craving for Coke. She opened the first can and handed it to her aunt. "I don't know what else to do," she admitted. "I've been talking to people, asking questions . . ."

"I know, I know." Her aunt patted her arm. "You have a good heart, Rachel. I told your mother. You may have strayed from the flock, but you won't go far, and you always know where home is. Maybe you should try doing as your uncle does. Trust in God that right will prevail. Maybe it is not meant for us to fix this but to wait on Him."

Rachel took a long sip of her Coke. She rarely got a headache, but she'd never felt this helpless before. It was as if she was standing in the center of the road, a lumber truck was bearing down on her, and she was paralyzed to move, or even scream. Disaster was headed toward her family. This wouldn't end well. She could feel it.

"Be at ease, child," her aunt said, pressing the cold can against Rachel's temple. "Some of your worries are for nothing. You will see. Whatever you've thought about me . . . about what mischief I was up to with Eli Rust . . ."

Rachel looked up into her twinkling eyes. "I didn't—"

"Shh, shh, do not tell an untruth, Rachel. I would think the same if I saw so much evidence of wrongdoing. But it is not what you think. I have never been unfaithful to your uncle—not by word or by deed. And not in my heart. He may be a stiff, difficult bear of a man, but he is *my* bear."

Rachel was so touched by her aunt's tender words that she couldn't speak.

"Now start this red monster and drive me down the mountain and on to State College. You will see. And do it now, before I lose my courage and tell you to turn back for home."

A half hour later Rachel pulled the Jeep into the parking lot of a diner on the outskirts of the college town. What they were doing there, she had no idea. Maybe her aunt had decided she was hungry, or maybe she wanted to use the public phone to make a call. Aunt Hannah was suspicious of cell phones, and although she did use the kitchen phone at Stone Mill House to make doctor or dentist appointments, she'd never consented to use Rachel's cell.

"Are we both going in?" Rachel asked when she'd parked the vehicle. The diner looked busy; the parking lot was more than half full. It was one of those restored '50s eateries with red booths and midcentury décor. They wouldn't likely meet any Amish inside.

"*Ya,* we both go in," Aunt Hannah said. She was so relieved to be back on flat ground that she was positively beaming. "There is someone I want you to meet here. Someone you know from a long time ago."

"Someone I know?"

"*Ya.*" Aunt Hannah fumbled with the seat belt, found the clip, and unfastened it. She got out with the ease of someone half her age and half her size and strode toward the chrome entrance. Rachel hurried after her.

Rachel was surprised to see Eli when she walked into the diner. He must have been watching out the window, because as soon as they entered, he stood up and waved from a booth halfway down the eating area. "Come," Aunt Hannah ordered. "Eli is here, and his son Rupert."

"Rupert?" Rupert was Eli's second or third son, a youth who'd left the Amish sometime before she returned to Stone Mill to live. She did remember him vaguely: a baby-faced boy with a sweet smile. Rupert had always seemed a little backward to her, definitely not someone who would break away from the faith and become English. But it was hard to tell which Amish would stay and which would go. As a child she certainly wouldn't have suspected *she* would leave some day.

A tall young man stood up as they approached the booth. Rachel's mouth dropped open, and she had to catch herself to keep from staring. Rupert Rust was wearing a U.S. Marine uniform. Eli's son had apparently joined the military, an act so un-Amish that she couldn't imagine what the bishop or the church elders would say.

"Rupert goes over the seas," Aunt Hannah whispered. "To one of those foreign countries where they make a war with guns. Eli's heart is broken, but he cannot let his son go away without giving him his blessing."

"Oh," Rachel said, suddenly understanding. Rupert had

left the church after his baptism. He was shunned. His father, Eli, and his mother and brothers and sisters were not allowed to eat with him, to speak with him, or to welcome him into their homes.

"Eli might be thrown out of the church if anyone knew he had been meeting his son," Aunt Hannah confirmed aloud. "He and I . . . we were always friends. He asked me what I would do, if Rupert were my son. I have been counseling him."

"And you told Eli that he should make his peace with Rupert," Rachel said.

"*Ya,* I did." Aunt Hannah said. She smiled at Rupert and Eli. "So you see now what your uncle cannot know, and who Eli was meeting late on the night that Willy O'Day disappeared."

"Eli was with Rupert that night when he was seen near your place?" Rachel asked.

"*Ya,* he was. So you can rest your heart, Rachel. Eli did not kill anybody. The worst he has done is to be guilty of having a father's heart."

Rachel didn't sleep well that night. She tossed and turned, falling asleep, then waking, then drifting off again. When she was *awake,* she kept going over conversations in her mind: conversations she'd had over the last two weeks with Dawn, Buddy, Eli, Aunt Hannah, Hulda, Mary Aaron, Alvin, Teresa, Blanche, Steve, Uncle Aaron, George, and Ell. Obsessing over them, really.

And when she *did* sleep, she had crazy dreams. Willy came to her like one of the ghosts in Dickens's *A Christmas Carol.* Only Willy wasn't there to lead her to some sort of Amish redemption; he was the Ghost of Murders Past. In the dream, she and Willy stood on the road that ran by the Hostetler farm. He kept pointing with a long finger, with his glistening diamond ring, to her uncle's cow pasture. But it wasn't his grave he was trying to show her; he was pointing at someone. Only she couldn't see who it was. She could just make out a vague form. In the dream, she kept looking away and he kept drawing her attention back to the figure in the mists. Willy, whose pants and coat and shirt pockets were bulging with wads of money wrapped in rubber bands, was trying to tell her something . . . but what?

She'd gone to bed thinking her investigation had been a total failure. And she *felt* like a failure. She had promised Mary Aaron that she would help Aaron, whether he wanted her help or not. She had promised her family that she would prove Uncle Aaron hadn't killed Willy.

She'd coerced Evan into giving her criminal evidence, an act that could get them both in a lot of trouble, possibly costing him his job. She ended up with lists of suspects, which, to her shame, had even included Aunt Hannah and her neighbor Eli, who'd risked everything to make peace with his son. She'd pried into people's secrets and lies, and all for nothing. *Admit it,* she told herself. *You're just no good at this.*

Was it time to just give up? Give in, and pray that the legal system worked the way it was supposed to? That's what Evan wanted her to do, no doubt . . . what Aunt Hannah had advised her.

Completely awake now, Rachel punched her pillow and rolled over to stare at the bedside digital clock. It said 4:43 a.m. She groaned and rolled onto her back and stared at the ceiling fan.

What had she missed in her investigation?

All day she had gotten the feeling that the answer was right there . . . she just couldn't quite see it. Where had she made her mistake? Surely she'd misinterpreted some crucial piece of information.

Rachel had a logical mind: her Wharton business school education, no doubt. She had investigated logically, tracking Willy's movements that last day, talking to people who had interacted with him in his last hours. What *hadn't* she done? Maybe Willy's killer really had been a stranger who robbed him, like so many in the town had suggested. The problem with that idea was that no one had seen him with a stranger. Though plenty of people had come in contact with Willy that day, no one had seen anything odd. The police had determined that the previous October when he went missing, and she'd confirmed it over the last three weeks.

So what had she and the police missed? She thought about Willy's journal. Was the answer there?

She was already sure that the entry "Fencing Fred" meant Willy had meant to meet with Fred about fencing in the pond. Fred had confirmed it. She was also convinced that Willy had noted he was to see Alvin Herschberger—to collect what Alvin owed him on the personal loan. And "stamp collecting" was a reference to a simple stop at the post office. So what about the last entry? "Sophia Loren" . . . Sophia Loren . . . It made no sense. She was an Italian actress. Willy had no connection to Hollywood or Italy or . . . She groaned, out of ideas.

Rachel lay in bed for a few more minutes. She closed her eyes. She tried not to think about Willy's notebook. Or Willy's body the way she had seen it that day. Or her uncle. Or George's sad eyes. But it was like the elephant in the room. The more she tried not to think about the journal, the more she thought about it.

At 5:05 she surrendered. She turned on the bedside light.

Bishop, who had been sleeping on the corner of her bed, protested loudly, then curled into a tighter ball and went back to sleep. Rachel padded barefoot, in her white-and-pink PJs, to the whiteboard on the wall. She turned on a desk lamp and stared at the board. It seemed to stare back.

In the center of the board, inside the rectangle she'd drawn, she'd written out the entries on the last page of Willy's journal. She took a red dry-erase marker and crossed off *Fencing Fred*. She added a question mark beside *Bearded A*. Then, after thinking about it for a moment, she crossed it off. She didn't care what the police thought; she knew it wasn't a reference to her uncle.

She stepped back and stared at the board, then crossed off

Stamp Collecting. She chewed on the cap on the pen and studied the names written on both sides of the rectangle. *Dawn:* crossed out. *Buddy:* crossed out. *Steve:* crossed out. *Verna & Alvin:* crossed out. *Blanche:* crossed out. Several other renters she'd tracked down whose names she'd added were also crossed out.

She turned on her electric teakettle and dropped a tea bag into a mug on her desk. While she waited for the hot water, she went back to the board. She crossed off Eli's name and Teresa's. No names were left but Willy's and George's.

When the kettle whistled, she poured hot water into her mug. She tugged on the tag and the tea bag bobbed. When the tea was sufficiently strong, she removed the tea bag and added a big squirt of her sister's honey. She couldn't find a spoon, so she used a pen to stir the tea. Taking the mug with her, she went back to the dry-erase board.

She stared at it. Everything was crossed out but *Sophia Loren* in the center . . . and *Willy* and *George*. Sophia Loren . . . Sophia.

She sipped her tea and thought and stared.

Sophia . . . *Sophie?*

She closed her eyes as she vaguely remembered George referring to the dog as Sophia Lazzaro. Where? When? In the bookstore, maybe? Right after Willy had been found? Was that the dog's AKC name?

It had to be.

She went to her laptop and did a search on Sophia Lazzaro. She got multiple hits. Sophia Lazzaro was one of Sophia Loren's stage names. She got up to look at the white board again. Wasn't Willy clever? He had been referring to George's Sophie.

So what account did Willy have to settle with a fluffy white dog? The dog certainly hadn't owed him money.

She took another sip of tea and dragged her desk chair over in front of the board. Willy hated the dog. George had said so himself.

George. She stared at his name. His was the only name besides Willy's that hadn't been crossed off. She'd added it to the board when she started the list of everyone who had seen him that day. He'd had breakfast with him. He had never seen him again.

Or had he? She rubbed her forehead, thinking back. She cupped the warm mug between her palms and stared.

In a murder involving a husband, the wife was always a primary suspect first, and vice versa. The person closest to the victim was always interviewed first.

She took another sip of tea. Swallowed. She had a dreadful feeling.

Sophia Loren. Sophie. George. It wasn't possible. It couldn't be. Tears filled her eyes.

As she let her mind go in that direction, more things, more terrible, awful things, fell into place: The pile of cash George had given her for her uncle's bail had been in a rubber band. George said Willy never came home that night, but he hadn't reported him missing until Monday. Ell said she heard Willy's truck that night, but George said Willy never came home.

Rachel's gaze shifted to Buddy's name, crossed off in red marker. George had let Buddy into his place with Willy's keys. Willy's keys, missing from his pocket, missing from his truck . . .

She didn't have all the pieces, and she certainly didn't have them in the right place, but suddenly she knew she was right. Rachel closed her eyes and clutched the warm mug of tea. "How could you, George?" she whispered. "And what does that spoiled little dog have to do with it?"

Chapter 22

At four minutes after eight Rachel walked out to the grape arbor with a cup of tea. Because she had no guests arriving until the next afternoon, when she had a family taking five rooms, she'd given Ada and the other women the day off. There would be plenty of time the next morning to get ready for their twelve guests. And twelve would be a relief. If she was going to make a go of Stone Mill House, she needed to fill her rooms. She was worried that too many stood empty too many nights. She'd put all her hopes and energy into this venture and she couldn't bear to think of failing, because the town's new rebirth was still a fledgling dream. If the B&B went down, would other family-owned businesses follow?

Rachel knew she needed to concentrate on the few things that needed to be done today to prepare for so many guests coming in the following day. She tried to. She truly did. But she couldn't. She sat down on the glider, placed her still-too-hot-to-drink mug of tea on a wrought-iron table and held her cell phone in one hand. She stared at the contact name on the screen. *George.*

Between six and seven, she'd lain in her bed, debating who she should call first. Evan? The police? Or George? The right thing, the responsible thing to do, was to call law enforcement. She hadn't figured out many of the details, but she was positive that Willy had come home that night, that the two brothers had gone out to the Hostetler farm and only one had come back. She didn't know what George's little bichon had to do with the whole thing, but her gut feeling was that the dog was the linchpin.

So the right thing—the responsible thing—was to call the police, give them the information she had, and let them take it from there. It was the right thing to do for Uncle Aaron. For Willy. But . . . she and George had been friends a long time. He had been her strongest supporter when she returned to Stone Mill. He had been the one to stand up at the first town meeting and tell his neighbors that Rachel's idea of turning Stone Mill into a tourist attraction was a feasible idea. A good one.

She stared at George's name, then glanced out over the property. It was going to be a beautiful day: warm and sunny. The smell of freshly cut grass was in the air, and she heard the steady hum of a mower. It sounded like it was coming from Hulda's.

Rachel heard Thomasina bleating. She'd found a bucket of milk on the back step this morning; one of her brothers had come early. She was sure whoever had been there had fed the goats. She imagined Thomasina was just getting impatient because she and the kids wanted to be let out into their new pasture.

She looked down at the phone again, now fighting tears. She owed George the first phone call. To do less than give him a chance to explain away these awful suspicions would be disloyal. Choosing his home number rather than the bookstore, she hit *Call* before she chickened out or dissolved into a puddle of tears.

The phone rang in her ear. She sniffed. Took a sip of tea. It continued to ring. When she got his voicemail, she hung up. What kind of message could she leave? *Sorry to bother you so early, George, but yours is the only name left on my whiteboard of murder suspects. Did you kill Willy?* She tried

George's cell next, but got the *please leave a message* recording there, too. Again, she hung up without leaving a message.

She finished her tea, drinking it down when it was still so hot that it burned her tongue. She barely felt it, then walked barefoot out to the barn. The rich, heady scent of well-cared-for animals comforted her, as it always did. How many times in her life in the outside world had she tried to explain the peace that could be found in a farmyard . . . in the simple life? Usually, people simply laughed, certain that they knew better . . . but they didn't. She'd always found joy in quiet places.

She entered the goat stall; sure enough, there was fresh water, and a few crumbs of sweet-smelling goat chow remained in the feed box. Whoever had come had even cleaned the stall and thrown down fresh wood shavings. She was touched by the effort . . . and realized with a rush of emotion how lucky she was to have so many people who loved and cared for her.

As she made her way to the back wall of the stall, where there was a door that led outside, the two kids pranced around her. Thomasina pushed her velvety nose into Rachel's hand, making little goat sounds. She was probably hoping for a treat.

Rachel smiled as she swung the old iron rail up and opened the door to the small field Fred and his crew had fenced in for her. It was barely half an acre; she'd have to continue to supplement the goats' diet with grain and hay. But this morning she was glad she had the goats. They were friendlier than most barnyard animals. She had grown up hearing about them in the Bible. They were smart and brave. Yes, she decided, she liked them, usually better than she liked dogs.

At nine, Rachel tried George's house again . . . then his cell at nine fifteen. She still didn't leave messages. In the kitchen, she sliced herself a piece of raisin bread that Ada had left in the bread box. While it toasted, she went into the pantry to get a pint of strawberry jam. She took note that there were only three jars left. Fortunately, strawberry season would be here before you knew it. She loved Ada's jam because it wasn't overly sweet. She made it the old-fashioned way, using only strawberries and sugar, no pectin, and cooked it for a long time to thicken it.

Rachel ate her toast and drank another cup of tea while she sat at the laptop in the office. She checked Stone Mill's website and printed off orders placed over the weekend. Then she did a little shopping of her own, on impulse, ordering a new pair of running shoes. This morning, while lying in bed trying to decide what she would say to her dear friend, who might also be a murderer, she'd made the impulsive decision to start running again. She'd been a runner for years, but then, when she'd returned to Stone Mill, she'd been so busy with restoring the B&B and . . . life that she'd just stopped. But this week, she decided, she'd start running again. Just for fun, just for . . . herself.

At five after ten, Rachel again brought up George's contact information on her phone. This time, she called the bookstore.

"Good morning, The George, this is Ell speaking."

She sounded so cheerful . . . and . . . confident. It was a tone in her voice that Rachel had never heard before.

Rachel groaned inwardly. Ell would be devastated when she found out that George had murdered . . . her . . . her father.

"Hello, may I help you?" Ell said.

"Ell . . . I'm sorry. It's Rachel."

"Rachel! Oh, gosh, can you believe it? Can you believe *any* of it? George is my uncle. You think I should start calling him Uncle George?"

"Ell—"

"Or do you think that would be weird? Maybe I should just keep calling him George, you know, because nothing has really changed. I mean *everything* has changed, but—"

"Ell, is George there?" Rachel interrupted.

Instantly, Ell picked up on her urgency. "No. Are you okay?"

"Do you know where he is?" Rachel ignored her question. No, she wasn't okay. "I tried his home *and* his cell and he's not picking up."

"He has that appointment with the lawyer this morning. In Harrisburg. He wasn't planning on coming in today. I'm in charge," Ell said proudly. "I think he has plans to meet with some of his book cronies this afternoon."

Rachel exhaled. She really needed to talk to George as soon as possible. Now that she knew what she knew, the secret was burning a hole inside her. Uncle Aaron needed to know that the charges against him would be dropped, that his life would return to normal. Blame needed to be laid at the feet of the guilty. Suddenly, she was so angry and hurt that tears filled her eyes again. How had George let her spend weeks running all over the place, making a fool of herself questioning people, when he'd known all along who had killed his brother? When the body was discovered, why hadn't he turned himself in instead of letting the police take their lead that her uncle had done it? It was true that George had insisted he knew Aaron didn't do it and he'd put up the bail. But he hadn't confessed.

"Rachel?" Ell said.

"Thanks, Ell." She forced a smile, hoping it would lighten her tone. There was no need to upset the young woman right now. There would be time enough for that later. "I'll catch up with him this afternoon."

After hanging up with Ell, Rachel called George's cell again. This time, she left a message: *George . . . it's Rachel. I need you to call me when you get this.*

Ell hadn't said what time George was meeting with his and Willy's lawyer, so when one o'clock passed and she didn't hear from George, Rachel assumed it was an early afternoon appointment. She kept busy around the house: doing her personal laundry, sorting files, caulking a shower stall. She was relieved everyone had the day off; she didn't think she could have been with other people today. Not carrying this awful secret.

When George didn't call back by three, Rachel thought maybe the appointment had been midafternoon. By five, she was beginning to become uneasy. Had she made a mistake calling George? Did he know she knew? Had he fled the state? The country? How ridiculous was that? Stone Mill was George's whole life . . . but Willy had been his whole life, too.

At five thirty, she called the bookstore. Mindy answered, but then Ell picked up when Rachel asked for her. "Hey," Rachel said into the phone. She was taking her laundry off the line. It was clouding up. She smelled rain. "You see George today?" she asked, trying to sound casual.

"No, but I wasn't expecting to," Ell said. "Rachel, what's going on with you today? You're acting kind of . . . weird."

Rachel dropped a wooden clothespin into the calico bag that hung on the line. "Is that Sophie I hear?" She didn't hear the dog. She was just wondering if George had left her at the bookstore. He did that occasionally.

"No dogs here. He took her with him. Said she'd be fine in the car while he was in the lawyer's. It's cool outside today."

"Ah." Rachel pulled a towel off the line. "Well . . . if he stops by on his way home, can you ask him to give me a call?"

"Sure. You leave him a message? He's got his cell with him. He called me back a little while ago. Minor glitch with one of our distributors."

Now Rachel was *really* suspicious. George had taken the dog with him . . . and he was calling Ell back, but not her?

"Don't worry about it. We're probably just missing each other," she assured Ell. "Thanks."

Rachel left the laundry basket in the grass and went to the barn. She scooped grain out of a metal trash can. The goats heard her and came running. It was still a little early to put them up, but with the coming storm, it was already getting dark. She gave each goat a scratch behind the ears, and closed and secured their stall.

Outside the barn, she called George. *Again.* "George, I really need you to call me," she said when the phone beeped.

She took her laundry into the house, then poked around the refrigerator. Realizing she wasn't all that hungry, she left the kitchen without getting anything to eat and wandered from room to room.

Had George skipped town? Was it time to call Evan?

She went into the gift shop and rearranged a table of jams and jellies. Bishop came to the doorway and sat down to supervise. He switched his tail.

"Don't say it," she said to the cat. "I should have called the police this morning. George isn't going to call me back. He's moved money into a Swiss bank account and is on his way to an undisclosed foreign destination, as we speak."

Her cell phone rang in her back pocket. She pulled it out and was stunned to see that it was George. "Hello?"

"Rachel. Sorry I didn't get back to you. Busy day. I was in Harrisburg. Saw the lawyer, then—"

"George," she interrupted softly. "We need to talk."

He was quiet long enough on the other end of the line for her to say, "George?"

"I'm here." He sounded so . . . sad. "You know."

Tears filled her eyes, and she looked out the big window in the gift shop. Branches of the oak trees on the front lawn were swaying, the new leaves turning up. In the distance she heard a very faint rumble of thunder. "I know," she repeated. She wiped under her eyes. "You have to turn yourself in."

Again, he was quiet for too long.

"George?"

"I . . . Rachel, I know I don't have the right to ask this, but . . . would you go with me? To the police station?"

A tear rolled down her cheek. "Sure, George. I can do that."

"Did you . . . have you said anything to anyone?"

"No. I wanted . . ." She took a breath. "I wanted to talk to you first."

"Okay, dear. We'll talk. I should be back in Stone Mill in about an hour and a half. I'll come by and you can take me. I have—" His voice cracked. "I have Sophie with me. What am I going to do with Sophie?" Now *he* was crying.

It was funny how neither needed to say what was obvious. That Sophie couldn't go with him where he was going.

"It's okay, George. Maybe Ell—"

"No, Ell doesn't like dogs. She's a cat girl. And she thinks she's allergic. I can't send Sophie to a shelter. You know I can't do that. I'd sooner have her put down."

"George, don't worry about her." Rachel couldn't believe she was saying this. But how could she not offer? What George had done didn't negate who he was or who he had been to her. "I'll take Sophie."

It was nearly two hours before George arrived . . . driving his brother's pickup. Rachel was waiting for him and saw him through the dining room windows. It was almost dark.

She ducked out of the house, her bag on her shoulder, her raincoat on her arm. She was still in jeans and a long-sleeve tee. What did you wear to escort your friend to turn himself in for the murder of his brother?

He kept the engine running.

She opened the passenger door. Sophie bounded across the seat toward her, but at least she had enough sense not to jump out of the truck.

"You . . . you want me to drive?" Rachel asked, petting the dog. "We can take my Jeep."

"I'd like to take Willy's truck."

"You want to leave Sophie here, George?"

He gripped the steering wheel, staring straight ahead. He was wearing his The George ball cap and a blue canvas jacket. He shook his head. "I thought we'd go for one last run, my girl and I . . . before . . . Jump in."

She hesitated. Was this foolish? Getting into George's truck with him? She hadn't told anyone she was meeting George. Had that been Willy's mistake?

But George would never hurt her. Would he?

She slipped her phone out of the outside pocket of her leather bag. "Let me answer this," she said, acting as if she had gotten a text. She texted Evan. *CALL ME. NOW!* All in caps. She got into the truck. George pulled out of the circular drive, but instead of going left, toward the police station, he turned right.

Rachel had just fastened her seat belt. She kept her hand poised over the buckle. The hair bristled on the back of her neck. For the first time in her life, she was afraid of George. Did she open the door and jump? "George—"

"Don't worry, I'm not kidnapping you. I just wanted to ride out . . . to *the property*. I want to explain." He glanced at her, then back at the road. His eyes were teary. "Sophie and I want to show you what happened."

"George, you don't have to do this." Rachel had her phone in her right hand. Evan hadn't called or texted her back. They were almost there. This time of evening, there should have been people on the road: a wagon, a buggy, a boy on a push-scooter, a car, someone headed home. But they hadn't passed a soul, Amish or English. A few raindrops fell on the windshield.

Rachel glanced at George. Sophie sat on his lap, looking out the window.

Rachel's brain, her *logic,* told her that she had no reason to fear him, but her *logic* had never suggested that he could have killed Willy. This wasn't the kind of thing she wanted to be wrong about.

"Tell me why, George," she said quietly. "It had to do with Sophie, didn't it?"

He didn't answer.

"I saw Willy's journal. I know what it said. I know you saw it, too." She looked straight ahead. He had turned on the windshield wipers, but it wasn't raining hard enough to really need them. The wipers squeaked as they moved across the semidry glass. "What's Sophie's AKC name?" she asked.

He turned off the windshield wipers. "Sophia Lazzaro."

"Sophia Loren's stage name," she said.

They were on her uncle's road. She could see his cow pasture up ahead. But instead of continuing toward the Hostetler farm, George surprised her by signaling and turning into the dirt driveway of the property beside the Hostetler property. There was a gate. He stopped there and turned off the engine. They sat in the semidarkness, quiet for a few moments. "He was going to kill her, Rachel." He stroked the dog on his lap. "Willy was going to kill my Sophie. She chewed the corner of Mother's dresser in his bedroom. Chewed right through the wood. Willy always loved that piece."

Rachel was still gripping the phone. Wondering why Evan hadn't called her. Wondering if she would answer if he did. George wasn't acting like a killer, but she suspected he hadn't acted like a killer that Friday night when Willy returned home about nine thirty.

"Do you really think he would have done it, though?"

He turned slowly to look toward her. He looked so sad, so . . . resigned. "You saw the journal. He planned to *reconcile* his affairs with her. Besides . . ." He looked away. "I knew he'd do it because that's what happened to Ell's cats."

"What?" she stared at him.

"Three cats last year. One the previous, but that one wasn't Ell's. That was before she moved into the barn. I don't know who it belonged to. Orange. It was big and orange. Willy didn't like cats. He said they dug in our flower beds and did their business there. Ell's cried to get into her apartment at night, and sometimes she wasn't so quick to let them in." He shook his head slowly. "I knew Sophie would just . . . disappear like the cats."

"So what did you do, George?"

He stroked the dog's little head. "That morning, I saw his notebook when we were at breakfast. I knew I had to do something before he . . . took her away from me forever. So . . . that night, when Ell thought she heard his truck . . ."

Rachel nodded expectantly. Darkness was falling quickly; she could still see his face, but not as well as a few minutes ago.

"When Willy came home, I had locked poor Sophie in her kennel in my room. I put her muzzle on her so she wouldn't bark."

Rachel couldn't stop staring at George. What he was talking about now was premeditation. He hadn't killed his brother in a moment of anger. He had laid out a plan and . . . gone through with it.

"When Willy came home, I was crying. That was real," he assured her. "But I told him I was crying because I had taken Sophie to the veterinarian and she'd diagnosed her with cancer. I told Willy I had put my Sophie down." He sniffled. "I even had a cardboard box that looked like the kind they give you at the vet if you want to take your beloved home with you."

In cartoons, when something came to a character, a lightbulb appeared over his head. Rachel felt as if someone had just drawn a lightbulb over *her* head. "The cardboard box the police found in the back of Willy's truck, this truck," she said. "With a ham in it."

He shrugged. "It had to have something about the right weight . . . in case Willy picked up the box. He had to think Sophie was inside." He hesitated. "Pork butt."

"I'm sorry?"

"It was a pork butt," he said quietly. "Not a ham. I put a pork butt in the box. It had been in our freezer."

"Okay . . . so then what did you do?"

"I asked Willy to ride out with me. To come here." He

nodded, indicating the property where they had parked. "I told him Sophie always liked it here. I told him I wanted it to be her final resting place." He turned his head slowly to look at her. "Only really, I intended for it to be Willy's final resting place."

Chapter 23

Rachel frowned, thinking before she spoke. "But . . . I don't understand. Willy's body was found on my uncle's property, not yours." She was beginning to lose a little of her fear. Her morbid curiosity was getting the best of her, and she didn't believe George would really hurt her.

"I thought I had it all planned out." George tugged on his ball cap. "I was sure it would work. Because I owned this property with Willy, I figured there wasn't much chance anyone would find him. Not, at least, until after I was gone. What I didn't count on," George said, "was Willy not cooperating once we got here."

He opened his door, and the overhead light came on. "Let's take a little walk. Sophie probably needs to do her business. There's a flashlight in the glove box." He climbed out of the truck, taking the dog with him.

Rachel sat on the front seat of the truck for a minute. Take a walk? In the dark? With a man who had just admitted to her that he *planned and executed* the murder of his own brother? A tiny trickle of fear returned. *Are you stupid? Is this the place in the horror movie where the girl knows that a psychopath is loose in the neighborhood and opens the door anyway?*

"Good girl, Sophie," George said, closing his door, leaving Rachel in darkness again. "What a good girl."

Rachel checked her phone. The ring volume was off, but it was on vibrate. Evan still hadn't called. Slowly, she opened the glove box. Should she go with George?

It was dark in the truck cab, but she could see the outline of a big ring of keys hanging from the ignition. They were Willy's keys, she noted. Which creeped her out even more.

She wondered if she should just slide across the seat and drive away. She could call the police once she got down the road.

As her fingers closed around the flashlight, her door opened, startling her.

"I hope it works. I haven't checked the batteries since I put the thing in there at Christmas."

Rachel looked at George. Swallowed. He seemed so sweet. So sad. He looked like the same George he had been before she knew he had killed his brother. The George she had known her whole life.

He smiled, his face so poignant. "Don't be afraid, Rachel," he said gently. "I would never hurt you."

Guilt washed over her. "No. No, of course not." Nervously, she climbed out of the truck with the flashlight in her hand. With the other hand, she slipped her iPhone into the back pocket of her jeans. "After . . . you did it, how—" She didn't know how to ask. No matter what George said or did, he was still her friend. She didn't want to see him hurting any more than he obviously already was.

"How did I get away with it?" he said for her. "I don't know." He shrugged and closed the truck door behind her. "I guess I didn't leave too much evidence for the police." He pointed into the darkness. "Let's take a little walk. That flashlight working?"

Before Rachel could flip the switch, George had the flashlight in his hand. The flashlight was a big red metal one. A Maglite. Heavy. Heavy enough to hit her over the head and knock her out. Heavy enough to kill her. She slipped her hand around to her back pocket and felt for her phone. That made her feel better, though why she wasn't sure. If he hit her over the head with the flashlight, she wouldn't be calling anyone.

"I took the money from Willy because it just seemed like such a waste. You know, to bury it. I thought it might come in handy . . ." George switched on the light. The beam was strong. "Turned out, it did." He chuckled, though his voice was still thick with sadness.

"It did *how?*" She shivered. Did she really want to know?

He aimed the beam ahead of them, and they walked toward the fence that ran between the O'Day property and the Hostetler cow pasture. Sophie trotted in front of them in the wet grass. "That was the ten thousand five hundred dollars I gave you for Aaron's bail."

She turned to look at him, certain her mouth was hanging open. "I knew whoever killed him had the money. It just didn't occur to me it was you. When I found out Buddy showed up at your place that Saturday morning with cash to pay his rent, I thought maybe—"

"He paid it with his landlord's money? Oh, goodness, no. Of course not. He would never have killed my brother. Buddy's a nice guy. Just . . . a little lost." Sophie stopped so George stopped. He was quiet for a minute. "Is that how you figured out that I had killed my brother? Buddy? The keys?"

"Not entirely, but that was a big part of it." She hung her head, feeling so damned guilty and not sure why. "Evan told me right after Willy was found that the truck had been abandoned, but with no car keys inside. Then Buddy said you took the padlocks off his trailer the day after Willy disappeared. And when I asked you about it. The second time . . ."

"I told you I had used Willy's keys," he finished for her.

"Yes."

"I should have thought to take Willy's key ring apart, made copies of the ones I needed and thrown his keys away. That morning when Buddy came with the rent money, though, I felt bad for him. He had the money to pay Willy the previous day, just not the cash. It was illegal of my brother to lock Buddy out of his place. Worse than that for me, is that it was wrong. I just grabbed Willy's keys off the rosewood table. That's where I put them that night. It was where Willy always put them."

Rachel didn't know what to say. Fortunately, George didn't seem to expect her to say anything.

He sighed. "I should have known I'd never get away with it. But I couldn't stand the thought of him doing to Sophie what he'd done to Ell's cats." George was quiet again for a moment, then went on. He reached the fence. "I should have known my brother wouldn't go along with my plan. I should have known he would disagree with something. Willy never liked doing things any way but his own."

Sophie shot under the fence.

"Come on, girl," George called after her. He turned back and pointed. "See that tree? That's where I was going to bury my brother. It's pretty there, next to the pond. Sophie!"

Rachel could barely make out the white ball that was the little dog.

"Come here, girl." Again George turned to Rachel. "We got the shovel and the box out of the back of the truck, but Willy wouldn't have it. He insisted I couldn't bury Sophie on our property. He was worried about selling it and the . . . *remains* being an issue."

"So Willy said you had to bury Sophie in Uncle Aaron's cow pasture?"

"Exactly." George looked out over the dark field. "Sophie, don't do this. Come on, girl." He exhaled. "So, anyway, when Willy said we couldn't bury Sophie on our property, I had no choice but to follow him over to Aaron's. We walked just this way. It was dark, just like it is tonight. But later."

A lump rose in Rachel's throat.

"Willy actually started the digging. Somehow he ended up with the shovel and I had the box. Willy was a hard worker. Always was. He dug a big hole."

"Big enough to bury a man," she said softly.

"Almost. Guess it ended up being not quite deep enough." George's voice took on a far-off sound. "When Willy put down the shovel to pick up the box, I picked up the shovel and I . . . I hit him. I took the money and the keys out of his pocket, rolled him into the hole, and buried him." George drew in a long breath. "I buried my brother," he murmured so quietly that she could barely make out his words. "Then I took the box and the shovel, climbed into Willy's truck, and drove back into town."

"Where you left the truck parked in front of the post office," she said, unable to imagine George actually doing what he said he had done. Except she knew he had done it—all the evidence she'd found had pointed to just that scenario.

George moved the flashlight, looking for Sophie, leaving Rachel and himself in darkness. "I didn't mean to leave the pork butt in the box in the truck. That was silly. Such a waste of a good piece of meat, but I was so upset, I guess. I forgot. I *did* remember the shovel."

"Made by Eli Rust."

"The murder weapon."

"So then you just walked home?" she asked.

"I did, carrying my shovel. No one saw me. Sophie and I went to bed. Maybe I should have called the police Saturday and reported Willy missing, but I was in shock, you know?"

She didn't say anything.

"Looking back," he continued, "I guess I should have taken his wallet and the ring. And the notebook." He glanced at her, moving the flashlight as he spoke. "The notebook." He shook his head. "It didn't occur to me that anyone would think they could understand any of Willy's gibberish. I rarely did. I didn't think they'd arrest someone based on anything in the notebook. I never meant to hurt your uncle."

"I know you didn't," she said.

"He's a good man," George mused. "He gave Sophie a

piece of his sandwich one day at the farmer's market. He likes dogs. You can tell."

Rachel glanced over her shoulder. She could still see the shadowy outline of Willy's truck. It was beginning to rain again. Lightly. She put up her hood and looked at George again.

"I can't see her. Can you see her?" His voice took on a panicked tone. "Sophie? Sophie, come, girl!"

Rachel couldn't see her, but the flashlight beam only went so far.

"I guess we'll have to go after her." George held the flashlight with one hand and parted the wire fence with the other. He motioned for Rachel to go first.

What he wanted Rachel to do was bend over and step through.

And leave herself completely vulnerable.

"Sophie!" George continued to call, while waiting for Rachel to climb through the fence.

Rachel's face felt warm, but her palms were cold and sticky. She wasn't really in danger from George . . . was she?

Her phone vibrated in her back pocket, and she almost exhaled audibly in relief. She fumbled to get her phone out of her pocket.

"There you are," George cried. "Get over here. Silly girl."

As Rachel answered her phone, she saw a white blur speeding toward them.

"Rache?"

"Evan."

Before she could speak, he went on. "It's okay if you just bring George into the station. There's no need to send a car, flashing lights, and make a fuss. Unless you're not okay with that?"

Rachel turned her back to George. "I don't understand. You . . . know?"

"George didn't tell you? He called me as he was pulling into your place. He confessed and said he was coming in. He said he just needed a few minutes with you to explain. I think he feels like you're kind of a daughter to him. I didn't call you right away when I got your text because I wanted to have something to tell you. I had to put in a call to the lieutenant on duty." He paused. "I'm so sorry, Rache."

Tears welled in her eyes.

"That's my girl," George called. "That's my Sophie." He handed Rachel the flashlight and scooped the wet dog up into his arms. "Now Papa needs to talk to you." He started toward the truck, speaking to her as if she were a child. "Papa has to go somewhere Sophie can't go, but you're in luck because you're going to a very special place. You're going to love Stone Mill House . . ."

George's last words were lost in the wind and the rain that was now coming down harder.

"Rache, you still there?" Evan said in her ear.

She wiped at her tears. "You'll meet us at the station?" she asked. "Because . . . I don't think I can do this without you, Evan."

"You know I'll be there. I'll always be there when you need me."

Three weeks later, Rachel tentatively entered The George. She'd been wanting to see Ell, to see how the young woman was dealing with everything, but her own concerns and her reluctance to face Ell had kept her away.

Of course, she'd spoken to Ell on the phone several times and seen her once at the courthouse, but that wasn't the same. And the fact that the B&B had been booked solid the past two weeks was no excuse for not being there to support Ell. Rachel supposed that having Stone Mill splashed all over the news again had brought in the tourists . . . or maybe it was just the time of year. June had come, and Stone Mill had become a wonderland of green mountains, sweetgrass, and blooming wildflowers.

Not that Rachel could complain about her booming business. Other than the loss of George, the town was pretty much back to normal. Charges against Uncle Aaron had been dropped, and the Amish community had breathed a huge sigh of relief. Her uncle had even consented to invite her to her aunt's birthday dinner on Sunday. Her own mother and father would be there, as well as her brothers and sisters and most of the church families. Being asked to join them, when she hadn't been welcome at her uncle's table for many years, made her smile every time she thought about it.

But this still had to be dealt with. She felt so sorry for Ell, and a little guilty that she was responsible for George's arrest. There wasn't any doubt in her mind that he would be convicted and would be going to prison for many years . . . perhaps for the rest of his life. It was so sad. Stone Mill wouldn't be the same without George. And—she had to admit it—in some perverse way, there would be a hole where Willy had once stood. This wasn't a community that expected violence. George's brother might not have always been a pleasant or a kind person, but he had been a thread that, woven with many others, formed the strong and enduring fabric of the valley.

Having such a large family, Rachel found it hard to imagine what it must be like for Ell, who'd had only her mother, then suddenly found out that she had an uncle she knew and cared for, and then lost him just as quickly. It wasn't fair. Somehow, Rachel would try to see that the young woman had a network of friends and neighbors who would be there for her.

"Good morning," Rachel said to the figure behind the checkout counter. "I—" She broke off in midstatement and stared. She'd expected to find Ell here where she always was, but instead, Blanche Willis was beaming at her. And Blanche wasn't in her wheelchair. With the aid of a walker, she stood behind the cash register, clearly in charge.

"Blanche?" Rachel tried not to stare. "Are you working here?" Clearly, she was. A name tag bearing her photo and stating *Associate* hung on a cord around her neck. And furthermore, Blanche's hair was styled; she wore a hint of makeup and large clip-on earrings.

"This is my second week," Blanche declared proudly. "I'm part-time; that suits me, four hours a day. My Chelsea, she's coming on for a few hours a week. Of course, she won't be at the register. Stockroom and cleaning for now. She's moving back in with me so we can take turns watching Justin. It didn't work out with that worthless boyfriend. This time, Chelsea's had it with him; she's talking about taking night classes and getting her GED. It's good of Ell to give her a chance here. Nothing like a job to teach a young person responsibility."

"Wonderful." Rachel nodded, smiling. "Is Ell here?" She glanced toward the stacks. It was a beehive of activity, customers perusing the books and enjoying coffee in the reading area. She even saw two Amish girls polishing the woodwork on the stage. But she didn't see Ell.

"Upstairs. Getting a book ready to go out. One of those fancy books, going to San Francisco." A tall woman in designer jeans and a blue T-shirt moved to the counter with two oversized children's books, and Blanche said, "You'll have to excuse me. I can't keep this lady waiting."

"No, of course not," Rachel agreed.

She found Ell upstairs, sliding a slim volume into a padded box. "Hi, Rachel," she said. "Come in, if you can find a place to sit. There. That chair." She waved to a leather desk chair currently occupied by a familiar-looking kitten. "Just move her," Ell said.

Rachel scooped up the kitten, the one Blanche had gifted to her. Ell had taken the kitten, relieved that she didn't have to take Sophie. Rachel deposited the fluffy animal onto the floor. The kitten yawned, gave her a curious look, and then dove under the desk after a cat toy shaped like a mouse. "How are you?" Rachel asked as she settled into the chair. "I'm sorry I haven't come by sooner."

"Busy," Ell said. "You, too, so I hear."

"I'm going up to visit George next week. I wondered if you'd like to ride up with me . . . unless you'd rather not . . ."

"Oh, I'll go. Just let me know when. I have a list of questions for him." Ell sealed the box and added it to a stack of two others. "Thank goodness he thought to leave instructions." She pointed to a green leather-backed ledger that lay open on the desk. "Really detailed. About what was coming in and where it had to go. The bookstore doesn't make all that much money." She shrugged. "Okay, so it barely breaks even. The real money is in the rare book business, but I've got a lot to learn before I can start buying. Meanwhile, I have George's client list and . . ." She folded her arms and perched on the corner of the desk. "It's a real bummer, isn't it? Like something out of one of Charles Dickens's novels. Secret heiress. Dastardly deeds."

Ell sighed again, and Rachel noticed that her eyeliner was smeared just a smidgen, as if she'd been crying. "It's George I'm going to miss. I've loved him for a long time, you know. Not in a creepy way, but . . . like a father. Finding out he was my uncle was probably the best thing that ever happened to me." She grimaced. "I could have done without all the other drama . . . and without having him go away."

"He did a terrible thing."

Ell nodded. "I know. It's hard to imagine, George hurting anyone. But he loves Sophie so much. And if he really thought Willy would . . ." She blinked, and Rachel saw moisture glisten in the young woman's eyes.

Rachel smiled sadly. "You've forgiven him, haven't you?"

"Maybe . . . The Bible says that it's not for us to judge. I know that I pray for him. A lot."

"Me, too," Rachel admitted.

"I don't mean to sound callous," Ell continued, "but it's hard to be grateful to Willy for leaving me all this money when I didn't really feel anything for him. He was okay, never weird or anything. He never made me feel uncomfortable around him, but he wasn't warm and fuzzy, you know?"

"I know." Rachel waited for a moment while Ell regained her composure. "You're going to keep the bookstore open? For George?"

The girl nodded. "And for me. He signed it over to me when he went to Harrisburg that last time. He knew that I love working here, and I have scads of ideas. I'm opening another shop next door, Ell's Attic. Vintage stuff, some Victorian antiques, but mostly bags, jewelry, and accessories. I love Edwardian stuff. Mom's going to manage the actual store, but I plan to design a Web page and try to do most of the selling on the Internet."

"You're not considering going away to college? You have the money now."

She shrugged again and flashed a shy smile. "Not for me. I can afford to hire some educated geeks, but I don't have the time or patience to sit in a classroom somewhere and listen to lectures. I know I'll make mistakes, but I want to try it the hard way. Maybe I've got a little of Willy in me, after all."

She got up and went to a wooden filing cabinet, pulled open the top drawer, and removed a folder. "George did something else when he was in Harrisburg." She handed Rachel the folder.

Puzzled, Rachel opened it. Inside was a copy of Rachel's mortgage contract stamped *PAID IN FULL*. "What is this? I don't understand." Her hands were trembling as she pushed the folder back toward Ell. "I can't accept this."

"There's a note taped to the back. From George."

Rachel turned the contract over and found the sheet of velum with George's scrolling handwriting.

My dearest Rachel,

Don't think too badly of me. I know what I've done is unforgivable, but I couldn't bear to see my little Sophie go the way of the others. Accept this small token of my gratitude for what you've done for our town, for my Ell, and for my precious Sophie. I know you'll take good care of them all. And if you're tempted to refuse this offer and try to weasel out of it, which you can't since the loan is already paid off, just consider Sophie a silent partner in your B&B.

Your loving friend,

George

P.S. Sophie likes her chicken breast poached, not baked.